DIAL M
FOR
MEAT LOAF

By Ellen Hart
Published by Ballantine Books:

The Jane Lawless mysteries:
HALLOWED MURDER
VITAL LIES
STAGE FRIGHT
A KILLING CURE
A SMALL SACRIFICE
FAINT PRAISE
ROBBER'S WINE

The Sophie Greenway mysteries:
THIS LITTLE PIGGY WENT TO MURDER
FOR EVERY EVIL
THE OLDEST SIN
MURDER IN THE AIR
SLICE AND DICE
DIAL M FOR MEAT LOAF

DIAL M FOR MEAT LOAF

Ellen Hart

FAWCETT BOOKS • NEW YORK

For Claire Lewis and John Schroeder,
two dedicated gourmets. Meat loaf *may* have passed their lips,
though it is not a topic they would ever discuss in polite society.
It is my fondest wish that they will be instructed,
entertained, and ennobled by this book.

Every saint has a past,
Every sinner a future.
—ANONYMOUS

There are no whole truths; all truths
are half-truths. It is trying to treat them
as whole truths that plays the devil.
—ALFRED NORTH WHITEHEAD
English philosopher
(1861-1947)

CAST OF CHARACTERS

SOPHIE GREENWAY: Owner of the historic Maxfield Plaza Hotel in downtown St. Paul. Restaurant reviewer for the *Times Register* in Minneapolis. Wife of Bram. Mother of Rudy.

BRAM BALDRIC: Radio talk show host: *The Bram Baldric Show*, on WTWN in the Twin Cities. Husband of Sophie.

JOHN WASHBURN: Ex-mayor of Rose Hill. Husband of Mary. Father of Bernice and Plato.

MILTON WASHBURN: Brother of John. Uncle of Bernice and Plato.

MARY WASHBURN: Retired grade school teacher. Wife of John. Mother of Bernice and Plato.

BERNICE WASHBURN: Food editor at the *Times Register* in Minneapolis. Daughter of Mary and John. Sister of Plato.

PLATO WASHBURN: Owner of the *Rose Hill Gazette*. Son of John and Mary. Brother of Bernice.

KIRBY RUNBECK: Handyman. Husband of Cora.

CORA RUNBECK: Housewife. Wife of Kirby.

ANGELO FALZONE: Bernice's friend from New York.

DIAL M
FOR
MEAT LOAF

Leavenworth, Kansas
June 22, 2000
J. D.—

I'm the last person you expected to hear from, right? What's it been? Ten years? I figured the rest of my buddies on the outside would forget I existed, but not you. We got history, pal. But then, I suppose if you tried to find me, maybe you struck out.

I was transferred from Jeff City three years ago. I'm in Leavenworth now. Can you believe it? Man, I remember hearing about this place when we were kids. Never thought I'd end up here. I've made some bad moves in my life, J. D. Very bad. You probably haven't heard, but I knifed a guy at Jeff City. It was self-defense, but how the hell was I supposed to prove it? I'll never be anybody's punk. That's why I had to carry. After the guy died, I was transferred here. There's no chance of parole now. Two murders on my ticket and the only way I'll get out of here is in a coffin. So, I guess I've had to do some rethinking about my life. Truth is, I've come to some pretty amazing conclusions.

The worst mistake I ever made—other than killing two unarmed men—was getting you involved in my crazy schemes. You were like a brother to me, man. I'm afraid I sent you down the wrong road and I'm sorry. I know I've never said it before, but I admit that what happened to us back when we were nineteen was mostly my fault. I'm glad you never got in trouble. You felt guilty about the way it worked out and you shouldn't have. Hey, we're both old men now. We got to live and let live. I wouldn't be writing except, well, I kind of got saved. It happened just before I left Jeff City, and I'm glad it did. See, I spent a lot of time talking to this one guy, another lifer, and he helped me see some stuff differently.

Don't laugh. I figure I'm going to meet my maker soon and I better get right with Him before I die. I'm truly sorry for the crap I've pulled, especially how I hurt you. That's why I'm sending you back some of the letters you wrote me over the years. I kept most of them, but some got lost. I wondered a lot about the kind of life you were leading on the outside. Now I'm not wondering anymore. I'm scared for you, J. D. I've done some bad things, but so have you. I never wanted to believe ill of you, man, but—all I can say is, read the letters and then get down on your knees and plead with the Good Lord to forgive you! You got to do it! You've been as twisted and sick as me. But the trick is, you got to be really sorry. Are you sorry, J. D.? God help you if you're not.

Your friend,
Gilbert Struthers

1

Rose Hill, Minnesota

"How could you do something so . . . so hideous!" declared Cora Runbeck as she stood in her kitchen, gazing at the walls. She was utterly amazed. No, not just amazed more like dumbfounded. Tugging angrily at her apron, she whirled around and nailed her husband with her eyes. "It's egg yolk, Kirby! How could you paint our kitchen walls egg yolk?"

Kirby, who had just come in with the afternoon mail, muttered something inaudible as he sat down at the kitchen table.

"For Pete's sake, speak up. You know I can't stand it when you mumble."

"I said the color's called Golden Sunrise. I like it. And you did, too. Before the damn cataract surgery," he added as he swiped a hand across his mouth.

Cora adjusted her hearing aid, then peered down at him with her hands on her hips. "Land sakes, Kirby Runbeck. When I get my left eye done, what other horrors am I going to discover around this place?"

"A body in the freezer," he said, snickering. He opened the water bill.

"What?"

"Just chill, Cora."

"Don't use that kind of language around me. This isn't *NYPD Blue*."

He rolled his eyes. "Do I get some lunch, or what? Maybe I should take my truck and go visit Mabel Bjorn-staad. She's always more than happy to see me."

"You just do that, you old goat. Maybe you'll have a surprise waiting for you when you get home."

Cora was a no-nonsense kind of woman. Norwegian to the core. She'd grown up on a farm near Le Suer. By the time she was ten, she'd been baking the family bread, feeding chickens, milking cows, washing clothes, taking care of her three younger siblings, and nursing an ailing mother. That was the late thirties and times were tough. She understood work and she understood responsibility.

Kirby, on the other hand, was a lazy man. Always had been. And he was cheap. He probably got the paint on sale. Or free from one of his buddies. Now that her eye was getting better, she would have to examine the entire house. It had been a good two years since she'd been able to see well. If there were other problems, she felt it was partially her fault. Being a Lutheran, Cora understood guilt. She should have had the eye surgery years ago. She was deeply embarrassed by the thought of what her friends must think when they sat and drank coffee in a kitchen with egg-yolk colored walls. She assumed they'd been painted a nice off-white. Tasteful. Understated. Cora admitted to a certain pride about her home.

As she busied herself making a pot of coffee, she heard Kirby mutter again. When she turned around, she saw that he was standing now, his hands squeezing the back of the chair. "What did you say?"

He cleared his throat. "I said, I want a divorce."

She blinked. And then blinked again. "A what?"

"You heard me. I need passion in my life, Cora."

She turned her hearing aid up to high. "For God's sake, man, you're seventy-five years old."

"So?"

For the first time in years, she was speechless.

"I don't love you anymore. You can keep the house and the Chevy. I'll give you enough money to make sure you're comfortable. I just want my clothes and my truck. Oh, and my tools. You got no use for those."

"Kirby, what are you saying? You don't love me?"

"I'm not changing my mind."

For the second time this morning, she was dumbstruck.

The coffeemaker began to gurgle and groan, adding a kind of vulgar background music to the marital trauma. Kirby glared at it. "I'm goin' down to the Prairie Lights Cafe to buy me a meat loaf sandwich. When I get back, I'm gonna pack my stuff. I don't want no scenes, Cora. Before I get old, I want to enjoy life a little. Kick up my heels."

"But Kirby—"

He held up a hand to silence her. Without another word, he turned and pushed through the screen door. His truck was parked under the carport next to the garage.

Cora closed her mouth. She turned to stare blankly at the flour canister on the kitchen counter. Her hearing aid was nothing but static this morning, so she turned it off. Divorce? The word flopped around inside her head like a wet sock in a dryer. Nobody in her family had ever been divorced before. The embarrassment would kill her. She'd never be able to show her face in Rose Hill again.

She even suspected she might miss Kirby. After all these years, they were just a habit, but a habit was hard to break. And she did love him, in her own way, didn't she?

Suddenly, Cora heard a thunderous roar. The floor rumbled so ominously beneath her pink terrycloth slippers that she had to grab hold of the counter to keep from falling backward. When the rumbling finally stopped, she rushed out to the back porch. There, where the carport used to be, was a huge smoking hole. The truck was gone. So was the garage. And so was Kirby.

Rose Hill Man Dies in Bombing

Kirby Runbeck, age 75, died yesterday at his home on the outskirts of Rose Hill, the result of a mysterious bombing.

According to the local sheriff's department, Mr. Runbeck had just left his house to drive into town when his wife heard a loud explosion. Authorities are still piecing together the facts, but preliminary evidence suggests that the ignition on Mr. Runbeck's Ford truck had been wired with an explosive. When questioned later, the police had no comment about a motive for the murder.

In a statement given by Runbeck's wife, Cora Runbeck said that her husband had been acting strangely yesterday morning. Pressed to give more details, all Mrs. Runbeck would say was, "Kirby once told me he loved his Ford Bronco so much he wanted to be buried in it. I guess he got his wish."

Rose Hill Gazette
August 10

John Washburn, Beloved Ex-Mayor, Suffers Stroke

Late yesterday evening, John Washburn, age 67, a resident of Rose Hill for the past forty-five years and mayor of the town for four years, suffered a massive stroke while having dinner at his home. Mr. Washburn ran for mayor of Rose Hill after retiring from his position as district manager of Midwest Optical. Before being promoted to that position, Mr. Washburn was a salesman for the company. His wife, Mary, brother Milton, and his two children, Plato and Bernice, are by his side at St. Matthew's Medical Center. No further word is available at this time on his condition.

Rose Hill Gazette
August 11

2

One Week Later

"For those of you who've just tuned in," said Bram Baldric, adjusting the mic a little closer to his mouth, "we're talking food in our final hour today with two home grown experts. First we have the talented, beautiful, and always opinionated Sophie Greenway, the new restaurant review editor at the *Times Register*—otherwise known around the house as my wife."

Sophie grinned at her husband, and said, "Always a pleasure, dear." This was the first time Bram had invited her to be on his afternoon radio show since she'd taken on the top reviewer spot at the paper. She knew all his food peccadilloes, so the hour was destined to become a classic.

"And our second guest is Bernice Washburn, author of the forthcoming *All That Glitters*, a study of cafe society in America. Bernice is also the food editor at the *Times Register*." Bram nodded to her.

"I'm delighted to be here," said Bernice, her tentative voice betraying her nervousness.

Sophie gave Bernice's hand a reassuring squeeze. They'd both worked at the newspaper for many years, Bernice as a full-time employee. Up until recently, Sophie wrote an occasional restaurant review, but she was just a guest columnist. She couldn't exactly say that she and Bernice were close friends. It was more of the work-related variety. Still, she respected Bernice enormously. Bernice had also written six books on various food-related topics. While she was a fascinating thinker and writer, she tended to grow a bit formal and pedantic when talking to a group, which only cemented her dislike of public speaking. Radio interviews terrified her. She would never have agreed to come on the show today if Sophie hadn't promised to be part of the ordeal.

Bram glanced at the clock on the wall. "So, before we start talking about cafe society and the denizens of that particular deep, tell me, ladies, what's new out there in foodie-land? What are gourmets eating today? What's 'in'? Trendy? Cutting edge?"

Sophie could see Bernice struggling to form an answer, so she jumped right in. "Believe it or not, meat loaf."

"You're joking."

"It's all the rage," said Sophie. "Come on, fess up, honey. Isn't it secretly one of your favorite foods?"

"Well . . . okay. I suppose. If it's made to my exacting standards."

"See. And *you're* a man of taste and refinement."

Bram tugged at the knot in his silk tie. "Not to mention boyish and sexy."

Bernice gave a little cough, signaling that she wanted to speak. "It may sound silly, but Sophie's correct. So many of our food choices today, especially for baby boomers like the three of us, are based on nostalgia. I'm currently doing research for a new book about that very subject. Boomers have an incredible ambivalence about

appetite, about bounty. We are the wealthiest, most edu-
cated, most powerful, plugged-in, well-fed, sheltered,
and pampered generation in history, and we're always
hungry. In fact, I believe that hunger and loneliness define us in some basic way. There's no better place to see
that reflected than in our uneasy relationship with food.
One minute it's our friend, it's going to help us live forever; the next minute it's a drug, getting us through
the day. And finally, it's the enemy. Food is going to kill
us. Even with all the abundance surrounding us in this
country, our nutritional intake is woefully deficient.
Why? Because we try to combine minimal meals with
excess—the rich dessert followed by days of lunching on
nothing but a Diet Coke and a cigarette. Excess is the
fashion in all age groups—either excessive indulgence or
an excess of denial."

"Where does meat loaf fit in to all that?" asked Bram,
scratching his chest through his Egyptian-cotton shirt.

"A perfect example of boomer food," Bernice continued. "It's where nostalgia and culinary evolution
meet. More than any other country in the world, Americans are constantly reinventing what they eat. Old ideas
are given a modern twist. Perhaps nothing reflects our
fragmented, multicultural, contradictory, patchwork society more than the simple meat loaf. Instead of the
more traditional beef, or beef, pork, and veal, it's often
made today with lean ground turkey, lentils, tofu, spiced
Mexican or Oriental, Greek or Italian, or a million other
ways. Meat loaf is such an old standard, such an integral
part of the American culinary psyche, that we can't leave
it alone. Each generation tinkers with it, while at the
same time demanding that someone, somewhere, cook it
just the way mom used to make."

Sophie nodded to her husband. "Tell me about it. When Bram and I first got married, one of his favorite foods was—"

Bram cut her off. "My listeners aren't interested in ancient history, *dear*."

Sophie regarded him patiently, and then continued, "One of his favorite foods was tuna noodle casserole."

The woman inside the control booth tossed her head back and laughed, pointing at Bram through the glass.

"Another American standard," said Bernice.

"I wrote to his mother," Sophie continued, "and asked her to send me her personal recipe. Bram would go into raptures about how wonderful it was. He used the same words to describe it that other people reserve for life everlasting."

Bram groaned.

"I was thrilled the day I finally received his mother's recipe in the mail. That night, I made it for him. It was going to be one of his birthday presents. I used Campbell's Cream of Celery soup, just like my mother-in-law said. Mixed it with sour cream. I chopped up onions and celery and sauteed them before adding them to the glop. I covered the mess in orange cheddar cheese and topped it with crushed potato chips. And then I baked it."

"I'm ruined," said Bram, shaking his head, refusing to look up. "No maitre d' will ever seat me in a four-star restaurant again."

"I lit candles. Obsessed over the wine. What does one serve with tuna noodle casserole?"

"One of life's imponderables," muttered Bram.

"When my husband got home that night, I presented him with the casserole. Was he pleased? Was he?"

"Yes," said Bram, about to hit the button and turn off her microphone. "He was."

"No," said Sophie, grabbing his hand. "He wasn't. And why? Because I'd failed to use the right noodles. I'd bought the flat egg-noodle variety. Bram insisted his mom always used the kind of noodle you could blow through."

The woman in the control booth nearly fell off her chair.

"You make me sound like I'm eight years old."

"You are."

Bernice was laughing now, too. "That's a marvelous story. I'd like to use it in my next book. It illustrates my point beautifully."

"But back to meat loaf," said Sophie.

"This should be a lesson to all you other talk show hosts out there." Bram rested his chin on his cupped hand. "Never bring your wife on your show. Somewhere along the way, I seem to have lost control."

"We were talking about meat loaf," said Bernice helpfully.

"I think we've done that topic to death."

"But one last comment," said Sophie. "The *Times Register* is currently running a special statewide competition. Everyone in Minnesota is invited to send his or her favorite meat loaf recipe to the paper. New or old, it doesn't matter. The deadline is next Friday. In early September the winners will be announced. We're giving out a first, second, and third prize, as well as three honorable mentions. The winning recipes will be published in the paper. The winners will spend a weekend at the historic Maxfield Plaza in downtown St. Paul. They'll be wined and dined at some of the finest restaurants in the Twin

Cities, and will be featured with their winning creations on WTWN's *Good Morning with Bailey Brown*."

"Such a deal," said Bram, peering at Sophie over the top of his reading glasses. "Now, since we're doing promos, I'd like to remind my Minnesota listeners that next Monday my show will be broadcast live from the Itasca County fair in Grand Rapids, Minnesota. I like to get out of the studio every now and then, and county fairs give me a great opportunity to meet and greet my audience."

"I'm sure the cows and chickens are lining up to get good seats," said Sophie.

"You're in rare form today, *darling*." Bram cleared his throat. "Now, I think we'd better talk about that book of yours, Bernice. Otherwise, your publicist will have my head on a plate."

"I'd stay away from culinary metaphors on this show." Sophie took a sip of coffee. She was surprised to see Bram pop a couple of antacid tablets into his mouth. She hoped the tuna casserole revelation wasn't giving him heartburn.

Bernice jumped in. "Sophie and I were talking about cafe society on the way over here this afternoon." She glanced around the claustrophobic studio, her eyes drawn to the gray honeycombed soundproofing material covering the walls. "It's a fascinating topic."

"In your new book," said Bram, "you discuss such subjects as roadhouses and speakeasies in the Roaring Twenties. Cafes in the Jazz Age. Gay cafe society in San Francisco during the seventies."

"But interestingly," Sophie interjected, "you wrote nothing about the role of the cafe in rural, small-town America. That's always fascinated me."

"Me too," said Bernice. "But that will have to wait for another book."

"Actually," Sophie continued, "since we're on the subject, I'm planning to feature small, Main Street cafes in my restaurant reviews for the next few months. If anybody out there knows of a great cafe, drop me a line and give me the details."

"On that note," said Bram, acknowledging a signal from his producer, "we need to break for weather and traffic. Steve Hardy, take it away." Bram removed his headphones and leaned back in his chair.

The "On Air" light went out.

"Are we doing okay?" asked Bernice tentatively. "It's not too boring, is it?"

"Listening to my wife deconstruct my life is never boring."

"Come on," said Sophie, "I was just having some fun." Over the rim of her coffee mug, she watched him press a hand to his chest. "Are you okay?"

"Sure. Why wouldn't I be?"

"It's just . . . you look like you're in pain."

He coughed a couple of times. "I had a greasy grilled cheese sandwich for lunch. I think it's stuck somewhere between my lungs and my backbone."

The woman in the booth held up one finger.

"Wait until I tell all my listeners about your wine and popcorn diet," said Bram. "That was your finest hour."

"You wouldn't."

He made his eyebrows dance.

The rest of the hour went by quickly. At five, when the local and regional news came on, Bram took the opportunity to walk Sophie and Bernice to the elevators. "Thank you, ladies. That was fun."

"It . . . I mean, I wasn't too . . . dry, was I?" asked Bernice. In high heels, she was several inches taller than Bram, who hit the mark at just over six feet. Tall, plain, large-boned, and string-bean thin. The heavy horn-rimmed glasses she wore made her look even more like the egghead intellectual she so clearly was. Her hair was shoulder length and brown, mixed with a touch of gray, and no matter how hard she tried to style it, wind and humidity always returned it to an unruly mass of curls.

"No, you were just fine. It was an interesting hour."

"Was I fine, too?" asked Sophie, blinking innocently.

Bram smiled, kissing the top of her strawberry-blond hair. "You're always fine." Sophie was as short as Bernice was tall. Short, and—staying with the bean analogy—more of the Great Northern variety. Both she and Bram fought their weight constantly. Bram, however, could hide a great deal more under his suit coats than she could hide in a dress. Most everyone thought he was the spitting image of the more mature Cary Grant. He generally milked the likeness for all it was worth.

When the elevator arrived, Sophie and Bernice stepped on. "See you tonight," said Sophie, blowing Bram a kiss as the elevator doors closed.

When they were finally alone, Bernice said, "You have such a handsome husband."

"Bram would agree with you."

"Oh? Is he . . . conceited?"

"Actually, no. A little vain perhaps, especially when it comes to clothes, but he's really a sweet guy."

"You're lucky."

Sophie recalled that Bernice had been engaged once, but she'd been in the process of disengaging when they first met. That was ten years ago. As far as Sophie knew, she hadn't dated much since.

As they approached Sophie's silver Lexus, the cell phone in Bernice's purse gave a beep.

"I need to take this,"she said, her expression clouding over. "It may be about my father. He had a stroke last week."

Sophie hadn't heard. "I'm so sorry."

"My mother and my Uncle Milt have been at the hospital just about round the clock since it happened." She clicked the phone on and said hello. After a few seconds, she raked a hand through her hair, and said, "Slow down, Mom. I can't understand you. You say he opened his eyes?" Again, she listened. "Can he talk? What? Just calm down, okay? You need to remember what the doctor said. Take it one step at a time." She listened a moment longer. "Okay, I'm leaving right away. Maybe I can beat the rush hour traffic out of town. I'll be there by . . ." She glanced at her watch. "Seven-thirty. Eight at the latest. Tell Dad I love him. And stay strong, Mom. This is a good sign. I love you, too." Bernice's hand shook as she stuffed the cell phone back in her bag.

"Where do your parents live?" asked Sophie.

"Rose Hill. It's out near Marshall. Dad's at St. Matthew's Medical Center."

"Are you sure you're okay to drive?"

"I'm fine. Just get me back to the paper. My car's parked in the lot across the street."

The radio studio was located north of St. Paul. Once they were on the freeway flying back to Minneapolis, Sophie looked over at Bernice and saw that she was crying. "Are you sure you're all right?"

"No," she said, sniffing into a tissue. "I'm not. I'm a

mess. I've been driving back and forth between Rose Hill and Minneapolis all week and I'm exhausted. I'm also scared to death."

"But it sounded like good news. Your father opened his eyes?"

"But he can't talk. And his blood pressure is still through the roof. It's not good, Sophie. Even if he survives, he might never—" Instead of finishing the sentence, she broke into tears.

Hesitating for just a moment, Sophie said, "Why don't you let me drive you to the hospital? I don't have anything on my agenda for the rest of the day. Please, Bernice. In your condition, it's not safe for you to drive."

Bernice glanced at her wristwatch again.

"If we stayed on the freeway and didn't get off in downtown Minneapolis, you'd save half an hour."

Closing her eyes and leaning her head back, Bernice relented. "Maybe you're right. But I hate to impose."

"It's settled. You navigate and I'll drive."

3

Mary Washburn hung up the receiver, then turned and rushed down the broad corridor to her husband's hospital room. As she pushed softly through the closed door, she found her brother-in-law, Milton Washburn, and her son, Plato, standing on one side of the bed. On the other side a doctor bent over her husband, shining a tiny light in his eyes. Mary stood silently in the doorway and watched. "Is it true?" she asked finally. "Is he really awake?"

"So it seems," said the doctor. "Can you hear me, John? Can you give us a sign?"

They all waited, but no sign came.

Looking up, the doctor continued, "I'll need to order more tests, but this is good news. We should all be hopeful."

Mary sagged against the door and started to cry. Ever since her husband had been rushed to the hospital last Thursday night, she'd been holding so much guilt and fear inside, she felt the weight would crush the life out of her. Now it looked as if he might recover. Or, at the very least, there was hope. And that meant she had another chance to be the wife he deserved, the wife he would need to help him get better. She had to put the last year of her life behind her, no matter what it took.

"Are you all right, Mom?" asked Plato, rushing to her side. Milton followed, and together they helped Mary over to a chair.

"I need to go see about those tests," said Dr. Hoffman, moving around the end of the bed and striding to the door. "But before I leave, I want you all to understand that I need your help. So does John. Now more than ever, it's important that you talk to him." He gave them all a stern look. "Read to him. Sing to him. Touch him. Tell him about the weather, the fish you caught this summer, the stock market. Anything you think might engage him."

"Of course," said Milton, casting a glance at his brother's still body lying under the covers. "We'll do everything we can."

"Mary, will you be all right? Perhaps you should go home. Get some rest. John needs your strength right now more than ever, but if you get sick yourself—"

"I'm fine," she said, sucking back her sobs. "I have to stay." She looked at the cot she'd been sleeping on for the past week. How could she leave now, when her prayers finally had been answered? "I'm just so glad—"

"We all are," said Dr. Hoffman.

He couldn't understand, Mary thought. He was a young man. His whole life was ahead of him. How could anybody his age truly understand the complex emotions she was experiencing right now? He had no idea what her life had been like.

After the doctor left, Milton walked back over to the bed. "Hey, Johnny," he said, taking firm hold of his brother's hand. "It's Milton. Your little brother. Mary and Plato are here, too. And Bernice is driving down from the Cities. Can you hear me, Johnny? Can you say something? Come on, just one little insult to let me know you care?"

Mary got up and went to his side. "I love you, sweetheart." She kissed his forehead. "John? Do you hear me?" She was startled to see him look straight at her. "John, I'm here." She glanced up at her son. "He looked at me."

"I don't think he moved his eyes, Mom," said Plato.

"No, I saw it. He recognized me." She took his right hand and lifted it to her lips. "Honey, you've come back." That's when she felt it. A slight pressure. He was reaching out to her! "He squeezed my hand."

Milton and Plato exchanged glances.

"John, can you say something? Please try. I need to know you're okay." Was his mind still intact? Had the stroke taken it away from him?

This time, his hand moved. It pulled away from her. As it did so, his arm dropped back onto the bed.

They all watched in hushed amazement as John struggled to move his lips. At first, nothing came out. Then, soft as the brush of a bird's wing . . . air. He was forcing air out of the right side of his mouth. Finally, closing his eyes and concentrating, he said, "Phh . . . ahhh."

"John!" Mary cried. "Oh, John. You've come back!"

"He's trying to say something," said Milton, shushing her.

John moved his eyes. This time, they came to rest on Plato.

"Dad, it's me. Sarah and the kids aren't here, but they'll come by later. They'll all be so thrilled to see that you're awake."

John's gaze rose to the ceiling. "Pah . . . pahh," he said

again, lifting his right hand a few inches off the bed and making a tiny circling motion.

"He wants his papa," said Mary, clasping her hands in front of her.

"He never called our dad Papa," said Milton, scrutinizing his brother's face. "He's saying . . . paper. He wants to write something to us. Is that it, John? You want to try and write?"

"Here's a notepad," said Plato, retrieving one from the vest pocket of his rumpled tan suit. "And a felt-tipped pen."

Milton carefully placed the pen in his brother's hand, the notepad underneath. "Go ahead, John. If you can't talk, maybe you can write."

Everyone waited as John's hand began to move. Slowly, with great difficulty, he scratched out:

i dying?

"No, no," said Mary, assuring him with great vehemence. "You're going to be just fine." She had no idea if that was true or not, but she had to be positive.

His hand moved again.

don lie

"I'm not lying," said Mary. "Tell him, Milton. He's going to get better now."

"Sure, Johnny, you'll be fine. Why, before you know it, you'll be back making those yummy carrot juice cocktails, just like before." He smiled and shuddered at the same time.

John turned his eyes on his son.

"Say something to your father," said Mary, encouragingly.

"I . . . ah." Plato smiled. "It's hot out, Dad."

Mary gave him a disgusted look.

John's eyes swung back to Milton.

"Sorry for that crack about the carrot juice, John. You know how much I hate health food."

Again, John's hand began to move. This time he wrote:

krby runbek

"What's he saying now?" asked Milton.

"He's talking about that handyman who did some work on our garage," said Mary. "The one who died last week in that awful bombing."

"Weird," said Plato, watching his father's hand continue to move.

Everyone stared in shocked silence at what John Washburn wrote next.

4

"You have a brother, don't you?" asked Sophie, watching the road ahead, but still enjoying the panorama of farms and fields as they whizzed past. As soon as they'd left the city limits, she'd called Bram on her cell phone. He hadn't returned to their apartment at the Maxfield Plaza yet, so she left him a voice mail message explaining that she was driving Bernice to Rose Hill and not to expect her back before ten.

"Yes, his name is Plato," said Bernice, one hand trailing through the ends of her curly brown hair.

"Unusual name."

"It was Dad's idea. He loved it. It's strange, but it actually kind of fits my brother. He's a philosopher at heart, an odd guy. He worked in banking for years. He and his family lived in a house right across from Lake Calhoun. Very posh. Between you and me, I lusted after it from the day they moved in, but it was too ritzy for my limited budget. Then about five years ago, his wife, Sarah, got a bee in her bonnet that they should buy a hobby farm and leave Minneapolis behind, raise their two boys in the country. Plato didn't seem all that enthusiastic about it at first, but he eventually quit his job and they moved to a ten-acre place just south of Rose Hill. The local paper, the *Rose Hill Gazette*, happened to be up for sale at the time, so Plato bought it and became a journalist—or publisher, as Sarah insists everyone call him. Odd transition, if you ask me, but then my brother never felt comfortable in banking. He said it was just a lot of men sitting around in suits trying to fake each other out."

"Does he have any training as a journalist?"

"None. He majored in philosophy at UMD, minored in political science. I can't say that he seems particularly happy with his new profession, either. Quite honestly, I don't know what would make my brother happy."

"How old is he?" asked Sophie.

"He's forty-four. Three years older than me."

"Are you two close?"

Bernice thought about it. "Not really. I mean, we don't talk about what's really important in our lives. The personal stuff. Feelings. We discuss ideas a lot. Politics. Current events. But never our hopes and our disappointments. I suppose it's kind of sad. I love my brother, and I know he loves me, but I'm not sure who Plato confides in. His wife, I guess. He doesn't have many friends."

Sophie adjusted the air-conditioning, making it a little cooler inside the car. Outside, the sweltering summer heat baked the fields. It had been an unusually dry summer. Good for vacationers, bad for farmers. "Sometimes I think emotional stoicism is a cultural thing. Bram calls it the Minnesooota Mule Manifesto: stubborn and silent; don't moan and for God's sake, don't brag; just suck it up and keep going. Bram has a sign above his desk that says 'Thou shalt not snivel.' "

Bernice laughed.

When Sophie glanced over at her, she saw that her

friend's good spirits were only temporary. She was back to chewing on her lower lip again.

"You're still very worried about your dad, aren't you."

"I'm worried about a lot of things," mumbled Bernice.

Sophie got the impression that the problems in the Washburn family ran deeper than John Washburn's recent stroke.

Sighing, Bernice continued, "My mother was diagnosed with breast cancer a year and a half ago. It's been a tough battle, but she's healthy now. I'm terrified that my father's stroke could change all that. She's suffered so much—the radiation, the chemotherapy, the hair loss, the nausea, and the fear that she'd never get better. Nobody who hasn't been through it could understand. That's why Dad asked Uncle Milt to come stay with them. He needed help with Mom. Uncle Milt's wife, Aunt Doris, died many years ago, so he was able to drive up from St. Louis right away. He's been staying with my parents ever since."

"Your Uncle Milton is your mother's brother?"

"My father's. He's part owner of Home Built Inc., a St. Louis company that builds and sells trailer homes. Believe it or not, it's made him a millionaire many times over. He ran the company until he retired in '97. Way back when, Milton convinced my dad to buy stock in Home Built. It's made my parents' retirement a lot more comfortable."

"He sounds like a great guy."

"He and my dad are so funny together. They're always insulting each other. Uncle Milt's been good to have around. He keeps everybody laughing . . . well, at least

part of the time. Before the stroke, Dad had become terribly moody and out of sorts."

Sophie glanced at a sign that said Rose Hill was seventeen miles away. "Do you know why?"

Bernice shrugged. "I asked Mom, but she said she
didn't know."

"Sounds to me like you're not sure you believe her."

Again, she sighed. "I don't know what to think."

Fifteen minutes later, Sophie pulled the Lexus up to
the curb across from St. Matthew's Medical Center.
"Seven-forty-five. We made good time." She left the
motor running.

"I can't thank you enough, Sophie. Really."

"I'm glad I could help."

Bernice hesitated. "Look, why don't you come in? I'll
see how Dad's doing. If everything is as hopeful as Mom
says, and if you don't mind waiting a bit, maybe I could
buy you dinner. It's the least I can do. There's a cafe
down the street. What do you say?"

Sophie rarely had to be cajoled into eating, especially
when her stomach was already growling. "Sure. I'd like
that."

Once they'd pushed through the glass front doors,
Bernice led the way. "Dad's on the fourth floor in a private room."

"Looks like the hospital is pretty new." The white ce-
ramic walls gleamed.

"The building was completed four years ago, while my
father was mayor."

"I didn't know your father had been the mayor," said
Sophie, folding up her sunglasses and slipping them into
her shoulder bag.

"He spent most of his life in sales, on the road selling sunglasses for Midwest Optical. But, yes, after he retired, a bunch of his friends talked him into running. He served one term."

Standing at last before the closed door to her father's room, Bernice's voice dropped to a whisper. "I'll be back out in a few minutes. Make yourself comfortable in the lounge. The coffeepot's always on, so help yourself." She nodded to a small waiting room directly across the hall.

When Bernice pushed through the door, Sophie caught a glimpse of the people inside. Everyone was sitting around the bed. Since there was only one woman in the room, Sophie assumed it was Bernice's mother, Mary. She was an attractive older woman, with a pretty, oval face and short, platinum hair. Her eyes seemed enormous, set against her pale face, and she looked exhausted. She was also terribly thin, no doubt a result of the cancer therapy.

The older man in the room, the one Sophie figured was Milton, was stocky and almost bald, with a full salt-and-pepper beard. He was dressed in a blue oxford-cloth shirt, rolled up at the cuffs, and dark-brown Dockers. Sophie guessed the younger man with the moon face was Plato. He appeared hot, wilted, and uncomfortable. His thick, overweight body was packed sausagelike into a wrinkled, tan summer suit and his shaggy blond hair was in need of a good wash and cut. In fact, everything about him seemed bloated and sagging.

Seeing Bernice in the doorway, her mother got up, pressing a finger to her lips.

Sophie retreated to the other side of the hall as Bernice disappeared inside.

*   *   *

"We have to keep our voices low," said Mary, drawing her daughter into her embrace, then nodding to the empty chair next to Milton. "Your father's asleep."

Before Bernice sat down, she bent over the bed, gave her dad a soft kiss on his cheek, then took a moment to study him. He looked exactly the same as when she'd seen him only two nights ago. Her mother insisted on combing his thinning gray hair straight back from his high forehead, the way he used to wear it when he was on the road. In the last ten or so years, he'd started to part his hair on the right side, because he thought it made him look younger. Bernice also noticed that the cot was still in the room, which meant that her mother was spending her nights at the hospital.

"I want to know everything," Bernice said, sitting down and dropping her purse to the floor, then leaning forward, her arms hugging her stomach.

"He's out of the coma," said Plato. "But he can't talk."

"But . . . is he out of danger? Will he get better?"

Plato shook his head. "We don't know."

Her brother seemed so restless tonight, Bernice thought. Usually, he was calm to the point of inertia. He could sit for hours in a chair, staring at the wall, never moving or uttering a sound. Tonight, one leg was twitching nervously and he kept crossing and uncrossing his arms. The strain was obviously getting to him, just as it was to everyone else.

"They did another MRI," said Milton. "Dr. Hoffman wants a specialist to look at the results."

"His vital signs are strong," said Mary, her eyes fixed

on her husband's face. "We should know more in the morning."

"The left side of his body seems the most affected," continued Milton.

"When he was awake, did he understand what you were saying to him?" asked Bernice. "Did he try to communicate?" When no one jumped in with an answer, her gaze shifted from face to face. "What's wrong? You're scaring me. If you know something I don't, tell me!"

"It's nothing like that, honey," said her mother, trying to sound reassuring. "It's just, we don't know anything for sure. And we're all so very tired."

"But, did you try to communicate with him? If nothing else, maybe he could blink his eyes. Once for yes. Twice for no. I've seen people do that in movies."

"This isn't a movie," muttered Plato.

"Your father did try to communicate with us," said Milton. "It's just . . . it didn't make any sense."

"Are you saying his mind is gone? Is that what you're afraid to tell me?"

"Bernice, please," said her uncle. "Whatever we tell you, it's only a guess. We'll know more when the test results come back."

"How long was he awake?" demanded Bernice.

"Not more than half an hour," answered her mother. "I know your father, and I know he wanted to stay with us, but he couldn't. He was too tired. Dr. Hoffman thought he'd sleep through the night."

They'd answered her questions, but Bernice still felt frustrated, as if they were holding something back.

"Listen, Mary," said Milton, placing a hand on her back. "I think I should stay here tonight instead of you."

"Absolutely not," said Mary, her voice firm. "He's my

husband. I can't leave. I want you to go home, Milton, before that thunderstorm they've been predicting hits. You too, Plato. Get a good night's rest. Bernice can keep me company for a while."

"What storm?" asked Bernice.

Plato squirmed in his chair, then stood and walked to the windows, looking up at the sky. "We've been under a tornado watch all afternoon. About an hour ago, the warnings started to pop up due west of us, so it's bound to get here sooner or later."

Bernice thought of Sophie. How could she send her off in the middle of a tornado? "Look, Mom, a friend of mine drove me down. She was planning to head back to the Cities after we had a quick dinner, but now I'm not so sure that's a good idea. If it's all right with you, I'd like to ask her to stay overnight at the house. She can follow Milton home, use the spare bedroom."

"By all means," said Mary. Hesitating just a moment, she added, "Is something wrong with your car?"

"No, it's nothing like that." Bernice didn't want to worry her mother with the state of her emotions, not when her mother's were so fragile, so she added, "My friend Sophie is the new restaurant reviewer at the *Times Register*. We had some business to discuss, so she offered the ride and I took it."

Plato stepped away from the windows. "Let's get going. I don't like the looks of that sky."

"We have some food in the house, don't we, something Sophie could have for dinner?"

"The refrigerator is packed to the gills," replied her mother. "Friends and neighbors have been bringing hot dishes, salads, and desserts over all week, but nobody's been home to eat it."

Bernice stood. "Then I'll just tell Sophie about the change in plans."

"Fine," said Mary. Rising from her own chair, she moved closer to the bed and gazed down at her husband.

In just those few seconds, Bernice could tell that her mother was already a million miles away.

5

After parking her car on the grass next to the Washburn's garage, Sophie slid out of the front seat and followed Milton past the clothesline and a wide patch of vegetable garden to the back door. Walking up the three steps, she glanced at a woodpile stacked in front of what looked like a small addition to the back of the house. The white stucco and green trim made her think of her grandparent's home in Grand Rapids. Luxuriating finally in the cool stillness of the kitchen, Sophie was grateful for the central air. Outside, the evening was thick with heat and humidity, just the kind of summer night likely to spawn a storm.

While Milton switched on the lights, Sophie scoped out the lay of the land. A long living room dominated the downstairs, with two picture windows capping off either end. Toward the front of the house, an archway opened onto the front hall. Peering into the dimness, Sophie could make out a beautiful old wooden stairway leading up to the second floor. It hugged the far wall, a remnant of the house as it had once looked, before the interior had been modernized. The furniture in the living room seemed comfortable and functional, neither antique nor modern. None of the furnishings were particularly tasteful. Two brown plush recliner rockers faced the TV, as did a nondescript gold-and-green couch. The dominant colors in the room were gold, green, and brown, with orange accents scattered here and there. Family photos and oil paintings of flowers lined the brown-paneled walls. All in all, the house seemed homey. It smelled of coffee and contentment.

Sophie didn't really want to spend the night in Rose Hill, but she saw the wisdom in not heading back to St. Paul in a potential storm. Still, she hated to impose on the Washburns, especially at a time like this. She could easily have found a motel for the night, but Bernice wouldn't hear of it.

"Hey, Sophie," Milton called from the kitchen. "You want a beer?"

"Sure," she said. She found him bent over with his head in the refrigerator. The small, round breakfast table behind him was overflowing with opened Tupperware bowls. The spread looked like a church basement feast, everything from deviled eggs to potato salad, coleslaw, fried chicken, carrots and green peppers pickled in a tomato sauce, Jell-O with canned fruit and Cool Whip, pickled cucumbers, tuna macaroni salad, cornbread, tiny bran muffins, the ubiquitous "overnight salad," and a cold ham loaf. Sophie did a double take at the couscous salad. Someone in town was clearly a budding gourmet. On the counter next to the table were paper plates filled with brownies, chocolate chip blondies, lemon bars, spice bars, two homemade berry pies, seven-layer bars, a rhubarb crisp, and slices of pumpkin bread.

"Help yourself," said Milton, handing her an un-capped beer bottle, then chugging half of his before he sat down. "Just thought I'd get out a few things for us.

I'm famished." He pointed to some paper plates and plastic forks on the counter, then bit hungrily into a chicken leg.

Sophie heaped a small plate with food. She sat down on the other side of the table and took a bite of a deviled egg. She'd always loved them, but rarely ate them anymore. Nobody did these days, what with eggs in general being frowned upon by the nutritional powers that be. Perhaps people in small towns weren't as impressed by "experts" as their fellow city dwellers.

"I'm beat," said Milton, scooping out some potato salad and pickled carrots.

"Have you been spending long hours at the hospital?"

"And then some. I'm worried about Mary. She's pushing too hard."

"Sounds like her husband made some major progress today."

Milton's eyes flicked to her, then away. "Yeah. At least he's out of his coma. Funny, you'd think that if anybody would have had a stroke, it would have been me. My eating habits are deplorable. Always have been. By all rights, I'm the one who should be lying in that bed, not John." He shook his head, then added, "He's worth two of me, Sophie. John was the good brother, the responsible one. He settled down with Mary, raised a family, and became a pillar of the community. I got lucky in life, but John made his own luck."

He seemed to want to talk. Sophie was more than happy to let him. "Are you from Minnesota originally?"

"No, Indiana. John and I were both born in Kokomo, but we moved to South Bend in '47 when my father changed jobs. John moved in with a buddy of his in Minneapolis after kicking around Indiana for a while. His first real job was here. He sold Camel cigarettes. Mary grew up in Marshall. They met at a party and were married a year later, in the spring of '58. That's when they bought this house. They've been living here ever since."

"What about you?"

He shrugged. "I kicked around a lot, too, when I was young. I didn't really settle down until I was in my forties. That's when I met my wife, Doris. I used to call her the mother superior. She really straightened me out." He laughed. "But sadly, she died a few years back, so I'm on my own now. John called me right after they got Mary's cancer diagnosis. I told him I'd do anything to help. A few months later he called again and asked if I'd come stay with them for a while. John was having a hard time dealing with Mary's illness. I think maybe his age was starting to catch up with him, not that any of us are that old. But the idea that he might lose Mary made him face his own mortality and . . . well, it was too much. On top of that, he had to take her to the hospital three times a week, do all the shopping, make all the meals, clean the house, hold everything together. Mary was too sick to help. And he had to stay positive, for Mary's sake. He tried to be a good soldier, but by the time I arrived, I could see he was in terrible shape. My brother's always been an in-charge, can-do kind of guy. He takes his responsibilities seriously."

Milton glanced up at a cupboard above the sink. "Look at this," he said, rising and opening the cupboard door, revealing shelf after shelf of vitamin and mineral supplements. "And this," he continued, bending over and opening a lower cupboard. "In case you're wondering, that big machine is a juicer. John began making vegetable juices for everyone in the family about a year ago, insisting we all drink it. He stopped eating regular food and started on a diet of organic raw vegetables, fruits, and supplements. No meat. No dairy. No sugar. No salt. He was going to get healthy. Live forever. He'd lost control of Mary's life; he wasn't going to lose control of his."

Sitting back down at the table, Milton added, "But he did. He exercised every day. Walked miles. He used to be a big man, but before the stroke, he weighed just over a hundred and twenty pounds. He read constantly, all these books on nutrition, health, additives in the food, the toxins all around us. He came to the conclusion that everything we eat is polluted in some major way. All this occurred just as Mary started to get better, as she began to want to go out again, have dinner in a restaurant, see friends, go to a movie, live a little. John demanded that they stay home and eat wheat grass. So much of the way we socialize is based around food, and John wouldn't give an inch. This may sound far out, but I think my brother was so deeply into control, he lost his ability to enjoy life. Everything was a threat. The air. The water. He told Bernice she couldn't stay at the house if she wore hair spray. He threw out all his aftershave and deodorant, made Mary get rid of her perfume. Before the stroke, he was just about starving himself. " Bowing his head, Milton said, "It was a nightmare. Something had to give."

It did sound like a horror story, Sophie thought, and yet she understood John's motivation. With his wife ill, possibly dying, he must have felt powerless. In similar situations, other people might have turned to religion or meditation or booze. John simply chose another route, one that on the surface might have looked like a good choice, except that he went too far.

Milton finished his beer, then wiped his mouth with a napkin. Stroking his beard for a moment, he said, "I think I better hit the sack. Would you mind putting the food away?"

"Not at all," said Sophie. She followed him into the living room, where he pointed out the guest bedroom and the bathroom, telling her that she would find fresh towels in the closet next to the sink. He also told her that several clean bathrobes were kept in the closet in the guest room, and any toiletries she might need could be found in the top of the bureau.

"Unless the roof blows off," he added, already on his way up the stairs, "I intend to sleep through the storm. Make yourself at home, Sophie. See you in the morning."

After finishing her dinner, she rearranged the refrigerator so she could stuff everything back inside. Selecting a lemon bar from the kitchen counter, she drifted into the living room and turned on the TV. The best way to keep track of the weather was by tuning in to a local station. After learning that a thunderstorm was supposed to hit the area within the next hour, she decided to call Bram. She wasn't supposed to be home until ten, so he probably wasn't worrying yet, unless he'd heard the weather report.

"I'm still in Rose Hill," said Sophie, as soon as he'd picked up the phone.

"Thank God," said Bram, sounding relieved. "You've heard about the storm then."

"I'm spending the night."

"Good. Did you find a decent motel?"

"No, I'm staying at Bernice's parents' house. They have a guest bedroom." She could hear glasses rattling. "Are you eating?"

"I'm mixing myself a Campari and soda."

"Ah." Being privy to his habits, she knew that this was a cocktail. Dinner would follow.

"I'm having a salad sent up from the Fountain Grill."

Last fall Sophie's parents had retired, leaving the ownership of the Maxfield Plaza, downtown St. Paul's most historic hotel, in Sophie's capable hands. A few months later, Sophie and Bram had moved into an apartment at the top of the north tower. It had taken Sophie the better part of the past year to feel she had a handle on the day-to-day running of the Maxfield. Thankfully, her parents had owned the hotel since Sophie was fourteen. She'd worked the front desk when she was in high school, so she wasn't a complete novice. When the position of restaurant review editor opened up at the *Times Register* last spring, Bram was initially against it. He thought Sophie was crazy to take on a second job, even if it was only part-time. But Sophie felt confident she was up to the task. As it turned out, her son, Rudy, was hired by the paper to be her assistant, giving her the best of both worlds. She not only kept her hand in at the hotel, but she also had the chance to work with her son doing something she loved.

After some initial grumbling, Bram finally had to admit that Sophie seemed to be handling the two jobs with remarkable finesse. And he adored living at the hotel. They both did. Not only did they admire the bold art deco architecture—which Sophie's father had worked hard to restore and maintain—but it quickly became apparent that they both appreciated having two exceptional restaurants and a famous theater bar on the premises. If Sophie didn't feel like cooking, they'd simply order in, or dine out. They never had to brave the winter winds or the summer swelter to have a delicious gourmet meal.

"How's Bernice's dad?" asked Bram.

"Better, although everyone's being pretty guarded."

"What time will you be home in the morning?"

"I've got a meeting at the paper at one, but I need to do some work in my office at the hotel first. Probably around eleven."

"If I'm not home, call me at the station to let me know you're back safely."

"Will do," said Sophie. "Say, how are you feeling?"

"Fine, why?"

"No reason," she said, deciding not to pursue the grilled cheese sandwich debacle. He was eating a salad tonight, and that was good news. "While I've got your attention, honey, your birthday's coming up soon. Got any ideas what you might like?" She could hear the door-bell ring.

"I'd like to have dinner."

"Okay, we'll talk about it later. I love you, sweetheart."

"Ditto, babe. See you anon."

After saying good-bye and slipping her cell phone back into her shoulder bag, Sophie rose from the couch and stepped up to the picture window overlooking the front yard. The sky had darkened almost to night during the last few minutes, and the breeze had died to a faint whisper. It was the quiet before the storm.

As she stood gazing through the heavy yellow twilight at the homes across the street, she noticed a hefty-looking man on the opposite boulevard. He was smoking a cigarette and leaning against an elm. In his dark suit, dark shirt and white tie, narrow-brimmed fedora and dark-rimmed glasses, he seemed completely out of place—sort of like finding one of the Blues Brothers in a lumber camp. Most disconcerting of all was the fact that he was staring at the house. Sophie supposed he could see her in the window, especially since the lights were on inside the living room. If so, he betrayed no awareness of her. He simply stood quietly, his hand rising with the cigarette, then falling away from his lips. Under other circumstances, she might have gone out for a short walk, or sat on the front steps and watched the storm approach, but the man's presence put her off.

Checking her watch, she saw that it was going on eight-forty. She wasn't tired, and she didn't feel like watching TV. Closing the front drapes, she sat down on one of the recliner rockers and spotted what she thought was a bag of knitting next to her on the floor. Closer examination revealed that a bunch of old photographs had been stuffed inside. Instead of leaving them where they should have probably stayed, she picked the photos up and began flipping through them. Most were old snapshots of John and Mary's kids, some at the beach, some in front of a Christmas tree, and a few with what must have been grandparents.

The last photo was a picture of a young man and a young woman standing next to a garage. Sophie recognized Mary Washburn immediately. Oddly, the man looked familiar too. Turning the photo over, she saw that someone had written, "Beauty and the Beast. June, 1959. First anniversary" on the back. Since Sophie had never met John Washburn, she flipped the photo over and studied it for a moment. John was slightly taller than Mary. He was also thin, wearing tight jeans and a white T-shirt under a wrinkled short-sleeved shirt. One arm was draped over Mary's shoulder, while his right hand was stuffed into the pocket of his jeans. He had a James Dean look about him. Squinty-eyed. Long sideburns and a slight pompadour. He might not be as handsome as James Dean, but the picture made him look every bit as sexy.

And then it struck her. John Washburn was the spitting image of another man, someone she'd known as a child.

"Morgan Walters," she whispered, feeling a prickle of excitement as she said the name. Morgan had lived up by Trout Lake, on the Iron Range, during the sixties. Every now and then, her grandparents used to drive out to his house in the country to buy fresh eggs. Sophie was only thirteen when they'd first met—a long time ago, though she'd never forgotten the encounter.

Morgan Walters owned a motorcycle. One summer afternoon, while her grandparents were inside the house talking to his wife, Morgan offered to give Sophie a ride. She still remembered the flush of excitement when she climbed on behind him, gingerly taking hold of his waist. It was the first truly sexual experience she'd ever had. In many ways, she still thought of him as the sexiest man she'd ever met.

When her grandparents came out of the house and found her gone, they were apparently quite worried; but as soon as they roared back into the front yard, everyone laughed, all anxiety forgotten. Morgan put everyone at ease with his disarming smile and his naturalness.

As Sophie sat in the chair now, thinking back about

Morgan, she grew increasingly confused. She knew that John Washburn and Morgan Walters couldn't be the same man. And yet, they looked identical. Sophie held the photo closer, scrutinizing every detail. And that's when she saw it. The tattoo on John Washburn's arm. It was partially obscured by the shirt he was wearing, but a small piece of it was visible. It was a snake, the very same snake she remembered staring at when she was riding behind Morgan all those years ago.

"Impossible," she whispered, resting her fingers on her temple. "Totally, completely, utterly impossible."

March, 1956

Dear Gilbert:

Hey, man! God, what a fucking mess, huh? I know we were supposed to meet up at the bus station in Terre Haute, but when I saw the cops pick you up outside, I took off. I waited around in my hotel room for more than a week. When I figured the coast was clear, I hiked back to the bus station, grabbed the bags from the locker, and hopped a bus for Chicago. But I followed your trial. Every day. I couldn't think about anything else. And then that guard died. What a nightmare. Man, I'm so sorry. Neither one of us wanted that. If there's anything I can do for you, you can reach me through my mom.

You're probably wondering what the take was. They lied about it at the trial, but that's bankers for you. Still, it was more than we ever hoped for. Two hundred thou. I feel guilty though. I'm out, free and clear, and you're in that awful hole. But what can I do?

I promise, I'll keep in touch. I figure, for now, I'll head north. See where it takes me. That money's got blood on *it, man. I don't even like to be in the same room with it. So much for our stupid dreams.*

    J. D.

6

By eleven, the worst of the storm was over. Bernice sat by her father's bedside, her gaze occasionally drifting out the window, watching the lightning fade in the east. She'd stayed late so that her mother could take a short nap. But the nap had stretched to almost three hours now, and she was still sleeping so peacefully, Bernice didn't have the heart to wake her. Her mother had seemed terribly anxious that somebody from the family sit with her father tonight. If he woke up, she wanted to know about it right away.

A nurse had come in around ten-thirty to check vital signs. While she was adjusting the drip on the bag, she mentioned that a tornado had hit Milroy, a small town about fifteen miles away. Thankfully, Rose Hill had been spared the worst of it. The last thing her parents needed was for their home of over forty years to be flattened by an angry, churning sky.

When Bernice was a child, probably no more than three, a storm had come through town late one afternoon and taken the screened porch off the side of the house. She didn't remember much about it, but she did recall her father grabbing her and carrying her down the steps to the basement as the back door burst open in the wind. Of course, she'd seen pictures of the destroyed porch, but her memory was of her father and his strong arms.

There were so many memories. The garage had always been her dad's special domain. He loved to wash the car in the drive, make the chrome shine and the wide, white-sidewall tires gleam. He used a chamois cloth to dry the car off, then he'd squeeze out the chamois and hang it over the fence to dry. He was careful never to let it touch the ground because it might pick up a small stone that could scratch the paint. Since he was a salesman, his car was very important to him. He called it a "company car." Every few years, he was issued a new one.

When Bernice got a little older, she would travel with her dad a few times a summer. He knew all the best bakeries in all the small towns. The best cafes. The movie theaters. In Rice Lake, Wisconsin, he'd bought her a ukulele and taught her how to play a few simple chords. From that point on, they sang together in the car, windows open, sailing over the country roads and past the corn fields, eating sugar cookies out of white bakery bags, stopping for gas and soda. Ever since, whenever Bernice caught the powerful scent of a skunk—or drank grape pop—she would think of those carefree summers. She still remembered the first time she'd eaten prime rib. It was in Red Wing at the St. James Hotel. She had her first lobster in the rustic dining room at Lutsen's, her first taste of beer in Thief River Falls on a hot summer evening.

Plato never wanted to travel with their dad. He always had more important things going on. Bernice couldn't re-

member what any of them were. Mainly, they were ex-
cuses. John Washburn expected a great deal from his
son. Plato once confided in her that he'd felt the heavy
hand of that expectation his entire life. Because of it, he
seemed ill at ease in their dad's presence. It was a sad
commentary on how boys were raised, but for Bernice,
whose only pressure was to be a good person, the time
she spent with her dad was golden.

Even though her father was what everyone considered
a straight arrow, Bernice had seen another side of him.
Since her dad called on drug stores, he'd made friends
with a number of druggists. Several of his friends in Rose
Hill regularly bought pills from him—mostly tranquil-
izers for their wives. He got the pills at wholesale prices
from his druggist buddies. It was all illegal, of course, but
Bernice figured her dad viewed it as nothing more than a
simple favor for a pal.

Her dad also kept a BB gun hidden in the garage.
Every now and then, he'd dig it out and the two of them
would take turns shooting at a telephone pole across the
street. Even as a kid, Bernice saw the potential danger.
Behind the pole were a bunch of bushes. And behind the
bushes was a yard. One stray BB at the wrong moment
could have put out an eye or hurt an animal. And yet, her
father never seemed to think about that. Not that Bernice and her dad weren't damn good at hitting the pole.
They rarely missed. She loved the sound of the BB hitting
and sinking into the soft wood.

So many memories. So much love. And now her father
lay in a hospital bed, fighting for his life. Bernice was just
about to get up and adjust the pillow behind his head
when she noticed his eyes flutter ever so slightly and then

open. She was so excited, she forgot about her mother's instructions to wake her.

Instead, she got up and bent down close to her father's ear, hoping he could hear her. "Dad. I'm here. It's Bernice."

His eyes moved to the side.

"Oh, Dad, I'm so happy you're awake. I've missed you so much."

The right side of his mouth moved.

He's smiling at me, she thought. Or, at least, he was trying to. "Don't exert yourself."

"Pah . . . " he said, his voice immensely weak.

"I don't understand," she said, her brow furrowing.

He closed his eyes, then tried again. "Pah . . . pah."

"Pah," she repeated, shaking her head.

She watched in amazement as he lifted his right hand off the bed.

"Pen," he said, his voice clearer this time.

Oh my god, she thought. He wants a pen and paper. He's trying to communicate. She quickly dug through her bag until she came up with a pencil and a notepad. Placing the paper carefully under his hand, she helped him get a feel for the pencil.

Staring up at the ceiling, her father scratched,

i dying

"No, no, no," said Bernice, kissing his forehead. "No. You're getting better." Again, she watched his hand move.

love you

Oh, God, her heart was breaking. "I love you too, Dad. So much. Please, you've got to believe me. You're going to get better. I just know it. You can't give up."

don be afraid

"I *am* afraid," said Bernice. "I'm afraid you'll stop fighting."

The pencil fell out of his hand. His eyes closed.

"Dad, listen to me. You're strong. You always have been. Stronger than all of us put together. You're the best part of this family. We can't lose you. Stay with me, Dad." She started to cry. "I need you now more than ever. I've done something . . . something I haven't told anyone about. And I'm so confused." She held her father's hand, squeezing it, trying to get him to respond.

After almost a minute, his eyes opened again. "Peh . . . " he whispered.

"The pencil? You want the pencil again?"

He gave a slow blink.

"Sure. Oh, Dad. Don't give up." She positioned the pencil in his hand.

This time he wrote—

kiby runbec

"What?" she said, staring at the words. She didn't understand. "Do you mean . . . Kirby Runbeck? The man who died in the bombing?"

At the same moment, one of the night doctors entered the room carrying a chart.

John Washburn kept his eyes focused on his daughter.

"What do we have here?" asked the doctor, seeing the pencil and the notepad. He stepped up to the bed and watched John write:

i Kil him   bomb tel poice   now

7

The next morning, Sophie made it to the hospital by eight. Milton had left her a note propped against the salt shaker on the kitchen table explaining that he'd set off for the hospital shortly after seven, and to help herself to anything in the refrigerator. Since no one else in the Washburn family seemed to be around, and the coffeepot was already on, Sophie poured herself a cup, ate a piece of pumpkin bread, and was on her way.

Last night's thunderstorm had blown in some cooler, dryer weather. After nearly a month of unbearable heat and humidity, Sophie welcomed the change. On the way to the hospital, she turned off the air-conditioning in her car and opened the windows all the way down. The breeze felt wonderful as it ruffled her short, blond hair.

Rose Hill was bisected by the Cottonwood River, placing St. Matthew's Medical Center on the south end of town. After parking in a lot across the street, Sophie entered the hospital and headed up to the fourth floor. She couldn't leave without saying good-bye to Bernice, nor without an update on her father's condition.

Before bed last night, Sophie had examined all the family photos scattered around the house, framed or otherwise. There were lots of pictures of Plato and

Bernice at various stages in their lives, a professional wedding shot of Plato and his wife, a wealth of pictures of their twin boys, and a recent professionally done portrait of John and Mary, but not a trace of the young John Washburn. The conundrum mystified her. Just before leaving the house this morning, she'd done a bad thing— to paraphrase Martha Stewart. She'd taken one last look at the snapshot of Mary and John Washburn on their first anniversary, but instead of putting it back in the knitting basket where she found it, she'd slipped it into the back pocket of her jeans. She knew she had no business stealing a family photo, and yet John's likeness to Morgan Walters had been too puzzling to let it drop.

Stepping off the elevator on the fourth floor of the hospital, Sophie found a crowd standing outside John Washburn's room, talking in a low buzz. She approached cautiously, noticing that the group included doctors, nurses, a police officer, and most of the members of the Washburn family. She could tell by everyone's serious expression that whatever had happened wasn't good news.

Bernice was standing between her mother and Plato, listening intently as Milton spoke quietly but heatedly to the officer. Since nobody had noticed Sophie's approach, she moved unobserved into the waiting room to pour herself a cup of coffee. She might as well hear firsthand what was going on.

"You can't possibly believe my brother had anything to do with that man's murder," said Milton, his hands rising in frustration to his hips. "He's been an upstanding citizen of this town for over forty years! Besides, he just had a stroke. He's not in his right mind."

The young officer rubbed his square jaw thoughtfully.

"I'll admit, I've never come across anything quite like this before."

"This is ridiculous," muttered Plato. "Utterly absurd. Tell me, Doug, were you planning to take my dad away in handcuffs?"

"No. But I thought maybe I should put a guard on his door. Just in case."

"Oh, right," said Plato. "I forgot. He's a dangerous man. Before you know it, he could be hopping a plane to Switzerland." The sarcasm appeared to be lost on the cop.

"I don't think a guard will be necessary," said one of the doctors, folding his arms over his chest. "I can assure you, John Washburn isn't going anywhere."

Doug, the cop, nodded. "Yeah, 'spose not. But the fact remains, he admitted to a murder."

Sophie nearly spilled her coffee.

"I'll bet a good lawyer—hell, even a crappy one— could get that confession thrown out of court." Milton wasn't even trying to hide his disgust.

Neither was Mary. "You get out of here now, Doug. Go keep the peace somewhere else. My husband could be dying in there." She nodded to the closed door. "We should be with him, not wasting our time standing out in the hall talking a lot of nonsense."

She must know him, Sophie thought. She was treating him more like a son than an officer of the law.

Looking around, Doug lowered his voice, and said, "You can't talk to me like that, Mrs. Washburn. You're not my teacher anymore."

Sophie shifted her gaze to Bernice. All during the conversation, she'd been silently biting her lower lip.

"There's no way I will allow my patient to be interrogated until he's stronger," the doctor continued. "You do what you have to do, but I can't allow you or anyone else from the sheriff's office into his room."

Looking frustrated, the cop removed his hat and scratched his blond crew cut. "Okay, okay. Maybe I better run this one by Sheriff Foley, just as soon as he gets back from his fishing trip."

"You do that," said Plato, shoving his hands into the pockets of his wrinkled, tan suit coat, the same one he'd been wearing yesterday.

Just then, a rangy young woman in black jeans and a red blazer stepped off the elevator and strode purposefully toward the group. Her dark brown hair was piled haphazardly on top of her head and fastened with two red plastic clips. The silvertipped cowboy boots she was wearing added three inches to her already tall frame.

"What the freaking hell are you doing here?" demanded Plato, moving away from the group to intercept her.

The woman's blue eyes were unusually wide-set and pale. "We just got word at the *Gazette* about your dad. I'm covering the Runbeck homicide, so Byron sent me over to get a statement from the family."

"You think I want this in my paper?" Plato exploded. "Have you lost your mind?"

"Keep your voice down," cautioned his mother.

"Tell Byron he needs to run everything about the Runbeck homicide past me before he prints it. Got it?"

The woman flashed her eyes flirtatiously at the officer. "Hey, Doug."

"Hey, Viv."

"*Is that understood?*" Plato fixed her with a lethal gaze.

Viv pulled out a stick of spearmint gum. As she un-wrapped it, she said, "Got it, Chief. Except, you know how word gets around a small town. If the paper doesn't cover all the news that's fit to print, isn't it going to look kind of suspicious? Like . . . maybe the publisher is trying to hide something?"

"Leave," said Plato. "Now."

After she'd gone, Bernice spied Sophie in the waiting room. She whispered something to her mother, then joined Sophie by the coffeepot.

"I suppose you've figured out what's going on by now," said Bernice, looking tired and ragged.

"Your dad confessed to a murder?"

"He can't talk, but he wrote a note to that effect late last night. Apparently, he wrote essentially the same thing yesterday afternoon, but my mother insisted on throwing it away. She also failed to tell me about it. That's my family in a nutshell. Instead of addressing the problem, they ignore it and hope it goes away. We didn't have that option last night because one of Dad's doctors happened to be in the room when he confessed."

"I'm so sorry," said Sophie.

"Thanks. But it's all a stupid misunderstanding. It has to be. My father isn't a murderer."

For the next few minutes, Bernice filled Sophie in on the details. Kirby Runbeck had been a handyman in Rose Hill ever since he retired from his job as manager at Bjorke Hardware ten years ago. He was in his mid-seventies, he was married, he had no children, and he was notorious for cheating people if he thought he could get away with it. Still, he was good at what he did, so he never went without work. He'd repaired the garage door opener for her parents several months ago, but

Bernice insisted that, other than minor house repairs, Kirby wasn't the kind of man her parents would ever associate with.

"How did he die?" asked Sophie.

"A car bomb—or, in this case, a truck bomb."

"Yikes."

"Yes, I know. Things like that just don't happen around here."

"Do the police have any leads?"

"They do now. That's why the deputy sheriff is here."

"But before your father confessed?"

"None that I'm aware of."

Sophie could read the anxiety in Bernice's eyes. "I'm sure it will all get sorted out. How is your dad doing this morning?"

"He woke up when Milton and Plato arrived, but he's been sleeping most of the time."

"Do the doctors have any more news?"

"They're guarded, but they think he's going to make it. They're giving him all sorts of drugs. He seems to have some paralysis on his left side, but he can move his right arm and his right leg. With therapy, the doctors think he may regain full use of his left side, too."

"Then, he's completely coherent?"

Bernice lowered her head. "I don't know. For Dad's sake, I hope so. But then, if he's in his right mind, why would he confess to a murder? It doesn't make sense. I'm sure our family lawyer will want to put his own spin on it."

"Does your lawyer normally handle homicides?"

"Heavens, no. I doubt he's *ever* handled a homicide."

"Then, you might want to find someone else. A good defense attorney is worth his or her weight in gold."

"That might be easier said than done. Sam Sullivan is a personal friend of the family. It's a typical small-town problem. On some level, everybody knows everybody. Mom probably thinks Sam would be insulted if he got replaced before he even had a chance to work the case. Fact is, he probably would be. And then it would end up being hard for our family to interact with Sam's family after that. Nola Sullivan is one of Mom's best friends. They're in the same garden club. They play bridge together every Wednesday afternoon. It just gets so complicated."

Sophie remembered now why her grandparents had hated small-town life. Checking the time, she said, "I'm sorry I can't stay longer. I've got to head back to Minneapolis. I take it you're planning on staying?"

"I can't leave now," said Bernice. "Not with everything so up in the air."

"Did you even come home last night?"

"No, I stayed at the hospital."

Sophie shook her head. "You take it easy, kiddo. If there's anything I can do—"

Bernice smiled. "You're a good friend."

"See you back at the paper?"

"Right. I'll be in touch with you soon about the meat loaf contest."

They said their strained good-byes to each other in the hall.

Just after lunch, a nurse came into John Washburn's hospital room and told Bernice she had a visitor.

Bernice didn't have a clue who it could be, but she excused herself and stepped outside.

The visitor, a fiftyish-looking man in a black suit,

black silk shirt, and white tie, sat in the waiting room, his narrow-brimmed fedora resting in his lap. Hurrying across the hall, Bernice blurted, "What are you doing here?"

Patting the chair next to him, the man said, "Can't you guess?" When he opened his mouth, his New York accent fell out like a brick hitting a dirt floor.

"But you promised. You said—"

"I changed my mind."

She stared at him for a moment, her heart thundering inside her chest. Finally, sitting down two seats away, she whispered, "You've got to leave. You can't be here."

"Why?"

"I don't want my parents to see you. I don't want them to know what happened."

"I already talked to your father."

"What?" Her eyes grew large.

"We met last week."

Now she was really thrown. "Last week? You were here last week?"

"I've been in Rose Hill for ten glorious, fun-filled days. What do you people do around here for fun? Watch the grass grow?" He leaned closer to Bernice and lowered his voice. "Look, just so you know, I called your parents' house last Wednesday and your dad agreed to meet me at this funky health food restaurant on Myrtle. Sprouts and tofu, the smell of B vitamins wafting through the air. You know the kind of place. It's just off Main."

"There's only one health food restaurant in town," she said testily.

"So sue me for explaining."

"What did you tell him?"

"Everything."

"Angelo!"

"I'm a bastard. What can I say?"

She dropped her head in her hands.

"I came all this way to get your attention. Do I have it, Bernice? Do I?" He cracked his knuckles.

"I can't have this conversation right now."

"I heard about your father's confession. It's all over the hospital."

"It's a mistake."

"What the hell. Mistakes happen. You made a big one in New York, babe. There I was, just a nice guy, trying to help you out with your book, show you the club scene. What did you call it? Cafe society." He laughed. "How could I, a simple good Samaritan, predict the future?"

"You're harassing me."

"I am? Sorry."

"You're not sorry at all."

"You're right, I'm not."

"I can't stay here and argue with you. I've got to get back to my father's room."

"Fine. But I'm not leaving town."

Rising, she said, "Stay away from me."

"No can do, doll." Placing his hat carefully on his head, he looked up at her and smiled. "See you around."

8

Sunday mornings at the Runbecks had followed a certain pattern over the past few years. Because Cora's sight had been failing due to cataracts on both eyes, anything that required extended reading had become Kirby's responsibility.

Cora kicked herself now about the surgery. If she'd only known it would be that easy, she would have done it years ago. But all her women friends had warned her to stay as far away from the doctor's office as possible. They told her horror story after horror story about cataract operations gone bad. Unleashed laser beams cutting off the tips of patients' noses. Eyeballs falling out. Things they'd read in the *National Inquisitor*, stories sandwiched in between articles on babies born with no heads and aliens visiting the Vatican. Cora never read the magazine herself, but she liked to know what was happening in the world. As a result of her friends' warnings, her life had become more and more restricted. And the Sunday morning *Times Register* was one of the casualties.

After trudging out to the mailbox to retrieve the extra-large Minneapolis paper, Kirby and Cora would sit at the kitchen table. Over pancakes and bacon, Kirby would read the highlights. First came the headlines on the front page. Anything that struck Kirby's fancy would be read in its entirety. If something struck Cora's interest and not Kirby's, he would grumble his way through the article, paraphrasing and skipping sections so they could move on to something he thought was more important. Cora hated him for his selfishness. There was no other word for it. She'd convinced herself that she loved him, but in the past few days she'd realized she never had.

The funeral had been a blur, but thankfully, her women friends had taken care of everything. After the service at First Lutheran, they'd brought food over to the house and encouraged her to eat, amazed that such a skinny little lady could pack away so much fried chicken. Cora had tried to work up some genuine tears for the graveside service, but all she really felt was regret. Regret at a life spent with a man she didn't even like. Secretly, she'd dreamed for years of a long widowhood. She would lie in bed at night listening to Kirby snore, and pray that he would go to his reward before she did. Even a year's peace and quiet would seem heaven-sent.

It was hard to talk about Kirby now without people getting suspicious. Everyone expected Cora to be in mourning, to cry and moan about how much she missed him. The truth was, she hardly knew he was gone. He had never really talked all that much. Oh, he did the grocery shopping and fixed little things around the house when they needed it, but he'd never been much company. That's what Cora's cat, Winthrop, was for. She doted on him, which made Kirby mad. Winthrop was a little Russian blue, with a sweet disposition and an even sweeter face. Most of the time, Kirby was either out in the garage working on one of his projects or sitting in front of the

TV with a beer in his hand. Cora thought Kirby was a cold-blooded reptile. Now that she could see again, being on her own was nothing short of bliss.

Cora had met Kirby when she was seventeen. Her mother had been dead for many years by then. Cora had lived with her father and four younger siblings on a farm in southern Minnesota. For all practical purposes, she was a mother to her brothers and sisters, and a servant to her father. When the Lutheran church in town got knocked flat by a tornado, several young men came down from the Cities to help rebuild it. The pastor had asked Cora's father if he had a spare room where one of the young men could stay. Kirby moved in the following weekend.

It wasn't exactly love at first sight, though Cora was definitely attracted to him. Kirby was young and strong, and back then, she figured his silence meant that he was deep. It took her many years to discover that she'd mistaken dull for deep, but by then they were married and living in Rose Hill. Fact was, when she was seventeen, she was sick to death of being her father's indentured slave, and Kirby offered a way out. Only problem was, she realized too late that she'd simply given up one form of slavery for another. At least with her dad, she didn't have to sleep with him. Cora suspected that Kirby wasn't very good in the lovemaking department. They'd never had kids. Cora wanted to find out what the problem was, but Kirby refused to go to a doctor. So, they remained childless, a source of great sadness for her.

When it came to life in general, Cora's expectations had never been high. Maybe that had been her problem all along.

It still bothered her that Kirby had talked about

divorce before he died. The nerve of a man like him wanting to divorce a woman like her. If anyone was going to demand a divorce, she should have done it. When it came to marriage, she always felt that men got the better end of the deal. All she knew was that she would never tell a living soul what he'd said. What would her women friends think? Cora assumed the old goat had a roll in the hay every now and then with that awful Mabel Bjornstaad. Mabel was the town whore. Then again, it was fine with Cora, especially if it kept him away from her. But divorce?

Cora was four years younger than Kirby. A spring chicken by some standards. Sure, she had hearing problems, and the cataracts, but she could still enjoy life. She walked a mile or two every day. Loved to garden. Maybe, down deep in her soul, she did understand what Kirby was talking about the day he died. Wanting some passion in his life, needing to kick up his heels a little before the end. Now that Kirby was gone, maybe she should take a cruise. Except, she'd scrutinized the bankbook the other day. Kirby's social security would come to her until she died, but there wasn't much extra money to pursue the good life. After years of scrimping and saving, shouldn't there be some reward?

"Divorce," she said, spitting the word out like it was a piece of gristle. "Ridiculous." She was sitting on the living room couch, the cat perched behind her, the Sunday Minneapolis *Times Register* resting on her lap, the television blissfully off.

For the second wonderful weekend in a row, Cora could start with the food section instead of the front page. She felt guilty for not feeling more guilty. Kirby was gone and someone should be sad.

"Mabel can handle that," she mumbled, snapping the food section out in front of her.

Cora had to squint with her right eye through her bifocals to see the small print, but it felt liberating not to have to rely on someone else to read to her anymore. Kirby never had time for the recipes. It was one of the small ways in which he liked to lord it over her. What a pathetic old man. She stopped for a moment and tried to think of his good qualities. Under the circumstances, it seemed the Christian thing to do. Acrimony wasn't God's way. After a couple of minutes, she gave up, shrugged her shoulders, and went back to the paper.

"Look at this," she whispered to Winthrop, finding an announcement in bold print about a statewide recipe contest.

!!!! RECIPE CONTEST !!!!

Do you love meat loaf as much as the editors at the *Times Register*? Everyone in Minnesota is invited to send a favorite meat loaf recipe to the paper. New or old, it doesn't matter. A first, second and third prize will be awarded on September 15. Winners will spend a weekend at the historic Maxfield Plaza in downtown St. Paul. They will be wined and dined at some of the finest restaurants in the Twin Cities, and will be featured with their winning creations on WTWN's *Good Morning with Bailey Brown*. Only one week is left, so make sure you get your recipes to us soon. Submissions must be postmarked by Friday, August 26.

The gears in Cora's mind started to spin. "I've got the best meat loaf recipe this side of paradise," she said, growing increasingly excited. This was just what she'd been looking for. A free way to enjoy life. A trip to the

Cities, a couple of nights at a fabulous hotel, great food, and fame and fortune on that morning TV show. Her women friends would die of envy.

"This was made to order!" she declared, rising from the couch and walking into the kitchen.

Winthrop followed.

After pouring herself another cup of coffee, she opened one of the top cupboard doors. All she had to do was retrieve her old, wooden recipe box with the duck decals on the front, find the recipe for which she'd won a blue ribbon at the county fair when she was sixteen, and send it off in the morning mail. She had no doubt that she'd win first prize.

But . . . the recipe box wasn't in the cupboard. "It's always been *right there*," she said out loud, her anger building. What had that old man done with it? She hadn't used it in several years, but that didn't mean Kirby had the right to move it or—horrors—throw it away. Her mother had given it to her on her eighth birthday!

"There was always room for your useless junk, but something as important to me as my recipe box—" It hurt so bad, she couldn't even finish the sentence. Without the box, she knew she wouldn't get the recipe right. She'd forget something. Or she'd get the measurements wrong. If she was going to win that contest, she had to find that box.

Even from his grave, Kirby was reaching out to thwart her.

Cora felt like cussing up a storm. If she'd been a weaker woman, she might have let fly, but Cora wasn't raised to use that kind of language. That was for tramps like Mabel Bjornstaad. Besides, Winthrop had never seen her behave like that and she didn't want to upset him. He was such a quiet, sensitive little fellow, sitting on the kitchen counter and licking the edge of a honey jar. Opening all the cupboard doors, Cora stepped back and peered over the top of her bifocals. Her heart leapt inside her chest when she spied it way up on the top shelf. The stepladder had been in the garage when the bomb went off, but a kitchen chair would do just fine. In a moment, the box had been plucked from its resting place and Cora was sitting at the kitchen table, staring for the first time in years at the decals on the front. Her mother had bought the box in the thirties at the local five-and-dime. She'd placed the duck decals on it herself. Cora couldn't work up much emotion about Kirby's death, but she still teared when she thought of her mom. Cora had used the wooden box all during high school. Some of the recipes inside came from her mother, some from her grandmother, some from her teachers, and some Cora had copied out of magazines. But the meat loaf recipe was all her own.

Opening the cover, Cora gazed at a yellowed piece of paper she'd stuck to the inside a thousand years ago. It said, simply: Cora Pauline Anderson. Rooms 3 & 5, Foods, Mrs. Hayes and Miss Brown.

Flipping through the cards, she found the meat loaf recipe almost immediately. But she couldn't stop there. She was too intrigued by her walk down memory lane. Philadelphia Dip for Chips. Lefse. Ice Box Cookies. Her grandmother's famous Nuts Cookies, and Floating Island. A favorite recipe for Angel Pie, and Beet Pickles. Her mother's favorite fish chowder, buttery and thick with potatoes and fresh corn off the cob. Everything came back to her with the patina of childhood attached— that innocent time before her mother had died.

At the back of the box, Cora found something she hadn't anticipated. It was a bankbook, and not one she recognized. A folded sheet of typing paper was attached to it with a paper clip. She figured it must be one that had expired years ago, but just to make sure, she opened it.

"Dear God," she said, her hand rising to cover her mouth. She stared at the numbers in utter disbelief. The bankbook was for a savings account that had been taken out in the name of Kirby Runbeck less then three months ago. Two deposits were recorded. The starting deposit was fifty thousand dollars. The second deposit had been made four days before he died. Another fifty thousand dollars.

"What on earth?" How had Kirby gotten his hands on that kind of money? And then it struck her. That's why he wanted a divorce. The little worm was planning to take the money and run away with that hussy, Mabel Bjornstaad. Sharing his good fortune with his wife wasn't part of the plan.

Thank the Good Lord there was justice in this world. The money would come to her now. "We're rich!" cried Cora, picking up Winthrop and hugging him to her chest. The cat seemed unimpressed. He wanted to get back to the honey jar.

After letting him go, she stared at the balance for a few more seconds. Only then did she notice a withdrawal at the bottom. Two days before his death, Kirby had withdrawn the entire hundred thousand dollars and closed the account.

"You bastard!" she thundered, pounding her fist on the table and causing the coffee cup to jump.

But what had happened to the money? If it wasn't in the bank, it had to be somewhere. Oh no, Cora thought. Her heart nearly stopped. Had it been in his truck? Or the garage? She closed her eyes and tried to think it through. Where would a secretive, naturally suspicious, not terribly intelligent man like Kirby hide a small fortune? Cora felt certain the place he'd pick would be absolutely secure. The truck and the garage didn't fit that criteria. No, it had to be somewhere else.

Pulling off the piece of typing paper clipped to the back of the bankbook, she unfolded it.

"What's this?" she muttered, looking at the lines her husband had drawn on the page. It was a map. "Sixteen paces due north of the Devil's Tree. East four paces. South twenty-two paces." What on earth was the Devil's Tree? Kirby had obviously hidden something there because he'd used an X to mark the spot.

"You greedy old pirate," she whispered. "That's where the money is."

It had been Kirby's tragic fate to die before he could spend his fortune.

"What a dirty shame," said Cora, an evil smile pulling at the corners of her mouth.

9

Sophie had a feeling Bram wasn't exactly thrilled to hear that she'd decided to accompany him on the drive up to Grand Rapids for his Monday afternoon radio show. For Bram it was a business trip. He wanted to leave early Monday morning, do the show in the afternoon, and be home for a late dinner on Monday night. Sophie convinced him to leave Sunday afternoon and combine the work with a little R and R, saying it would be good for them both.

Just over a year ago, Sophie's cousin Sulo had bought a summer cabin on Pokegama Lake. Since Sulo was forever telling her that she should come up and spend the weekend, Sophie insisted that this was the perfect opportunity. They could take out the houseboat. Enjoy a little twilight ride around the lake.

"You mean spend the evening swatting mosquitoes," Bram grunted. He wasn't known for his love of the great outdoors.

They'd just passed the town of Garrison on their way around the northern part of Lake Mille Lacs.

"While you do your live broadcast from the Itasca county fair," said Sophie, turning off the music they'd been listening to, "I'll spend the time scouting out the local cafes for possible review." Just because that wasn't the real reason she wanted to visit Grand Rapids didn't stop her from using it as a ruse.

"You're planning to make me eat some godawful small-town cafe food, aren't you?" muttered Bram, sulking. "Breaded pork chops. Chopped iceberg lettuce with that red, sickly sweet French dressing. Little Jell-O salads covered in Cool Whip. Canned green beans. And everything, absolutely everything else covered in cheese or deep fried." He shivered at the thought.

"Has anyone ever told you you're a snob?"

"Frequently. And I accept the title . . . with my usual grace. I repeat, I don't like eating in greasy spoons."

"You had a greasy grilled cheese last Thursday, before your show."

"I did not. I had a salad."

"You never eat salads for lunch."

"I am a man of many surprises."

"But you said the sandwich gave you indigestion. That's why you were popping Tums. And hey, don't change the subject. Why do you assume a small-town cafe would be a greasy spoon? Maybe they have someone in the kitchen who's an artist, a culinary wizard. You love good home cooking."

"Only when it's served by a restaurant with at least two stars."

She threw up her hands in disgust. The fact was, she probably wouldn't have time to visit the cafes anyway. She intended to spend as much of the afternoon as possible digging up information on Morgan Walters, the man who was the spitting image of John Washburn—right down to his tattoo.

Sophie had failed to fill Bram in about that little detail

because she knew he'd think she was either A, wasting her time, or B, meddling. But Bram didn't have the same history with Morgan as she did, so there was no way he could truly understand her fascination. Under the circumstances, a little plausible misdirection was the better part of discretion.

Just after seven, Bram pulled his Jeep into the dirt drive next to Sulo's cabin. "Not exactly the Ritz," he said, staring at the dilapidated log structure. Pokegama Lake spread out blue and hazy behind it.

"Sulo said he's been working on it little by little. He figures he'll have it in tip-top shape by next summer."

"Why didn't we wait until then to visit?"

Sophie could see that the dock was deep in a patch of weeds. The houseboat, the one Sulo had been raving about, looked as upscale as the cabin. "He said he'd leave the key above the door."

"Great," said Bram, pushing out of the front seat. "No burglar would ever think of looking there."

Lugging two disgracefully heavy overnight bags across a patch of dead grass, Bram waited for Sophie to unlock the front door. Once they were inside, he dropped the bags with a thunk. "Good thing your cousin wasn't planning to spend the night with us. Somebody would be sleeping on the floor."

Against the far wall sat two rusted metal bunk beds with sagging mattresses. That was the extent of the sleeping accommodations.

"I don't understand it," said Sophie. "Sulo's told me so many times how incredibly comfortable the place was."

"This from the same man who nearly killed me in his hand-built sauna. Sophie, if I've said it once, I've said it a thousand times: hyperbole is dangerous. It can kill."

They both stood for a few moments examining the dingy, claustrophobic interior.

"Hey," said Sophie, moving closer to her husband. "What's that scratching noise?"

"A mouse. Or, with our luck, a skunk."

Another few seconds passed.

"Call the Sawmill Inn," said Sophie, turning on her heel and marching out the door.

"I'm on it."

Later that evening, while Bram was taking a shower, Sophie looked up Morgan Walters's name in the Grand Rapids phone book, the one the motel conveniently provided. No Walters was listed. Morgan and his wife would probably be in their late sixties now—if they were still alive, and if they'd stayed in the area. Two big ifs. That's when Sophie remembered Dan and Cathy Greenberg. The Greenbergs had lived next to Sophie's grandparents all those years ago. They bought their eggs from the Walterses, too. They'd been in their twenties when Sophie knew them, so maybe they had some information on what happened to the Walterses.

Scanning down the G's, Sophie found a Daniel Greenberg on First Avenue North East. As Bram scrubbed away, Sophie punched in the number. Someone picked up on the second ring.

"Hello?" It was a man's voice.

"Mr. Greenberg?"

"Yes?"

"I don't know if you remember me, but this is Sophie Greenway. I used to be Sophie Tahtinen. You used to live next to my grandparents."

"Of course I remember you, Sophie," Mr. Greenberg

said warmly. He'd spent his life as a high school athletic coach in Coleraine. "You were just a child the last time I saw you. Gee, that must have been—"

"A long time ago," said Sophie, not wanting to get into the age thing. "I'm calling because I'm hoping you can help me with a question. Do you remember Morgan Walters and his wife? They lived out near Trout Lake."

"Sure, I used to go biking with Morgan. Nice guy."

"Do you know if he and his wife are still living around here?"

Now he hesitated. "I guess you didn't hear. Laura died four or five years after they were married."

"Died? How?"

"Suicide. I don't remember much about it, but shortly after it happened, Morgan took off. Far as I know, nobody's seen him since. If you're interested, you might try talking to Laura's sister, Dotty Mulloy. She lives out on Mishawaka Road. I'm sure her name's in the book."

Sophie could hear Bram's shower winding down. She could tell because he'd reached the next to the last chorus of "The Battle Hymn of the Republic." "Thanks, Mr. Greenberg."

"I hope you find the information you're looking for."

"Me, too."

As soon as she'd hung up, she pulled the phone book in front of her again and scanned the M's for Dotty Mulloy. There it was: Ben and Dotty Mulloy, 1748 Mishawaka Rd. She punched in the number. The line had just flipped over to an answering machine when a woman's voice answered. "Mulloys."

"Hi, is this Dotty?"

"Yes, it is."

"My name's Sophie Greenway. I'm the food editor for

the *Times Register* in Minneapolis. My husband is Bram
Baldric." She thought putting a little information up
front might be a good ploy to get the woman's attention.

"Say, I've heard of Mr. Baldric. He's the one with that
talk radio show."

"That's right. We're in town because Bram is doing his
show live from the fair grounds tomorrow afternoon."

"I was over at the fair today. He'll get a great crowd."

Sophie felt pretty confident she had her. "I was wondering if I could come over to your house tomorrow
afternoon. I was hoping to talk to you while I was in
town."

"Me? Why?"

Sophie was afraid that if she said too much, Dotty
might refuse. "I'd rather explain it to you in person."

For a few seconds, Dotty didn't speak. "Well," she
said, finally, "I guess that would be okay."

Sophie could hear the water in the shower stop. The
curtain was yanked back. "What time is good for you?"

"I have a doctor's appointment at noon. How does
two sound?"

"I'll be there. And thanks, Dotty."

10

Dotty Mulloy's home was an old white clapboard farmhouse nestled into a tall stand of jack pine, a good hundred yards in from the main road. A screened porch stretched all the way across the front, and that's where Dotty was sitting the following afternoon when Sophie pulled into the long drive.

Based on Dotty's white hair, arthritic-looking hands, and the cane resting next to her rocking chair, Sophie estimated Dotty's age at somewhere in her late seventies. Her eyes were lively, and she smiled broadly as she motioned Sophie to the wicker love seat.

"Lovely day," said Dotty, adjusting her cotton skirt carefully over her knees. One knee was wrapped in an Ace bandage, while the other looked swollen and sore.

Sophie sat down, noticing a pitcher of lemonade and two glasses resting on the table between them.

"Help yourself," said Dotty. "It's a warm day. I thought we could use a little refreshment."

"Would you like me to pour?"

"Go ahead. I was hoping my husband could be here to meet you, but he had business in town. While I was making the lemonade, I was listening to your husband's radio show. I think it's such fun that he's broadcasting live from our fair. He has the most wonderful voice. And he always sounds like . . . I don't know, like he's smiling at us—like he's up to something."

"He usually is," said Sophie, crossing one leg over the other. She'd worn a pretty yellow summer dress and matching heels today instead of her more comfortable jeans, sandals, and short-sleeved cotton shirt. "I'll pass on your compliment."

After taking a sip of lemonade, Dotty continued, "So, put me out of my misery. Tell me why the restaurant reviewer at the *Times Register* wants to see me."

Sophie wished she had a more pleasant answer. Instead of launching into a long explanation, she took the picture of John and Mary Washburn out of her purse and handed it to Dotty. "Do you recognize that man?"

All of Dotty's good humor faded instantly. "Of course I do," she said, her voice flat. "I don't know the woman, but that's Morgan Walters, my sister's husband."

"Look carefully, Mrs. Mulloy. Are you positive?"

Dotty held the photo closer. "Sure I'm sure. There's that hideous snake tattoo on his arm, and he's wearing those awful tight jeans, just like he always did. It didn't leave anything to the imagination, if you catch my drift. No," she sighed, shaking her head, "it's not likely I'd forget what my sister's murderer looked like."

"Murderer?"

"That's what I said."

"But, I thought . . . I mean I'd heard—"

"That Laura committed suicide?" She looked away, her expression growing steely. "That's what Morgan wanted everyone to think. He might have fooled the police, but he never fooled me or my husband. We always knew Morgan had done it. He was no good. Oh, he had a line with women that was smooth as butter, but if he cared about Laura so much, why did he isolate her out there at that godforsaken house? Why did he leave her all alone for weeks at a time?"

"When were they married?"

"April of 1960."

Less than a year after the photo had been taken, Sophie thought, and less than two years after John and Mary were married. That made John Washburn—or Morgan Walters—a bigamist.

"When did Laura die?"

Looking down at her hands, Dotty replied, "November 16, 1965. It was a Saturday. Her best friend, Rebecca Scoville, found her."

It was the same year Sophie had taken her unforgettable motorcycle ride with Morgan. "What did Morgan Walters do for a living?" she asked, afraid that she already knew the answer.

"He was a traveling salesman. Don't ask me what he sold. I don't think I ever knew." Dotty glanced at the snapshot again. "Who's the woman he's standing with in the photo?"

"A relative," Sophie answered. She hoped Dotty would leave it at that.

"Humph. He never was very forthcoming about who his people were. From the very first, my husband and I figured he had something to hide, but Laura was head over heels in love with him. Nothing we ever said made a difference."

"How did your sister die?" asked Sophie.

"The police said she hung herself. Tied one part of a rope around a pipe in the basement, put a noose around her neck, stood on a chair, then kicked it out from under her. But it was all lies. Why would my sister kill herself? The fact that she didn't leave a note should have been a red flag to anyone who was looking. Laura always told me how much she loved her life. Loved Morgan. Then again, I thought it was funny when I'd drive out to their place and she couldn't get rid of me fast enough. Why would she act like that with her own sister—unless she had something to hide, too?"

"What do you think it was?"

Dotty lowered her voice. "I saw lots of liquor bottles around that house. Laura didn't drink, so that left Morgan. I think she was trying to hide what was going on. There were times when I'd drive out to Trout Lake and Laura would be nursing cuts on her face, or bruises on her arms. Morgan did that to her. He had her so twisted around, so scared of her own shadow, that she wouldn't even confide in her own sister."

"Did you ever confront him about it?" asked Sophie.

She shook her head. "It's one of the biggest regrets of my life. I should have done more to help Laura get away from him." She wiped a tear from her eye.

"What happened to Morgan after your sister died?"

"He sold the house and left town. Far as I know, he's never been back." She removed a handkerchief from her apron pocket and dabbed at her eyes. "How come you're so interested in Morgan?"

Sophie'd been thinking about how she would answer that question. "The truth is, I ran into an old friend recently who used to know Morgan. He gave me the snapshot. My friend thought Morgan might still be living up here, so I told him I'd check it out when I was in town. Actually, I met Morgan myself once when I was thirteen. He took me on my first motorcycle ride."

"Did he ask you for a date?"

Sophie did a double take. "No."

Dotty snorted. "From small comments Laura used to make, I got the impression that he was a . . . well, a very highly sexed man." Dotty's face flushed. "Thank God, my husband was never like that."

"So, you think he was unfaithful?"

"I do."

"With women around town?"

Dotty considered the question. "I doubt it. He was gone so much, I'll bet he had a woman in every small town from here to Nebraska."

It was an interesting adjunct to Sophie's theory. A traveling salesman with more than one wife. Maybe even more than two. "You mentioned that Laura had a best friend."

"Yes, Rebecca Scoville. Nice woman. Laura and Rebecca were the same age—went to school together. Laura was nine years younger than me. I suppose I seemed like an old fuddy-duddy to her."

"Where does Rebecca live?"

"Down in the Cities. After her divorce, she started a small business. She still sends me a Christmas card every year."

"I wonder if I could get her address."

With great effort, Dotty got up. "I'm kind of slow. The arthritis in my knees is the worst."

"Can I help?"

"No, just drink your lemonade. I'll be back shortly." The screen door banged behind her as she entered the house.

Sophie finished her glass and was just about done with

a second when Dotty returned. "Here," she said, dropping a file folder in Sophie's lap.

"What's all this?"

Dotty didn't answer until she was once again seated in the rocker. "It's a copy of the official coroner's report on Laura's death. I stuck a copy of the police report in there, too."

Sophie was amazed. "How did you get your hands on that?"

Rocking slowly, Dotty said, "Well, the police report was public information, so that wasn't a problem. But the coroner's report, that was another matter entirely. See, the county coroner retired a few years after Laura died. He was a medical doctor and a friend of my husband's. Seems crazy to me, but nobody was interested in his files back then. That's the way the government was run. Maybe it still is. Anyway, he asked us if we wanted Laura's records. Of course we wanted them. I hoped that, one day, that file would help us prove what Morgan did to her." She sighed. "It's a terrible thing, being so powerless. I know the truth, but I'm helpless to do anything about it."

Sophie looked at the file. On the outside, Dotty had written Rebecca Scoville's home address.

"You take that with you," Dotty continued, looking off in the distance. "I'm an old woman now. I've got no use for it anymore. Maybe you'll find something in there I missed."

July, 1960

Hey, Gilbert—
Okay, so I'm not very good at this writing stuff. Neither are you. It's been at least a year since my last letter. Lots of changes. I was down in Jeff City about six months ago—thought of trying to see you, but I guess what happened really put the fear of God in me. I stay as far away from the police now as I can get.
You probably want to know what I did with the money. Maybe you'll think I'm a chump, but I couldn't stand to be around it, so I dumped it in the nearest gutter. I'm on my own now, and I'm learning some important things about myself. Believe it or not, I'm good with people. Really good. But I'm not so good at punching a time clock every day. I went that route for a while. Worked in a bakery. Man, those early hours are enough to kill your soul. Now I've found something better— something that gives me more freedom. I hate all the worn-out rules people try and make you believe. I'm still a rebel at heart, but a quiet one now.
I've taken a job as a salesman. My route includes what they call the "five-state region." South Dakota,

North Dakota, Minnesota, Wisconsin, and Iowa. Beautiful country.

You know how I always thought my brother was a jerk? Well, I've changed my mind. He's on to something, Gilbert. He's working hard. Making a good life for himself. When people looked at us, they always thought I was the smart one. People can sure get the wrong idea. What a guy looks like on the outside doesn't mean shit.

Hey, I forgot to tell you. I got married in April. Man, she's a peach. Her name's Laura, like the song. Raven hair. Beautiful blue eyes. I suppose it sounds sappy, but I'm so in love with her I could burst. I'll send you a picture next time.

If they let you read books, there's a couple I'd send you, books Laura got me to read. One is Catcher in the Rye. *Another was* Lord of the Flies. *That one was weird. But the one that really hit me hard was—*Too Late the Phalarope *by Alan Paton. Paton wrote* Cry, the Beloved Country *too, but this book is better. It's all about a man who doesn't feel at home—not anywhere. Not in his house, not in his body, and not in his mind. He has a deep longing for love, but he never quite finds it. He also has terrible bouts of depression because of what he calls "his lust." See, he's locked in this unforgiving, puritanical society, and because of that, he's doomed to destroy himself and everybody around him. But the point is, he's a good man . . . a loving man trapped in a society with a lot of unjust rules. It's a sad story. Tragic, even. For a man like that, maybe tragedy is the only possible ending.*

J. D.

11

"So," said Bram, flipping through the file on the death of Laura Walters, "you actually think Bernice's father was married to two women?"

Sophie was loading up the dishwasher. They'd returned home from their whirlwind trip to Grand Rapids shortly after nine. While Sophie attended to a bit of hotel business, Bram had occupied himself by preparing a couple of his famous Bruder Basil omelettes. And now, Sophie was cleaning up.

Over dinner, she'd finally thrown caution to the wind and confessed her real reason for wanting to visit Grand Rapids. She was entirely too excited by her conversation with Dotty Mulloy to keep it to herself.

First, she explained her personal connection to Morgan Walters. Bram took it all in with a small roll of his eyes. Next she told him that both she and Dotty were positive that the man in the picture, otherwise known as John Washburn, was none other than Morgan Walters. The tattoo on his arm proved it. But the clincher was, Morgan had murdered his wife and gotten away with it. He was a murderer as well as a bigamist.

Amazing as it might seem, instead of insisting she drop the matter, that she was a total busybody with no business prying into other people's affairs, Bram warmed to the subject. He'd read through the complete file while Sophie puttered in the kitchen. And now he was ready to talk.

"Sure, I think he's a bigamist," said Sophie. "Dotty said he was the kind of guy who probably had a woman in every town he called on. What if he had more than two wives, Bram? What if he had three or four. Or more!"

Bram held up a hand to quell her enthusiasm. He was sitting at the dining room table, a glass of ice tea resting next to the file. "Trust my instincts on this one, Soph. It gets to be a case of diminishing returns after awhile, especially if he had to support more than one household. Why not just have affairs? Why get married?"

Sophie leaned against the kitchen sink, tossing a damp dish towel over her shoulder. "Maybe he loved weddings, or maybe he harbored some ethical notion that he shouldn't sleep with a woman unless he was married to her."

Doing his best Orson Welles imitation, Bram said, "Who knows what evil lurks in the hearts of men?"

"It *is* evil," said Sophie, joining him at the table. "If he marries, then murders."

"He hasn't killed the wife he has now, and they've been together forever. What's her name again?"

"Mary."

Bram leaned back in his chair. "I don't know, Soph. It seems pretty clear you don't have all the facts."

"No, but I've got a police report on a death that should never have happened."

"Yeah, I'll admit that was pretty interesting." He ticked the salient points off on his fingers. "Laura Walter's body was found hanging in the basement of her home by her best friend, Rebecca Scoville, at approximately ten-thirty on the morning of November 16, 1965. A Saturday morning. Scoville said she'd stopped by because she and Laura had planned to do some Christmas shopping together that day. When she couldn't get a rise out of anyone inside, she used a key hidden under a flower pot to get in. After discovering the body, she rushed upstairs to call the police just as Morgan entered through the back door. At Rebecca's prompting, he ran downstairs and found his wife hanging from a water pipe. The police arrived a few minutes later. No note was found at the scene."

"Which is suspicious," said Sophie, drumming her fingers on the table. "Don't most suicides leave notes?"

"How the hell should I know? To continue: Morgan said he'd gone into town to a get haircut, but that he'd forgotten his wallet and had to come back to get it. He confirmed that his wife had been depressed recently, but he never thought she'd kill herself."

Again, Sophie interrupted him. "Dotty said her sister *wasn't* depressed. I figure it was just something Morgan made up to throw the police off the track."

"But, did you read Scoville's statement? She agreed with him. She said Laura had really been down before her death."

"Everyone is depressed now and then. I'd be good and depressed if my husband was gone two weeks at a stretch."

"But Laura knew he was a traveling salesman when she married him."

"It's one thing to know something in the abstract, and another thing entirely to live with it day in and day out."

Bram closed the file. "What really seemed like a major

problem to me was when the police searched Walter's car and found his bags in the trunk, packed and ready to go. I mean, it was a Saturday. If he was going out of town, he wouldn't be leaving until Monday, right? Why have your bags in the car so far in advance?"

"You think he was planning to take off?"

"Sure looks that way to me."

"Then why did he come back?"

"Maybe he really did forget his wallet. It's certainly possible. And he wouldn't get very far without it."

"But the police were never able to prove Laura's death was anything other than a suicide. That meant Morgan didn't have to run off. He was able to sell the house, move away and never look back."

Bram sipped his ice tea. "Okay, let's say you're right. Let's say he did murder her. What was his motive?"

Sophie had been thinking about that all afternoon. "Maybe Laura found out about his other wives and threatened to tell the police. He had to protect himself, and the only way to do it was to shut her up. Permanently."

"Sounds pretty cold."

"That doesn't stop it from being true."

"All right, granted. But when you come right down to it, maybe it *was* a suicide."

Sophie didn't buy it. Someone who broke the rules in one direction could easily break them in another. Besides, hadn't John Washburn just admitted to murdering a man in Rose Hill? Maybe it was all connected. "It drives me wild that we may never know the truth."

"Are you planning to tell Bernice about your suspicions?"

"Heavens, no. That's the last thing she needs."

"So, you're just going to drop it? Walk away?"

"Are you kidding?"

"I realized it was a ridiculous question the moment the words left my mouth."

"Is that a veiled comment?"

"I'd hardly call it veiled."

The fact was, Sophie had already begun to formulate a plan, one that might help her discover the truth. Tomorrow morning, she intended to set the wheels in motion.

Before Sophie left for the *Times Register* on Tuesday morning, she approached the concierge desk in the main lobby. Last night, after returning home from Grand Rapids, she'd asked one of her assistant managers to locate a photo shop that could make several dozen copies of the snapshot of John and Mary Washburn. She wanted them first thing in the morning. Sure enough, a white envelope stuffed with prints was waiting for her at the desk. Also waiting for her was a letter.

Sophie recognized the handwriting even before she looked at the return address. It was from Nathan Buckridge, her childhood sweetheart. Nathan had come back into her life last spring. It had been an emotionally charged time for them both, especially since their reunion had coincided with his explosive family problems. By June, Nathan was in jail. In return for his cooperation, the D.A. had given him a reduced sentence. With time already served and more time off for good behavior, he would be out of jail before the end of the month.

Over the summer, Nathan had left several voice mail messages for her at the paper, asking her to come visit him. He said they needed to talk. In his mind, what had transpired between them was still unresolved. And yet for Sophie, the situation was clear. She'd made a terrible mistake with an old love, a man she was still drawn to, but one with whom she had no future. She'd let matters get out of hand last May, but it wouldn't happen again.

Even now, she continued to be amazed at how easily she'd been seduced by the intense pleasure of an old romance. Secretly, she still daydreamed about the night she and Nathan had spent together, even though she'd made a firm decision. She loved her husband; her life was with Bram.

Before the trial, Sophie had explained all this to Nathan. She hoped it would be the end of it. But of course, it wasn't. When she looked at herself in the mirror now, she saw a different person staring back at her, a woman who could cheat on her husband and keep it a secret. Even more amazingly, a large part of her didn't regret what had happened. But the part that did had to live with the guilt every day. The experience had altered her in ways she didn't even understand yet.

Sophie sat down in the hotel lobby and opened the letter. It had been written in pencil on a piece of lined notebook paper.

Dear Sophie:
I'm being released at the end of the week. Thought I should let you know. I still want to talk. I'll be returning to New Fonteney, and will probably live in the main hall until I figure out what to do next.

New Fonteney was an old, deserted monastery a few miles north of Stillwater. Nathan had purchased the property last spring hoping to convince his mother to develop it into a Midwest campus for the Buckridge Culinary Academy. After his brother, Paul, nixed the deal, Nathan had toyed with the idea of starting his own cooking school. As a Cordon Bleu–trained chef with over twenty years' experience, he certainly had the credentials. But then he'd gone to jail. Everything had been put on hold.

I had the phone service restored, so you can reach me at 651-555-2095. I hope you're well. I miss you. And I love you.
Nathan

Sophie felt oddly flattened by the note. In all outward ways, her life was back to normal now. Nathan represented chaos, confused emotions, frustrated desire and potential disaster. Tucking the letter into her briefcase, she rose and and asked the bell captain to send someone for her car. She gave him her usual chipper smile, but today, it almost choked her.

12

Sophie finally made it to the paper by ten. She'd spent the last hour driving around, trying to clear her head. It hadn't done much good. In the end, she simply had to put Nathan out of her thoughts and get on with the day.

Once on the ninth floor of the *Times Register* tower, she headed for her office. Sophie usually put in about ten hours a week at the paper. Normally, the job would have required far more time. That's where her son, Rudy, came in.

Rudy Greenway had grown up in Montana, living with his father, a minister in the Church of the Firstborn. It was a long, heartbreaking story. Sophie hadn't been allowed to visit or even talk to him for a great part of his young life. After a nasty court battle, her husband had been granted sole legal custody. He'd quickly filled Rudy's head with poison. No wonder her son wouldn't even take her phone calls. But life—and the truth— eventually caught up with him.

When Rudy was eighteen, he appeared on Sophie's doorstep, asking if he could stay with her and Bram during his freshman year at the University of Minnesota. The fact was, he'd run away from his father and the re- pressive values he represented. Rudy was gay, not that he told Sophie that that was why he'd left. The church he'd been born into, and more importantly, the people he'd come to honor and respect, believed that homosexuality was a sin punishable by death. It was impossible for Rudy to be gay and at the same time be a good human being, loved by God as a part of His one and only true church. Rudy knew he'd either have to live a lie his whole life, try to press himself into a mold that would never fit, or leave. Coming to Minnesota, arriving on Sophie's doorstep basically penniless, leaving his home and family—all of this must have been terrifying, but he saw no other way out. For the past five years, he'd been coming to terms with his desire to be a Christian, and his knowledge that he was—and would always be— a gay man.

Last spring, Rudy had committed himself formally to another young man, one he'd met during his first few months in Minneapolis. John Jacoby, a few years older than Rudy, was an artist. To keep body and soul together, he worked at a brewery in St. Paul. Sophie had thrown a grand party for them at the hotel after the commitment ceremony. The next day, John and Rudy had left for Europe. They'd backpacked across Spain, France, Germany, Austria, and Italy. Rudy had just completed his degree in theater arts at the university. He'd lived such a sheltered life as a child, he was hungry to learn about the world firsthand.

When Sophie called him in Italy and offered him the job as her assistant at the paper, he'd jumped at the chance—both as a way to get to know his mother better and as a way to pursue a genuine interest. He was young. He could always pursue his passion for the theater avocationally. Or, if he found the job at the paper ultimately uninteresting, he could move on. Whatever the case, for now, Sophie was elated to be able to work with her son. While she put in ten hours a week, he put in thirty to forty. Her name might come first on the office door, but Rudy was the heart and soul of the operation.

Breezing into the office, Sophie found her son sitting at one of the two desks, staring at a computer monitor.

"Hey, Mom," he said, jumping up and giving her a kiss on the cheek. "You almost missed me."

"Are you all set to go?"

"I'm just about to print out my itinerary."

For the next two weeks, Rudy would be traveling around Minnesota, visiting small-town cafes for possible review. He planned to venture across the border into Wisconsin, as well.

Clicking the print icon, Rudy leaned back in his chair and stretched his arms high over his head. He was a handsome young man, with the same strawberry-blond hair, great smile, and diminutive height as his mother. While Sophie, in stiletto heels, hit the mark at five-three, Rudy, in his favorite Nikes, barely stretched to five-seven. Taller than his mother, to be sure, but not as tall as he'd like to be. Still, he worked out in the gym several times a week and kept himself fit. More than fit. Sophie was starting to notice some major muscle development. As far as she was concerned, he had the perfect constitution to eat ten cafe meals a day. That's what he'd have to do to canvass the region properly.

When the printout was finished, Rudy handed her a copy.

"You're going to call me and give me updates, right?"

"Yes, Commander." He saluted.

Ignoring his grin, she handed him the packet of pictures.

"What's this?"

"As you drive through the small towns, I want you to show this snapshot around, see if anybody recognizes the man in the photo. Try the cafes first, but I also want you to take the picture to hardware stores, feed stores, whatever you think looks like it's been around since the sixties. If you see a senior citizen center or a nursing home, try that, too. If somebody wants to keep a photo, or allows you to post one, that's even better. Leave them the number at the paper. I realize I'm asking you to do some extra work, Rudy, but it's important."

"Do you mind telling me why?"

Sophie gave him the highlights. She could see by the gleam in his eyes that he was as fascinated by the story as she was. A chip off the old block. Or perhaps, in this case, a wing off the old turkey? "You've got your marching orders."

"Aye aye, Captain."

"I thought I was a commander."

"To be honest, Mom, you remind me of General Patton sometimes."

"I don't find that amusing."

He gave her a peck on the cheek and was out the door.

13

Dour, fussy, and disdainful. That's what Plato Washburn thought of his managing editor. Byron Jenny was a pain in the ass. Still, the man knew his job inside and out. Plato could hardly fire him when his own knowledge of how to run a paper—even a small one—would fit into a shot glass with room to spare. Jenny was the soul of the *Rose Hill Gazette*. He'd been the managing editor for the past sixteen years. But that didn't mean Plato had to like him.

Mr. Jenny, as everyone was urged to call him, was elegantly thin, in his midfifties, and never without his bow tie and pipe. The look was studied Hollywood faux-newspaper kitsch, but nobody seemed to notice except Plato, who had never managed to have any sort of look at all. To Plato, "Mr. Jenny" sounded like the name of a gay hairstylist. If Mr. Jenny didn't knuckle under to Mr. Plato's wishes, he might have an opportunity to change careers.

Today the heat and humidity made Plato look as if someone had tried to suffocate him under a mattress. Mopping his brow with a crumpled white handkerchief as he trudged up the stairs to the *Gazette*'s conference room, Plato cursed the weather. "Might as well live in a rain forest," he muttered, pushing open the heavy oak door. Everything in the old brick building reeked of history. It was all so self-consciously historic, Plato had the urge to burn it down.

Jenny looked up sharply at Plato's entrance.

Ever since he had been a child, Plato had been determined to avoid disagreeable situations. His current life was a veritable Victorian tableau of where that kind of philosophy got you. Facing his problems for once, he'd decided to sit in on the biweekly editorial meeting, the place where reporters' assignments were handed out. It was only the second time he'd attended, mainly because Jenny had made it admirably clear that his input wasn't needed. Plato figured it was about time he sent his own message.

"Can I help you?" asked Jenny, watching Plato in that imperiously questioning manner of his, a look that no doubt sent lesser men running for their mommies.

"No, just continue." He pulled up a chair and sat down at the long table.

Jenny twiddled a pen between his fingers, calculating how to handle this unwanted intrusion. "If you need to talk to me, why don't you step into my office. I'm sure my secretary would be happy to get you a cup of coffee."

"It's too hot for coffee. I'm here to listen. As I said, just keep going as if I'm not here." Plato wanted to kick him.

The other heads at the table shifted back and forth, as if they were watching a tennis match, their attention switching between Mr. Jenny and Plato, not sure what was happening.

"All right," Jenny said finally, sitting back in his chair and pressing a match to the tobacco in his pipe. "What's next?"

After Plato had bought the paper four years ago, the former owner had offered him some advice. "Let Byron have his head," he said, speaking of the man as if he were a race horse. "He's temperamental, but he's a thoroughbred." Since Plato had been looking for a professional situation that wouldn't require a great deal of time and effort on his part, the idea that he had a ready-made editor who could run the shop at a profit appealed to him. Now, it irked him.

The *Rose Hill Gazette* appeared twice weekly—on Wednesdays and Saturdays. Clearly, organizing this sort of rag wasn't rocket science. It was about time Plato got his hands dirty, learned the ropes firsthand. Byron Jenny was just one more person who treated Plato as if he existed only marginally—like a bug, or a fungus, more a nuisance than a necessary part of life. That was about to change.

"Who's covering the funding for the new library?" asked Jenny, puffing away on his pipe, his manner entirely too urbane for the likes of Rose Hill.

"I am," said a woman with a face like a slab of concrete.

Jenny nodded, then wrote something down. "Do we have any new information on the Runbeck homicide?" When no one responded, Jenny looked up. "Where's Viv?"

"She got a phone call right before the meeting," said the woman with the concrete face.

"From whom?"

"She didn't say, but she raced out of here."

Plato raised a finger. "I'll be covering that story from now on."

With glacial deliberation, Jenny turned his gaze to

Plato. "Excuse me?" he said, removing the pipe from his mouth.

"I *said*, I'll be covering that story from here on out. Inform Viv of the change."

Jenny looked as if he'd been slapped. "You can't cover that story. Your father's just admitted to the murder."

"My father," said Plato, folding his hands patiently on the tabletop, "has just suffered a stroke. He's confused."

"But, it's a conflict of interest."

"I'm not a lawyer or a doctor. I publish a small-town paper. Newspapers take stands on issues all the time."

"In the opinion pages."

"Oh, come on, Byron, you know better than that. Newspapers can elect government officials, or get them fired. They shape opinion all the time simply by the way they report the news."

"The news is based on facts. Journalists deal in fact, not opinion."

"Fine. The facts are, my father is innocent. The Runbeck homicide will no longer be fodder for the bored and brutish among us."

Before Jenny could offer more objections, the door opened. Viv, dressed in bleached blue jeans, her ubiquitous silver-tipped cowboy boots, and a tight pink tank top, ambled into the room. "Boy, have I got a story for you." Seeing Plato, she stopped chewing her gum. "What's he doing here?"

"I've decided to start sitting in on the editorial meetings," Plato said casually. He could tell Jenny was about to rupture a vital internal organ. This was far better than kicking him.

"You mean," said Jenny, his voice dialed up to full dour, "this is going to be a biweekly event?"

Plato gave a curt nod. "Now, Viv, why don't you sit down and give us your news flash." He could see she was just bursting to tell.

"Sure thing," she said, looking a little hesitant. "It's just . . . with you here, Mr. Washburn . . . I mean . . . I feel a little funny. It's about your father."

Plato stiffened. "What about him?"

Viv glanced at Jenny again, then pulled out a chair. Instead of sitting down, she rested a knee on top of it. "Well, see, I was just talking to Doug Elderberg. It seems that before Kirby Runbeck's death, he made two deposits into a newly established savings account at the First Bank of Rose Hill. Fifty thousand dollars each time. That's one hundred thousand dollars," she said eagerly. "Where would a man like him get that kind of money?"

"Maybe he played the stock market," said the cement-faced woman.

Viv's eyes took on a fiery glow. "He closed the account the day before he died. Doug also told me that a month or so before his stroke, John Washburn withdrew fifty thousand dollars in cash from one of his accounts at Wells Fargo. Then, a week before the stroke, he closed out a bank CD for the same amount and took the money in cash. They can't prove it yet, but they figure Washburn was paying Runbeck some kind of hush money."

"Blackmail," said Jenny, a note of triumph in his voice.

"That's hogwash," said Plato, his fist hitting the table. "I'm sure there's another explanation."

"The sheriff's office thinks it was blackmail, too," Viv continued. "They've got a B.C.A. guy down here from the Cities helping them with Runbeck's murder, and he agrees. After John Washburn confessed to the murder, they went looking for a motive. They don't have all the specifics yet, but they figure it's only a matter of time before they do."

"That should be our lead headline on Saturday," said Jenny, glaring defiantly at Plato. "Runbeck obviously had some information on John Washburn that Washburn didn't want made public. So he paid for Runbeck's silence. Paid *twice*. I'll bet Runbeck was hitting him up for more when Washburn went tilt. Killed him instead of paying him."

Plato erupted out of his chair. "That's enough! What you're saying is pure speculation, with no basis in fact. I know my father, and I know beyond a shadow of a doubt that he's incapable of murder. I have no idea why he withdrew so much cash, nor do I know how Kirby Runbeck came by his money, but there's no connection. If you run that headline on Saturday, *Mr.* Jenny, or if there's mention of any of this in the paper, you're fired. You're all fired," said Plato, slamming the door on his way out.

14

"I'm truly sorry, Mrs. Washburn," said Deputy Sheriff Doug Elderberg. His eyes cast down, he turned and trotted back to his waiting squad car.

Mary stood in her front doorway and watched him drive away. Would this nightmare never end? John had been making good progress. One side of his body was still terribly weak, and his speech was garbled and slow, but the doctors assured her he was out of danger—for the moment. He was on medications that should help prevent another stroke, although nobody was issuing guarantees. If only his spirits would improve. But how could they? His brain function didn't seem to be impaired. He knew he'd admitted to a murder, and the sight of police officers outside his hospital room door couldn't have passed his notice.

Dragging herself back to the living room, Mary crumpled onto the couch to think. Doug had come by to inform her that her husband had withdrawn one hundred thousand dollars from two of their accounts at Wells Fargo in the last month, and that just before his death, Kirby Runbeck's personal worth had grown by exactly the same amount. Doug wanted to know if Mary was aware of her husband's actions. She assured him she wasn't, that all their accounts were set up so that only one signature was necessary to make a transaction, but she wasn't sure he believed her.

Tipping her head back against the cushion, Mary had a sinking feeling that the horrific events of the past few weeks were all her fault. John hadn't killed Kirby—that was never an issue—but if he hadn't, why admit to it? Mary had been with him the night he learned of Kirby's death; she'd witnessed his reaction firsthand. His blood pressure must have shot through the roof. Almost immediately, he began complaining of a headache and weakness on his left side. "Oh, John," she whispered, closing her eyes. "What have I done to you?"

The sound of a ringing phone interrupted her concentration. Instead of getting up to answer it, Mary let the machine pick it up. After a few clicks, she heard Bernice's voice say, "I'm leaving the hospital for a few hours, Mom. Thought I'd let you know. Plato's here now, so don't feel you need to come down. The nurse took Dad to physical therapy a few minutes ago, and they've scheduled him for more tests. He'll be busy most of the afternoon. So stay home and try to relax, okay? Bye."

Thank God for her family, Mary thought. Whenever there was a crisis, no matter what the current squabbles, everyone rallied. They were good kids. *Kids,* she thought, smiling at the word. You knew you were old when your kids were middle-aged.

Mary's thoughts turned to Milton. He didn't have any children. When he was in his twenties and thirties, he'd lived a nomadic existence. He barely had any photos of himself from that time, with the exception of the ones she and John had taken at birthdays, anniversaries, or when he just happened to stop by. After all these years, it was still amazing to her that two brothers, only two years apart, raised in the same home, could be so different. John took life—and his responsibilities—so seriously, while Milton was a free spirit. Even so, both of them were successful professionally, and both seemed to have a nature that required a great deal of personal solitude.

Over the years, John had grown to be a pessimist, always seeing the glass half empty, while Milton was still as optimistic as the day they'd first met. Social scientists used to insist that the way a person was raised was everything. If anyone was to blame for a bad outcome, it was the mother. But now, it seemed the experts had changed their tune. Mary had recently read an article that said modern social scientists felt human beings were far more a product of their genetics than anything else. In the battle of nature vs. nurture, nature had won. So how did that explain Milton and John? It was a useful theory, blaming your faults on your DNA, but before Mary swallowed it whole, she wanted to wait for the next study.

Picking up a framed photograph on the end table next to her, Mary examined the snapshot of Bernice and Plato, aged four and seven, flailing like starlings in a small plastic pool in the backyard. Even then, they were already who they would become, if only she'd had eyes to see. Bernice was such a secure little child, very confident of her abilities. She knew what she wanted and she knew how to get it. Plato, on the other hand, always seemed to be walking around in a fog of indecision, unsure which toy to play with, which TV show to watch. He instinctively understood life's infinite possibilities, and that knowledge seemed to confuse him into inertia. He was also far more concerned about pleasing his father than Bernice was. Both Plato and Bernice were unusually bright, even precocious, kids. Perhaps that's why Mary had such a hard time raising them. Most of the time, Bernice behaved as if she didn't need any help, while Plato was always awash in indecision. Again, two children raised in the same home, yet so different. And each one difficult to mother.

As she set the picture back down, she heard a car pull into the yard. Milton had returned. By the time she reached the kitchen, he'd come through the back door carrying a copy of the Wednesday *Rose Hill Gazette* under his arm.

"The police were just here," she said, feeling a rush of emotions so conflicting they almost took her breath away.

Milton moved to the counter and set the paper down. "What did they want?" he asked, keeping his back to her.

"It was Doug Elderberg. He said John gave Kirby Runbeck one hundred thousand dollars before he died."

Milton turned around. "Did he say why?"

"He didn't know. He thought maybe I did."

"Do you?"

"No!"

Seeing her distress, Milton put his arms around her. "The police asked me a bunch of stupid questions, too. But they're fishing, Mary. They don't know anything for sure."

"Neither do I," she said, breaking away from him.

Milton followed her into the living room. "Mary, I don't mean to sound like a broken record, but I'm worried about you. It won't do John any good if he gets better and you get sick again."

"I'm not sick."

"No, of course you're not," he said patiently. "But the stress you're putting on yourself isn't good for you."

"John's in that hospital bed because of me."

"Ridiculous."

"Is it?" She whirled around to face him. "When I found out about my cancer, it threw John into a panic. He went a little crazy, Milton, because of *me*. Everyone saw it. All those gallons of carrot juice, the hundreds of bottles of vitamin supplements. He was trying to control his world so that nothing else bad would happen."

"I realize that, Mary."

"That's why he called you to come stay with us. He knew he couldn't handle it on his own. He's a proud man, Milton. He's never lost control of his world before."

"I was happy to help."

She felt tears burn her eyes. "But you did more than help. While John was growing more and more distant, you were there. Why did you always have to be there, Milton? Why did you have to be so damnably kind?"

"Mary—" He stepped closer to her.

"I didn't mean to fall in love with you. How did that happen?"

"I don't know," he said softly. He reached out to touch her, but she pulled away again.

"John must have found out."

"Why do you say that?"

"Maybe he sensed it. Or—what if Kirby saw us? We were acting like teenagers, Milton. Picnicking in the woods. Going to motels."

Taking hold of her firmly by the arms, Milton looked her square in the eyes. "Do you think I wanted to hurt my brother? Do you think I planned this? You needed your life back, Mary. All John wanted was to stay home and figure out new ways to cook seaweed. I didn't mean to fall in love with you, either, but I did. I can't take it back."

"We should never have spent so much time together."

"Maybe, but the doctors all said you needed fresh air and . . . hell, some fun in your life. You were getting better every day, but you needed to get out of the house. Somewhere along the line, John forgot how to have fun, Mary."

"And you never did."

He held her eyes. "What do you want me to say?"

"I don't know," she said, tears rolling down her cheeks.

"Oh, sweetheart," he said, crushing her in his arms. "I'm so sorry. This has gotten so complicated."

"What are we going to do? I can't leave John. Even if I wanted to, I couldn't do it now."

"I wouldn't ask you to. But don't expect me to walk away either. Not when your life is in so much turmoil."

She relaxed into his arms, welcoming his embrace, but knowing at the same time that she had to stop leaning on him. "What if Kirby did see us? Maybe that's what he was blackmailing John about."

"John would never give a jerk like him money to keep quiet about an affair, not even one his wife was having with his brother."

"But this is a small town. You don't know what it's like here."

"Look, if John had suspected anything, he would have come to me and knocked my block off."

"Then why did he give Kirby that money?"

She could feel the muscles in Milton's back tense. "I

was alone with him for a few minutes today, Mary. I tried to get him to talk about it. I even gave him a pad and pencil and asked him some questions."

"And?"

"Nothing. Whatever he's thinking, he's got it locked up inside him."

"If it's not us, then . . . what?"

Milton kissed her gently, then stood back. "My brother isn't perfect, Mary, but the guy's a rock. Always has been. When we were kids, I thought he was insufferable. He tried to be both a brother and a father to me, and it didn't work. He was always so cool, so tough, and I tried to be just like him, but I'm sure he hated me sometimes, hated it when his little brother tagged along. I never understood John's kind of integrity, Mary. Plus the guy seemed to be blessed with this incredible Lady Luck." He turned around and smiled at her, adding, "He found you, didn't he?"

She could feel her face flush.

"If anybody's got skeletons in his closet, it's me. John's lived an exemplary life. I was the one who was the crazy kid."

"Tell me about your skeletons," she said, watching his reaction.

"Oh, no," he said, the old twinkle back in his eyes. "A man of mystery is far more intriguing."

"Really."

He nodded, but his good humor was already fading. "We've got to find a way out of this mess, Mary." He drew her into his arms again, speaking quietly into her ear, as if he was afraid to say the words out loud. "My brother isn't a murderer. He must be protecting someone. And the only people he cares about that much are you, me, Plato, and Bernice."

"Are you saying one of us killed Kirby?"

"We've got to face facts. If John isn't guilty, one of us is."

15

When Cora Runbeck entered the Prairie Lights Cafe on Wednesday afternoon, the place was packed with hungry diners. Ever since Sunday, she'd been wracking her brains, trying to figure out where Kirby could have hidden the one hundred thousand dollars. The police had stopped by to question her about it, but she said that Kirby had never mentioned it to her. That was the truth. She wasn't about to let them see the map Kirby had left behind in her old recipe box. If what Doug Elderberg told her was true—that her husband had likely been blackmailing John Washburn—well, too bad for John. If she found the money, as far as she was concerned, it was hers. She was due for a break in this life, and that money was it.

The key to the map seemed to be the location of the Devil's Tree. In a rather offhand, low-key way, she'd been querying her friends and neighbors about it. That nobody had a clue what it meant led her to believe it was something Kirby had made up. If that was true, if the location of the tree existed only in his head, then she might as well forget it. She could look for the tree for the rest of her life and never find it.

But Cora refused to admit defeat. That's why she was here today.

Easing into a booth, she waited for a waitress to bring her a menu. Kirby always raved about the meat loaf sandwiches with a side of mashed potatoes and gravy, but she was more of a Denver omelet person herself. Or sometimes she liked the pork chop dinner, which came with mashed potatoes and gravy, a vegetable, usually green beans although sometimes it was carrots, and a small red Jell-O, cranberry, and Cool Whip salad.

Decisions, decisions, she thought, glancing over at the lunch counter. Sitting on the stool closest to her was a middle-aged man laughing with one of the waitresses. Something about his voice struck a familiar chord. He was foreign sounding, like the people on *NYPD Blue*. She turned her hearing aid up to high, wishing she were just a little closer. With his classy pin-striped suit, expensive shoes, diamond pinky ring, and his black hair slicked straight back from a high forehead, he reminded her of a ballerina in a barnyard. In a small town like Rose Hill, he was totally out of place. And then it hit her. She'd heard that voice before.

Several weeks ago, just after her eye surgery, she'd been lying on the couch in the living room when she heard some fella talking to Kirby out on the front lawn. She was positive it was the man sitting at the counter. When Kirby finally came inside, he seemed shaken up. It was so unlike him that she asked him who the man was, but he just grunted, said he didn't want to talk about it. She'd forgotten about the incident until this very minute. Who is that man? she thought to herself, watching him take a fat money clip out of his pocket and toss some cash on the counter. Once he was outside, he dashed across the street to a dark sedan. Cora watched through the window as he drove away. She wondered what her husband had been talking to him about.

After she was served a glass of water, Cora concluded that she was in a pork chop mood today. The waitress took her order, then sauntered back to the kitchen. Cora hated the decor in the Prairie Lights. It was much too country for her tastes. This wasn't Texas, for goodness sakes; it was Minnesota. The man who owned the restaurant, Melvin DuCharme, was a transplant from Norman, Oklahoma, so maybe there was a reason for it, but it was still annoying. Melvin was an old buddy of Kirby's. They liked to drink beer together at the Timber Wolf Tap over on Myrtle. They also fished together in the summer and hunted in the winter. Kirby didn't have all that many friends. He wasn't a friendly kind of man.

As Cora sipped her water, she watched two young fellows from her church sit down in the booth directly across from her. They were talking so loudly, she couldn't help but overhear their conversation.

The man with the beard said, "I was up near Grand Maris last November. Shot six grouse one afternoon. Couldn't believe there were so many around the cabin."

"I've been mostly bow hunting," said the other man, the one with the longish blond hair.

"Yeah, I bow hunt, too," replied the first man, "but I'm not a very good shot. I'm better with a rifle."

"My uncle and I nearly got us a six-point buck last December, just south of Hibbing. It was standing behind this big old oak. When I aimed, I held my breath because I figured I'd hit the tree, but I got it in the haunch. Not my best shot. It took off and we ran after it, following the blood through the snow. But then I saw it run close to a tree and the arrow broke off. We tailed it a while longer, but we never found it."

"Too bad," said the man with the beard.

How utterly ghastly, Cora thought. The poor animal. Terrified. Running through the woods bleeding from an arrow in its side. She would never understand the pleasure men got from chasing animals around with guns and bows. Where was the sport in that? Her father had never been a hunter. Sure, he'd lived on a farm since he was a little boy so he understood that if you ate meat, you had to kill it first. He'd slaughtered his share of pigs and chickens, even a few cows, but he still couldn't fathom why men poured out of the city every fall heading for the big woods so they could blow their toes off, or cripple some poor critter in the woods. He always maintained it didn't really qualify as a sport unless you gave the animals guns, too. He usually got a laugh when he said it, but Cora thought it made sense.

She was glad her food finally arrived so she could think about something else.

Kirby used to pack his gear every fall, and he and Melvin DuCharme would drive up to Melvin's cabin on the Cottonwood River. Knowing them, she assumed they spent more time guzzling beer and peeing in the woods than they did sitting in a deer stand. Kirby rarely came back with anything other than a hangover. She wondered who Melvin would take up to his cabin this November. Might get kind of lonely for an old guy up there all by himself. Kirby said the cabin didn't even have electricity or running water. Melvin heated it with wood. Men certainly had a different idea of fun than she did.

The pork chop was a disappointment. It was tough

and the center wasn't cooked enough. She ate the vege-tables and the potatoes and gravy, but she left most of the chop sitting on her plate. Cora didn't like to spend a lot of money eating out. For the price of a meal in a restaurant, she could make three at home.

Wiping her lips daintily with a napkin, she waited for the check. Instead of her waitress, Melvin DuCharme pushed out through the swinging kitchen doors and entered the main part of the cafe. Just the man she was looking for. As he headed toward the cash register, he spied her sitting in the booth. She could tell he didn't really want to stop and say hi, but he was stuck. Unlike Kirby, he had some semblance of manners. She waved her hand, yoo-hooing at him pleasantly.

"Hey, Cora," he said, walking up to the table. "How are you?"

"I've been better," she said, taking a last sip of water.

"Sure, I understand. I was up at my cabin last weekend doing some repairs. Can't believe Kirby wasn't with me. I sure do miss him. I know how hard it must be for you." Glancing at her plate, he added, "Something wrong with the pork chop?"

She turned the plate around so he could see the center. "It's pink. I don't think a person should eat pink pork."

Melvin scratched his chin. "No, Cora, you're right. I'll have to say something to my cook. Hey, maybe you're still hungry."

She wasn't, but she nodded anyway. You never knew when somebody in a restaurant was going to feel bad for serving you inedible food and give you a deal.

"Why don't I buy you a piece of our famous apple pie?"

She looked up at him pitifully. "Why, that would be very kind of you." But she didn't smile. Not yet.

He cocked his head and stared at her a moment. "Ah, why don't I throw some ice cream on that. Apple pie needs a scoop of ice cream."

Now she smiled. As he motioned to the waitress to get her attention, then barked the order at her, Cora said, "Melvin, I wonder if I could talk to you for a minute. Privately."

"Me?" He shoved his hands into his pockets. "Well, sure. I thought that's what we were doing."

She nodded for him to sit down. He looked kind of uneasy, like a mouse sticking its head out of a hole, looking for the cat. Too bad. He could give her one minute of his time. "You know, Melvin," she began, picking up her unused spoon, dipping it in her water glass, then wiping it off with her napkin, "after Kirby died, I found a diary he'd been keeping."

"A diary," repeated Melvin, this time scratching his snow-white hair. "Kirby didn't seem like the diary type to me."

"I was surprised, too, but there it was, tucked inside his tool box in the basement. It was awfully sad for me to read through it."

"I imagine."

"He talked about a place that was very special to him. Said that before he died, he wanted to bury the diary under this special tree, so that there'd always be a piece of him there."

"Really." Melvin didn't look very interested. He was starting to get squirmy.

"In a way, I take it as a last request. Except, I don't

know where the tree is, Melvin. I thought maybe you might. He called it the Devil's Tree."

Melvin gave her a blank stare. "The Devil's Tree?"

She nodded.

He thought for a moment, crossing his arms over his thick stomach, then shook his head. "Can't say that I ever remember him talking about anything like that, Cora. Sorry."

Her spirits sank. A second later, the pie arrived. Wasn't that just like life, she thought. One minute you're up, full of hope, the next minute you're flat on the floor. And then somebody serves you pie. Cutting off a bite with her clean spoon, she thanked Melvin for his time.

As he edged out of the booth and started to walk away, he stopped. "You know, Cora," he said, turning around and resting his knuckles on the table. "There was this one tree. It's up near my cabin. The tree's dead but it's still standing, and you always see a lot of crows in it. Kirby wanted to build a deer stand in a tree about ten feet away from it once, but he was afraid that the crows would scare off the deer. Those birds make such a racket. Anyway, I could be wrong, but it seems to me that I remember him referring to it as a Devil's Tree once— because of all the black crows, and because it was still standing when by all rights it should have fallen over long ago. I thought it was kind of funny at the time, but also kind of true."

Cora thought it was creepy. "That's fascinating, Melvin. What kind of tree is it?"

"A weeping willow."

"You own that property, don't you? The cabin and the property surrounding it?"

He nodded. "Ten acres."

"I don't suppose you could tell me how to get there? If you wouldn't mind, I'd like to bury that diary just like my dear husband wanted."

"Sure, Cora. Anything you want." He grabbed a clean napkin from another table, pulled a pen out of his shirt pocket, bit off the plastic tip, then drew her a quick map. "You can't miss the tree," he said finally, pushing the napkin toward her. "It's due north of the cabin, right along the river."

"I'm sure I'll find it."

"You're welcome to use the cabin while you're there." He wrote down his secret hiding place for the spare key. "I only go there on weekends."

"Thanks, Melvin. You're a good friend."

"If I see some fresh digging, I'll know it was you burying your piece of Kirby. Well," he said looking over his shoulder, "I've got to get back to work."

"You do that," said Cora, tucking into her piece of pie, resisting the urge to jump up and shout Eureka!

April, 1964

Dear Gilbert:
   Thanks for your letter. Sorry to hear your parole was rejected. Maybe next time it'll be different. Also, sorry to hear you've been under the weather. I suppose those prison doctors aren't the best and the brightest, but they'll fix you up. I don't think too many people die of bronchitis. Hey, I'm joking. Of course they don't. But when something like that lingers a long time, it's hard to live with. If I could, I'd send you some of my wife's chicken soup. Viola's the best cook. I'm actually getting fat. Hey, didn't I promise to send you a picture of her? I'll include one before I seal up the letter. She's a little older than me, and maybe she's not the best-looking woman I've ever laid eyes on, but I think she's wonderful. She's just what the doctor ordered after a long stretch on the road.
   Life's been pretty good to me lately. Got a new company car. It's a Chevy station wagon, but it's got a lot of zip. Handles real well. I love being out in the country. Who would have thought a city boy like me would end up traveling the back roads to a bunch of hick towns.

Believe it or not, Viola's got me real interested in classical music. Every now and then I can pick up a radio station in the car that plays the classical stuff. You know, Beethoven, Brahms, Bach? Viola gives piano lessons. She's also the town librarian. I suppose you could say she's refined. I like that. And I've really grown to appreciate Chopin's etudes, and Wagner. Man, that Wagner had some major darkness in him to write the way he did. And you know me. I was born angry. That music makes me want to drive a hundred miles an hour, roar like a banshee. When I listen to it I feel powerful, strong, like I could live forever.

I guess it's hard to explain about the music, how it makes me feel, but when you grow up thinking you're nothing, that your dad didn't care enough about you to even stick around and see how you turned out, things get to you in a way they don't get to other guys. I never thought music would help me, but it has. My brother seems to be able to live with what our dad did, but for me it still hurts. I could never just abandon someone, just walk away and never come back. I remember thinking in high school that I hated my dad's guts so bad, if he showed up, I'd beat him to death with my bare hands. I still would.

Hey, here I'm going on about my childhood and yours was even worse. Kids are so important, man. But you have to teach them right from wrong. Hell, if anybody knows about wrong, it's me and you, right?

Hang tough,
J. D.

16

Sophie sat behind her desk in her office at the Maxfield Plaza, punching in the work number of Laura Walters's best friend, Rebecca Scoville. She'd found Rebecca's home number in the Minneapolis area phone book and had left several messages on her answering machine to no avail.

Earlier in the day, she'd driven out to Deep Haven, the suburb where Rebecca lived, hoping she might talk to her in person. Pulling up in front of an attractive two-story brick home on a quiet, tree-lined street, she hopped out of the car and proceeded up the winding walk to the front door. After ringing the doorbell she waited, but when nobody answered, she took a pen and a notepad out of her purse. She was composing the message when a woman popped out of the neighboring house and headed in her direction.

"Morning," said the woman, tucking her T-shirt into her running shorts. "You looking for Becca?"

"That's right." Sophie backed up so that the neighbor could pull the mail out of the slot.

"I'm Sandy Revas." She flashed Sophie a friendly smile.

"Sophie Greenway. Is Rebecca out of town? I've left

her several phone messages but she hasn't returned my calls."

"You a friend or a client?"

"Neither," said Sophie. "We've never met. I was hoping to ask her a few questions about a woman we both used to know."

Sandy brushed a lock of brown hair away from her forehead. "Becca's out of town on business right now. That's why I'm taking her mail."

"If you don't mind my asking, what does she do for a living?"

"She owns an investigation and security agency. Northstar Investigations."

"She's a P.I.?"

"Yeah, but don't call her that to her face. She loathes the way books and TV portray people who do professional investigation for a living. It's nothing like *Magnum, P.I.*—or Kinsey Millhone."

Sophie smiled. She already knew that. But she'd never give up her crime novels. "Do you know when Rebecca will be back?"

"I don't," said Sandy. "Call her office. Someone there will probably know."

"Northstar Investigations," repeated Sophie.

"It's in Minneapolis, near the Art Institute."

Sophie thanked her, then returned to her car and headed back to the hotel. She made it just in time for a staff meeting. An hour later she was in her office punching in Rebecca's work number.

Three rings later, a male voice answered, "Northstar Investigations."

"I'd like to speak to Rebecca Scoville, please."

"She's not in. Can I take a message?"

"When do you expect her?"

"Well, I thought she'd be in this afternoon, but now I hear it may be the end of next week. If it's urgent—"

"No," said Sophie. She left her name and number and asked that Rebecca call her as soon as possible. Feeling thwarted but still hopeful, she sat at her desk and worked on hotel business until six, when she finally quit for the day and headed up to her apartment.

She found Bram ensconced on the balcony overlooking downtown St. Paul, with Ethel, their elderly mutt, lying next to him. In his gym shorts and T-shirt, he looked hot and sweaty, as if he'd been working out. It wasn't like him to use the fitness center on the eighth floor. Generally, when the elevator passed the dreaded spot, he'd close his eyes or make the sign of the cross to ward off evil vibrations. Exercise was so unlike him, Sophie wondered what was up. His shoes and socks were resting next to his chair, and his bare feet were propped up on the iron railing, the only part of him in the sun. He was also drinking a beer. Grabbing her own beer from the refrigerator, she joined him. "How was your day?" she asked, giving him a quick kiss and Ethel a quick ear rub, then lowering herself wearily onto the chaise.

"Are you asking me or the dog?"

"Whoever cares to answer."

Without raising her head from the terra-cotta tile, Ethel looked up at Sophie with unusually baleful eyes.

"She's in an ugly mood."

"She isn't the only one."

"What's wrong, honey?"

"Don't ask."

"No, really. I want to know."

"I am *so* out of shape."

She laughed, glad that it wasn't something more serious. "Join the crowd."

"But it looks good on you."

"Please. I need to lose ten pounds before Christmas. Otherwise—" she drew a finger across her throat. "—it's curtains for all my slinky holiday outfits. I'll have to walk around in a tent."

He sipped his beer, looking morose.

"Bram?"

"What?"

"Are you really concerned about your weight? You're a gorgeous, handsome hunk of a man. There are guys out there who'd kill to look as good as you do."

"*At my age.* Why didn't you finish the sentence, Sophie?"

"You can't be serious."

"Don't humor me." He sat up, then leaned forward in his chair, looking uncomfortable.

"Are you feeling all right?"

"I'm fine."

"You know, honey, maybe you should get a physical. You haven't had one in years."

"I hate doctors."

"And I hate dentists, but if I don't go see one occasionally, my teeth will fall out."

"Let's change the subject."

He really was in a rotten mood. "Okay," she said, not sure what else to do. "Did you interview someone today, or was it the usual Baldric-inspired free-for-all?"

"Don't you remember?"

She'd been so preoccupied for the last few days, she was ashamed to admit she didn't. Then it struck her. "The governor?"

"Give the lady a cigar."

"How did it go?" Finally, she felt she'd hit on a topic that could pull him out of his funk.

"It was a blast, Soph. Jesse Ventura is the best guest I've ever had on. He's funny, quick, and he says what he thinks. I mean, the guy doesn't sound or act like any politician I've ever known. The phone lines were lit up like a Christmas tree for the entire hour."

Bram had first interviewed the governor last spring. The program had gone so well and they'd had so much fun together that they agreed to meet for lunch the following week. From there, they'd struck up a friendship. Sophie felt they were an unlikely duo since Ventura was so rough-and-tumble, and Bram was, well, more . . . sophisticated. But in this case, their opposite natures seemed to complement one another. And since they both enjoyed the good life, loved a good laugh, and had similar political views, Ventura had agreed to make Bram's radio show a regular event. This was the third time he'd been on.

"The gov told me he's thinking of having a white-tie ball at the mansion next December. If he does, he wants me to be in charge of the artistic elements, as he put it. He thinks I have impeccable taste. I do, you know, in case you've forgotten."

"Have you ever told him you didn't vote for him?"

"No," he said, wiping a hand across his sweaty forehead. "It hasn't come up. And it won't, if I have anything to say about it." He gave her stern look.

"Mum's the word."

"I'll vote for him next time—when he runs for president." After chugging the rest of his beer, he continued, "I've got some other news I think you'll be interested in. I talked to Al Lundquist this afternoon. He stopped by the studio before I went on air."

Al was one of St. Paul's finest, a buddy of Bram's from way back.

"And?"

"I asked him about the Runbeck murder case. Thought I'd see if he knew anything we didn't."

"Did he?"

"Are you going to drink that beer or just hold it against your cheek?"

Taking a quick swig, she handed him the bottle.

"Thanks. Okay, here's the scoop. The Bureau of Criminal Apprehension sent some hotshot out to Rose Hill because the local sheriff's department has never handled such a high-profile homicide before. They did some testing back in the B.C.A. lab and figured out that whoever blew up Runbeck's truck did it with nitrogen tri-iodide."

"What's that?"

"It's a chemical compound that's often used by terrorists because it's so easy to make. Al said you could even find recipes for it on the Internet."

"Can they trace it?"

He shook his head. "If the murderer had used dynamite, I guess it is traceable. But this stuff isn't. Al said the B.C.A. guy figured that the perp mixed up a bunch of the stuff, crawled under Runbeck's truck and found a spot where the exhaust pipe and the fuel tank are relatively close to each other. Heat sets the compound off. The murderer probably figured that Runbeck would start the motor, back out of the drive, and a little way down the street the heat would cause a chemical reaction, and pop—the explosion would hit the fuel tank and the truck would go up like a firecracker. Runbeck's home is on the edge of town. The closest house to it is maybe half a mile away. Only thing is, Runbeck must have sat in the drive for a minute or two, so it detonated in his backyard."

Even on a warm summer afternoon, Sophie felt herself shiver at the thought. "Somebody must have really hated him."

"Al said that the local sheriff would already have arrested John Washburn if Washburn wasn't still in the hospital recovering from a stroke. They don't think it will be long before they have a strong enough case to convict."

Sophie petted Ethel's head. "Could a guy John Washburn's age crawl under a truck and do all that?"

Bram shrugged. "Why not?"

"Poor Bernice."

"Yeah," said Bram, blowing over the top of his beer bottle, "I feel sorry for the entire family. And, if what you suspect is true, Washburn could be a double murderer."

The phone inside the apartment began to ring.

"Want me to get that?" asked Bram.

"No, I will," said Sophie, glad that his mood had improved. She'd eventually have to dig it out of him—whatever it was that was wrong—but not right now. Grabbing the cordless phone off the coffee table in the living room, she clicked it on. "Hello?"

"Mom?"

"Rudy, hi! I was hoping it might be you. How's the cafe search going?" She sat down on the couch.

"Okay, I guess. My main impression is that real cafes are a dying breed. Most of the small towns I've visited have a pizza parlor and a Chinese takeout, but the old-fashioned cafes are few and far between."

"But you have found some."

"Oh, sure. One place served the best chocolate pecan pie I've ever tasted."

Sophie smiled. "Where are you now?"

"Well, I headed west on Tuesday, and now I've worked my way up almost to Fargo. I'm in Loomisville at the moment, about to have dinner at Dub's Lounge."

"Sounds kind of sleazy."

"Well, let's just say it's not much like the Chatterbox Cafe in Lake Wobegon. A lot of the places I've found have attached bars. I'm sure it's the only way they can make a go of it financially. Hey, but there's one bright point in all this."

"What's that?"

"The coffee house craze hasn't made it into *every* nook and cranny of the boonies yet. At least there are a few places in this world where you can still get bad coffee." He laughed.

Sophie looked through the double French doors leading out to the balcony and saw Bram pick up Ethel and cuddle her in his lap. She was getting to be such an old dog. They wouldn't have her much longer. "What about that photo of John Washburn? Has anybody recognized him?"

"Actually, that's why I'm calling. I've shown it to dozens and dozens of people, but nobody knew a thing. Until today. When I drove into town, I stopped at a gas station. The man behind the counter inside the office—his name was Morey—looked like he was in his seventies. So I pulled out the picture and asked him if he'd ever seen this guy before." Rudy paused.

"Don't keep me in suspense!" Sophie cried. "This is no time to use your dramatic skills."

"Okay, do you have a pencil and paper?"

"Just a minute." She went into the kitchen. Finding some scratch paper and a pen in the drawer next to the sink, she said, "Shoot."

"The guy at the gas station, Morey Hall, said that the man's name was Jim Newman. He married a woman who used to be the town librarian. Her name was Viola Little. They lived in house that was torn down about ten years ago. I guess there's a Wal-Mart store there now."

"What happened to Viola?" asked Sophie.

"Morey said he thought she was still alive, in a nursing home somewhere, but he wasn't sure. I guess she was quite a few years older than Newman. No other family around. If she is still alive, she'd be in her eighties. I left the photo with him and he said he'd try to find out more information. I wrote the number at the paper on the back."

"Good work," said Sophie. She still had so many questions. "Was he positive he recognized the man in the photo?"

"Absolutely. He said he used to play horseshoes with Newman—until Viola had to go into a home. Newman sold the house and moved away. "

"He deserted her?"

"That's what Morey said. He thought Newman was scum."

"What did he say this Newman did for a living?"

"He was a salesman. Look, Morey seemed to be a nice old guy. There's no reason he'd lie to me."

"No, I'm sure he wouldn't."

"I'll keep showing the snapshot around, and I'll let you know if I find out anything more. I better get going now, Mom. My dinner reservation is for seven."

"Dub's Lounge takes dinner reservations?"

He laughed. "In my dreams. But I am pretty hungry. I've only eaten seven meals today."

"The restaurant critic's cross."

"Yeah, it's a hard life, but somebody's gotta do it—preferably a man with a high metabolism and abs of steel, like me. Later, Mom."

17

Bernice hefted her heavy leather bag over her shoulder and pushed through the hospital doors out into the early evening sunlight. The scorching heat and the brightness were almost too much for her tired eyes to bear. The grass was brown and burnt and the trees had that late August look about them—dry and lusterless.

She'd spent part of the afternoon at the library, trying to get some work done. The *Times Register* had FedExed her over forty new meat loaf recipes people had sent in since last Friday. She was glad it was just about over. She'd been working hard, testing recipes at her parents' house, trying to select the three prize winners and the three honorable mentions. She also had to finish an article she'd started on American fall food festivals—everything from the National Hard Crab Derby in Maryland to the Okra Strut in South Carolina. She'd made plans to personally attend the Feast of San Esteban in New Mexico this year, but wondered if she'd still be able to make it. If her father's health took a turn for the worse, she couldn't leave Minnesota.

Bernice assumed that everyone in the family had taken a private shot at her dad in the last couple of days, trying to get him to open up, to explain why he'd admitted to killing Kirby Runbeck. Bernice had been alone with him for the past two hours. He'd slept most of the time, but he did wake briefly before her uncle arrived. She asked him some pointed questions, but as usual, what she wanted from him was what he refused to tell her. What she wanted was certainty.

And now she was wilting in the early evening heat as she walked the half mile back to her family home. Every morning when she got out of bed, she hoped she would be one day closer to finding an answer to her father's predicament and to her own.

As she rounded the corner and headed down First, she heard a horn honk. Turning around she saw that Angelo had pulled his rental car up to the curb.

"Hey, doll. Want a ride? I got air-conditioning in here. Nice and cool."

She turned and kept on walking.

He drove beside her, matching her pace. "Just think how hot and tired you're gonna be when you get home. And that shoulder bag—what you got in there? Bricks?"

Realizing her nose was in the air, she lowered her head and forged on.

"Got some sweet jazz playing in here, Bernie. Cool air and jazz? What more could a girl want?"

"Don't call me Bernie. And I'm not a girl." She quickened her pace.

"What should I call you?" he asked, turning up the music so she could hear.

It was Duke Ellington. Her favorite.

"I got some Count Basie, too. Come on, Bernice. Quit being so stubborn. You're gonna die of heatstroke out there. Who would've thought Minnesota was so freakin' hot."

"You should have stayed in New York."

"Like I said before, babe, no can do."

He was so infuriating. "I suppose you think you're making me an offer I can't refuse." It was the only kind of offer he ever made.

"Huh? Look, I'll even let you drive. I'll put my life in your hands, Bernice. You can take me anywhere you want. Total control."

"Like I was ever in total control." She turned to glare at him and saw that he was grinning at her. Sweat trickled down her back. She was hot and miserable and being stalked by a relentless jerk from New York City. Life didn't get any better than this.

"Look at it this way, Bernie. It's either me or the paramedics."

She stopped. Very slowly, she turned. "If I agree to let you drive me home, will you promise to shut up? Not say a word?"

"If that's what you want."

What she wanted was of no consequence and he knew it. Still, he wasn't an ax murderer. If he was going to take somebody out, he'd probably do it with a quick bullet to the head.

She climbed into the seat beside him, glancing at him briefly. His eyes were so large and round and blue. They reminded her of a doll's eyes. And his aftershave smelled spicy and inviting. It made their current proximity seem way too intimate.

Angelo took the long way back to her parents' house. And he was driving about fifteen miles an hour, but he wasn't talking. At least he kept his word about that. Except, his silence was beginning to bug her.

"Why don't you say something?" she demanded.

"You told me not to."

"So? Like you always do what I ask?"

"Okay. How's your father?"

"Fabulous. He's dancing a jig in his hospital room."

"Don't do that," said Angelo. "Don't start with the sarcasm."

"How do you *think* my father is?"

"I talked to his nurse this morning. She said he was doin' better."

"His nurse wouldn't talk to you."

"I told her I was family."

Bernice turned her head away and stared out the side window. "Do you always get what you want?"

"Not always."

As they pulled up to the house, the conversation hit a dead end.

"Thanks for the ride," said Bernice, opening the door.

"You wanna have dinner?"

She was torn. She hated eating alone, and she'd been forced to eat alone so much lately. But wasn't that exactly what had gotten her into trouble the first time round? "I don't know," she said hesitantly. If she said yes, he might take it the wrong way. It was just like a man, wanting things to mean more than they did.

"Come on. Aren't you sick of eating that garbage in the refrigerator?"

She whirled to face him. "How do you know my parents' refrigerator is filled with garbage? You broke into the house, didn't you! You picked the lock. How dare you invade our privacy like that!"

Now he seemed angry. "Why do you always jump to such wild conclusions about me, Bernie? Most people's refrigerators are filled with junk."

Just then, a squad car pulled around the corner and headed straight for them. It came to a full stop in front of the house.

Bernice watched it silently, sensing that Angelo's uneasiness matched her own. "I better see what they want," she said, climbing out.

Angelo cut the motor and followed her across the street.

"Evening," Doug Elderberg said. Sitting next to him in the squad car was a small man who looked like a pelican. Long neck and nose, beady black eyes, and a tuft of white hair on top of his head. "This is Bill Fordam," Doug said, making introductions. "He's from the Bureau of Criminal Apprehension in St. Paul."

"Nice to meet you," said Bernice. "This is a friend of mine, Angelo Falzone."

Angelo shook Doug's hand, then nodded to Bill.

Pulling a piece of paper out of his shirt pocket, Doug continued, "I've got a search warrant here, Bernice. We need to get into your parents' house."

Bernice couldn't believe her ears. "You can't be serious. I can't give you permission for something like that."

"They don't need your permission," muttered Angelo.

"That's true," said Doug. "We don't."

"My father didn't murder *anyone*," Bernice said defiantly.

"I know you believe that, and I'd like to believe it, too, but the fact remains—"

"You wouldn't know the facts about my father if you fell over them."

Looking impatient, Bill got out of the front seat. He

rested his arms on the roof of the car. "Do you have a key to your parents' house, Ms. Washburn?"

She glanced at Angelo for help.

"You better do what they say," he said softly.

"But what do you expect to find?"

"Evidence," said Doug. "We can't be any more specific."

Feeling as if the entire world had just landed on her shoulders, Bernice searched for the keys in her bag and handed them over.

As the officers entered the house, she remained by the squad car, drooping against the rear fender.

"It's gonna be okay," said Angelo, his lips barely moving.

"How can you be so sure? My father's had ample opportunity to recant his statement, but he hasn't. And he won't. I just know it."

"Don't worry, Bernice. I'm here." He put his hand on her back. "They won't find anything."

She looked up at him. "What's that supposed to mean?"

"There's nothing in that house to tie your father to Runbeck's murder. You trust me, don't you?"

"Of course I don't trust you! Are you crazy?"

He smiled, socking her on the arm. "That's my girl."

18

Plato was a man who lived his life in slow motion. Or maybe he existed in a parallel universe. Whatever the case, the people he lived with seemed to be moving at a different speed than he was. Plato had come to believe that, because of this phenomenon, he was essentially invisible at home. He was like an odd smell in the kitchen. His wife and two sons knew the smell was there and that it signified something, but because it had no particular meaning to their everyday lives, it was largely ignored. Ever since Plato and his family had moved to the hobby farm just outside of Rose Hill, he had watched his wife whiz past him to milk the cow, water the garden, attend to her charity work in town, visit her friends, play bridge, read magazines, gossip on the phone, attend church, and all the while he simply stood in a dark corner, stinking. People walked around him, past him, near him; sometimes they even stopped next to him and looked as if they might speak, but they never did. He even felt sometimes as if his family walked through him, an odd sensation indeed for a man as corporeally substantial as he was. He wasn't insane, so it had to be real. The more he considered it, the more he understood that his life had taken on the quality of a parable.

His identical twin sons, Kevin and Jack, had sailed past him years ago on their way to computer nirvana. They'd graduated from high school last spring. Nobody ever had trouble telling them apart because Kevin was a magenta-haired skateboarder, while Jack was a preppie in chinos. This fall, they were both planning to attend DigiPen Institute of Technology in Redmond, Washington. DigiPen was one of the first U.S. colleges to offer a bachelor's degree in video game programming. When Kevin and Jack weren't playing some ghastly piece of video trash, they were brushing up on their solid analytic geometry and algorithm analysis. To a man like Plato, it made as much sense as climbing the Himalayas or writing a poem in Sanskrit. Plato knew his sons were leaving for Washington soon not because they told him, but because he could enter a room and listen to a conversation without anyone knowing he was there.

The only one at the farm who lived at the same feeble-minded pace as he did was his dear friend, Astrid. And it was to see Astrid that he was headed at the moment, a plastic folding chair tucked under his arm. The day had been a long one, but it was finally over. As he walked through the field directly south of his house, the dead grass crunching under his loafers, the deerflies dive-bombing his head, his entire body felt swollen by the heat. He needed comfort, someone to understand him, to listen with undivided attention and offer, if not love, then at least genuine fondness.

He found Astrid standing by a patch of purple milkweed flowers. The evening light surrounded her in a golden haze. She wasn't afraid of him. She didn't move away. She simply stood and chewed, her tail swishing, her soft brown eyes welcoming him.

Plato set the chair directly in front of her and sat down. A light breeze cut across the field, and it cooled him now. For the first time all day, he was in the presence of someone who cared. His frayed nerves grew calm. His thoughts grew reflective. The world slowed to a manageable velocity. The milkweed flowers smelled sweet.

"Tell me, Astrid," said Plato, crossing his right ankle over his left knee, "why is the soul so often depicted as unconscious? That bothers me. It makes me feel like the deck is stacked against me. Like God only meant me to be half awake."

Astrid watched him, responding with a tiny moo.

"You're so beautiful, you know that? Black and white. I wish my life could be like you. People think cows are dumb, but that's because they've never known one, never loved one." He handed her an Oreo cookie, her favorite.

She chewed it slowly, then bent her head to tug at a tuft of grass. There was no rush. She wasn't going anywhere. She was here for him, ready to listen.

"There's something I haven't told you," he said mildly. He valued her good opinion of him, so he didn't want to speak sharply or to add unusual emphasis to his statement. "Let me backtrack a moment. You remember that I'm reading that biography of John D. Rockefeller? Well, Rockefeller and me, we've got something in common. He loathed his dad. I don't exactly loathe mine, of course, but . . . I've always felt like such a fraud and failure in his eyes. It's hard being the son of a saint, Astrid. Bernice thinks I see him that way because I never really got to know him when I was a child, not the way she did. But why would I want to spend time with a man who made me feel small and, if not exactly bad, then at least irrelevant?" He paused, watching an ant crawl across his foot. "Turns out, my dad was a fraud himself, just like Rockefeller's father." Plato smiled, then threw his head back and let rip with a belly laugh.

Astrid chewed her grass.

"I don't mean to insult you," he said, wiping a hand across his eyes, "but I don't think you appreciate how important this is to me. It's like I've been given this amazingly great gift. For the first time in my life, I feel like I can freely love my father, no holds barred. He's a sinner, just like me. Flawed. Scared. He did something so bad once that he was willing to pay a man one hundred thousand dollars to keep it a secret." When Plato said it out loud, he felt such glee, the tips of his toes curled.

"I suppose you want to know how I found out."

Astrid's attention had switched to a red-winged blackbird, but Plato trusted her. She was still listening.

"See, it's like this. Two days before my dad's stroke, I stopped by the house. It was late afternoon. I walked in through the front door and was about to call out a hello when I heard Dad talking to someone in his study. It sounded pretty heated so I stayed in the foyer and listened. Dad was talking to a man named Runbeck. You don't know him, but he's a handyman. Has a reputation as kind of a weasel. He'd fixed my parents' garage door opener a few months back, and he'd taken his old sweet time about it, too. I remember Mom saying that Dad shouldn't pay him by the hour because he was so slow. At first, I thought they were arguing about the bill. It wasn't like Dad not to pay it, but maybe he was taking Mom's advice—dickering over the price. But then I realized they were discussing something else. Somehow or other, Runbeck had discovered information about Dad's past. Whatever it was, it was really bad. From what this Runbeck implied, I think my dad may have killed someone and then covered it up. I mean, I couldn't believe it. I was mulling it over when I heard Runbeck demand another fifty thousand dollars." Plato waited for Astrid's response. "Did you get that? He said *another.*"

The cow twitched.

"Yeah, I was pretty shocked, too. That meant Dad had already paid the guy money for his silence once before. If that was the case, and I had no reason to doubt it, there had to be truth in what the handyman had found out." Plato batted a fly away from his face. "Okay, so they argued for a few more minutes. Finally, Dad agreed to pay him what he asked. But he demanded that Runbeck give him back 'the letters' first. That really grabbed my attention. Dad said Runbeck had no business snooping around the garage. From that I guessed that my father must have hidden something in there and that Runbeck had found it. Dad asked, did Runbeck really want to ruin him? Runbeck said that Dad had already done a pretty good job of it himself.

"You know, Astrid, for the first time in my life I actually felt sorry for my father. Even though I'd never killed anybody, I felt this . . . this crudely visceral sense of kinship. It's what spiritual types call an epiphany. Do you know what that is, Astrid? An epiphany is when you learn something that changes the entire direction of your life. It's like God appearing to Paul on the road to Tarsus. Like the day Edison saw the light."

When Plato looked at Astrid this time, he saw two great startled eyes staring back at him. She understood, just like he knew she would.

"So I stood there in the front foyer, feeling as if I'd been struck by lightning. Like the burden I'd been carrying around all my life had just been lifted off my shoulders. I would have stayed a while longer, but I heard a noise in the kitchen. Someone was standing in there listening. I had no idea who was home. Bernice was in town, so it could have been her. Or maybe it was Uncle Milton or Mom—or maybe all three. I didn't stick around to find out."

Astrid was eating grass again. Apparently, shock in a cow didn't last as long as it did in a human being. What Plato appreciated about Astrid was her sense of proportion. In her own quiet way, he felt she was attempting to teach him something important.

"Thanks, Astrid. I get your point." He sat for a while enjoying the peace and quiet. Somewhere down deep inside him, he knew he should feel immense guilt for taking such pleasure in his father's fall from grace. But instead, he was grinning like an idiot.

"You know, Astrid, in that biography of John D., it said that he believed overeating rich foods stimulated the criminal organs in the brain. Do you think that's true?" He waited. "Maybe that was why my father was trying to starve himself to death before his stroke."

Astrid blinked one eye.

"Yeah, I'm with you, kid." He got up, folded his chair, and patted her nose. "I'm gonna find myself the biggest, meanest, baddest hot fudge sundae with whipped cream and *two* cherries this side of the Pecos."

He winked, then walked away whistling.

19

Cora rumbled down the country road in her '78 Chevy Malibu, kicking up a cloud of dust in her wake. She knew she probably shouldn't be driving, what with her one eye dimmed by a cataract and her other eye recovering from surgery, but it was pretty deserted out here, there wasn't much to hit, and her good eye was almost back to normal. Besides, it was Friday. If she didn't drive out to Melvin DuCharme's hunting cabin today, she'd have to cool her heels until Monday. She remembered Melvin saying he used the cabin on weekends, and for what she needed to do, she didn't want company.

Last night, she'd redrawn Melvin's directions so she could read them easily while she was on the road. This morning she'd packed a picnic lunch and started off around noon. Even with the map, she'd made a couple of wrong turns, but she was pretty sure the cabin was just up ahead now. She'd been toying with the idea of renting a metal detector, but felt it might look suspicious. Why on earth would an old woman like her need a metal detector? People would talk. It was better to use Kirby's map and pray for luck.

When she came to a fork in the road, she eased the car to the right. A few minutes later, the river came into view.

Just as Melvin had said, the road dead-ended at the cabin.

Cora sat in the car for a few seconds and looked around. It was quiet out here by the river. Quiet and green, and the air smelled of moss and earth and dry leaves. It reminded her of the years she'd spent on her father's farm. Even a small town like Rose Hill had become cluttered with noise. At this moment, all she could hear were birds and the faint whine of a cicada. Summer sounds. It felt good to be out having an adventure. She'd never been the adventurous type before. Funny, the twists and turns a life could take.

Cora lugged the picnic basket and the shovel up to the small wooden deck just off the front of the cabin. She located the extra key where Melvin said it would be and unlocked the door. The first thing that hit her was a stale, musty odor—like dirty laundry that had been sitting in the basement too long. Cora's face puckered as she muttered, "What a dump." It was what she'd expected, only worse. With just three windows, all covered by dingy, yellow curtains, there wasn't much light, but she could tell the floor was partially covered by a shabby, green indoor-outdoor carpet. Two cots rested along the far wall and a couple of battered wood chairs sat next to an old-fashioned Formica kitchen table. It was just one room, and not very large. Melvin had built a bookcase out of pine boards and bricks next to the door, but there weren't any books in it. Only magazines—and clutter. Cora couldn't understand why he didn't clean the place up. There wasn't any water or electricity, so it might not be real easy, but what kind of man would want to spend time in such a pigpen? Her opinion of him took an instant nosedive.

Leaving the picnic basket on the kitchen table, Cora took the shovel and went back outside. The first order of business was to figure out where the Devil's Tree was. Without that tree as the anchor, Kirby's map was useless. Cora climbed down off the deck and headed north along the river. She was glad now that she'd remembered to cover her exposed skin with sunscreen, but she hadn't thought to bring along any mosquito repellent. Big mistake.

Even though there was a cooling breeze coming off the water, the day felt sticky and hot. Cora was dressed in a pair of thin cotton pants and a sleeveless cotton shirt. Both pieces of clothing were pink. She loved pastels, although she knew they did nothing for her aging skin. The woman behind the cosmetic counter at Mansel's department store told her she was an autumn. She should be wearing lots of browns and oranges. But Cora hated brown and orange. Her friends would just have to cope with her in pastels. It was very little to ask.

Tramping through the brush, Cora finally spotted the weeping willow. Never before had she seen such a huge dead willow. She could understand now why Kirby had been so impressed. The leafless limbs looked like giant hanks of wooden hair drooping toward the ground. Way up at the top were several dark smudges. Cora couldn't see the crows very well, but she could tell by the way the smudges moved that they were ready to spring and destroy at a moment's notice. Crows were disturbing critters. She'd never liked them.

Pulling Kirby's map out of the pocket of her slacks, she pressed a finger against the bridge of her glasses, and read out loud, "Sixteen paces due north of the Devil's

Tree. Due east four paces. Southeast nine paces. X marks the spot."

Why hadn't she thought to bring a compass? As an adventurer, she was a flop. She'd simply have to use the sun and hope she got the measurements right. Except, the clouds were thickening. The sun was in and out, but mostly in. "Fudge," she mumbled. She'd just have to wing it.

Looking up at the sky, she placed her back flat against the tree trunk. The crows started to caw. They were laughing at her, but she ignored them. "This seems like north to me," she said, knowing full well that it was only a guess. As soon as she moved away from the tree, she realized that she had no idea what a pace was. "Probably the length of Kirby's big feet," she muttered. She stopped dead in her tracks when she saw movement up ahead of her, about thirty yards into the woods. It was a big dark form, hazy to her damaged eyes, but definitely there. What if it was a bear?

Standing absolutely still, she waited to see what would happen. If it *was* a bear, she'd have to run for it. But if it was a deer, she'd be okay. She kicked herself for not bringing along one of Kirby's rifles, not that she'd know what to do with it, or even how to load it. Her dad had kept a loaded shotgun in the barn, but that was a long time ago. Cora used to be a pretty good shot. She wasn't a wimp.

After waiting another minute, she decided she must have been mistaken. All was quiet. She was understandably jumpy. She'd never gone searching for buried treasure before.

"Okay," she whispered, backing up against the tree

again. The crows continued to laugh. Sixteen paces due north. She counted to herself as she put one foot carefully in front of the other, leaving a good five inches between each step. When she got to the end, she turned east four paces, then southeast nine paces. It was all so frustratingly inexact. Taking a deep breath, she placed the tip of her shovel on top of the spot and dug in. A few minutes later, dabbing a clean hanky at the sweat on her forehead, she stood back. She'd uncovered a hole the size of a twenty-inch television set, but she'd found nothing.

She paced it off again. This time, she ended up several feet away from the first hole. So she dug another. And again, she found nothing. Seven holes later, she was tired and frustrated. She needed to sit down and rest her weary shoulders. She wasn't giving up. Oh no. But she had to take it easy. Filling the holes back in, she stuck a longish twig on top of each. She didn't want to dig up the same place twice.

Checking her watch on the way back to the cabin, she saw that it was going on two-thirty. She should probably eat her picnic lunch, but decided to take a short nap instead. It was only supposed to be in the high eighties today, but Cora was sure it was already in the high nineties. She hated the dog days of August.

Returning to her car, she stowed the shovel in the trunk, then rolled down the driver's window and slid in. She adjusted the seat back and tried to get comfortable, but it was difficult because she was so hot and sticky. It wasn't the best place she'd ever napped, but at least it was cleaner than the cabin. The idea of lying down on one of those filthy cots made her very grateful indeed for the modern luxury of a '78 Malibu.

* * *

A crack of thunder woke her. Cora sat bolt upright and tried to get her bearings. She'd been dreaming about winning first prize for her meat loaf recipe. She was lying on a silk couch in her suite at the Maxfield Plaza, talking to reporters and drinking chocolate milk out of a martini glass. Her mother was there and so was Kirby. He kept calling her "cookie" and "sweetie," trying to ingratiate himself, to insinuate himself back into her life. Fat chance.

A sudden bolt of lightning cut directly across the river. Cora leaned her head out the window and looked up at the sky. The clouds had turned a yellowish gray, like heated metal. The air was so still, not a leaf fluttered. Cora had been a Minnesotan all her life. She knew the signs. This was tornado weather.

For a moment, she wondered if she should make a run for it. Try to get home before the storm hit. But being out on the open road wasn't smart. The cabin was old but solid. It had lived through many a Midwestern summer and was still standing. She could feel herself begin to dither. Make a decision, old lady, she ordered herself.

She rolled up the window and slammed the car door before rushing for the deck. Standing with her hand on the doorknob, she looked behind her and saw the wind moving up the river. The sky was churning now, with roiling black clouds that looked like fields of inverted haystacks, some dipping toward the water. Lightning ripped through the dark sky, sending her shrieking for cover.

And then it hit. First the roar of the wind, forcing the pokey tree branches against the windows. Then the rain came down with such ferocity that the sound of it pounding on the roof was almost deafening. Cora turned down her hearing aid and put her hands up to her ears. She cowered in the center of the room, not knowing what else to do. There wasn't a basement or even a piece of heavy furniture to get under. She closed her eyes and prayed. As hot as she'd been, she was shivering now.

But almost as quickly as it had come, the worst of it passed. The rain eased. The sky became lighter and the wind died down. That's when she noticed it. The picnic basket was gone. For a moment she was so surprised, she couldn't move. She thought she'd been completely alone out here by the river, but that had obviously not been the case. What kind of idiotic nincompoop would steal an old woman's food?

Feeling thoroughly disgusted and just a wee bit frightened, Cora opened the front door. She replaced the key where she'd found it, then marched down the soggy wood steps out to her car. "You aren't safe from hooligans *anywhere* these days," she muttered to herself. It was too wet to dig in the woods anymore, but when she returned, she'd have to be more careful.

Cora had just started the engine when she saw a vague form flutter out of the trees toward the rear of the cabin. Thick clouds still obscured the sun, and thunder continued to rumble. After locking all the doors, she pulled around back. A man dressed in a hooded raincoat was standing on his tiptoes looking into one of the windows. Startled by the sight of her car, he tipped backward, nearly losing his balance. Cora switched on the headlights so she could get a better look at him, but by then he was rushing toward the safety of the woods.

October, 1965

Dear Gilbert:

It's a gloomy day here. A cold wind's blowing the leaves across the front yard. Kind of reminds me of when I was a kid. It was always my job to rake the leaves, then burn them. I like the smell of burning leaves. And, I suppose, it was a quick way to get rid of them. I like solutions that are quick and easy. But the job of raking was endless. That's what I feel like today. Like my job is endless. This may seem dumb to you, but for the past few years, I've been trying to make up for the bad things I've done. Okay, so maybe I look at life a little differently than some. I admit I'm a maverick. But I've been sitting at the kitchen table for the past hour, staring at an empty bottle of Coke, trying to figure out what went wrong. Life was going so good, man, but I've hit a real bump in the road. And I don't know what to do.

It's Laura. We got problems, stuff I've never told you about. Something's gotta give before I go tilt. Last night I got so mad at her, I kicked a hole in the bedroom wall. And then I left. Took my car and went into town. I had to cool off before I did something I'd really regret. When

I got back, she'd locked herself in the bathroom. Wouldn't come out. God, she makes me insane. I had to break the door down.

I don't know why I'm writing you about this. It's not like you can do anything to help. But there's no one else I can talk to. Laura's sister is useless. She's nosy, and she hates my guts. I don't know what I ever did to her. Her husband's totally henpecked, so anything I say to him would go right back to her. And anyway, I don't like to tell people about our problems. That's our business.

Tomorrow I hit the road again. In some ways, I hate to leave, in other ways, I know I've got to get out of here. But more than anything, I'm scared. I've tried with Laura. I want to be a good husband, but sometimes it's so hard. I feel that same old anger taking hold of me, the way it has all my life. Anger has always been my demon, man. That's why I've got to go.

J. D.

20

Sophie had just bent over the drinking fountain in the hallway outside her office at the *Times Register* tower when a gray-haired man in a brown and tan state police officer's uniform stepped out of the stairwell and headed in her direction.

"Say there," he called, glancing at the numbers on the doors as he hurried along, stopping in front of Sophie's. "I'm looking for Sophie or Rudy Greenway."

He had a clipped, military bearing, his voice a low growl.

"I'm Sophie," she said, taking in his solid features, curious to know why he'd come.

"My name's Diamond. Frank Diamond. Could I talk to you a moment? It's important."

"Sure," said Sophie, opening the door for him. She followed him inside and motioned to a chair. As she sat down behind her desk, she wondered if his visit had something to do with John Washburn. "What can I do for you?"

Diamond leaned forward, clamping his large hands between his knees. "I'm here because of a poster I saw yesterday afternoon at a nursing home up near Fergus Falls. It was a snapshot of a man and woman, with a note attached that said if anybody recognized the man in the picture, would they please call you or Rudy. There was a phone number under the name of the paper. I assume Rudy is your—"

"He's my son."

"I see." He sat back in the chair and crossed his legs. "Well, the fact is, Ms. Greenway, I think I may know the man in the photo. I assume you've left these posters all over the state for a good reason."

"Yes," she said. His stern tone made her wonder if she'd done something illegal.

"Care to share your reason with me?"

She didn't want to lie to a cop, but she didn't want to advance a theory that hadn't been proven. She settled for something in between. "He's . . . a friend, a man I haven't seen in years. I'm trying to locate him."

"Why?"

"Well, you see . . . he was married to another friend of mine. It was a long time ago."

"And?"

"He took off on her."

Diamond nodded. "I figured it was something like that."

"How do you know him?" asked Sophie, hoping her question would put an end to his interrogation.

"I work for the LaPierre County sheriff's office, Ms. Greenway, but when I was a young man, I worked for the Hayward County sheriff's department in Claremont, Wisconsin. I believe the man in the photo was a neighbor of mine. His name was Glen Taylor."

"Do you remember what he did for a living?"

"He was a salesman." Watching her reaction, he

added, "If I'm not mistaken, that's exactly what you wanted to hear."

"It fits," she said. "Was he married?"

"Yes, to a wonderful woman. Her name was Bliss Milkowski. Bliss and I had known each other since first grade. She married Glen in May of '68. I was the best man."

With that kind of connection, it wasn't likely he'd made a mistake about the snapshot. "Do you still keep in contact with either of them?"

"I haven't seen Glen in almost thirty years."

"What about Bliss?"

"She's dead."

It took an effort of will, but Sophie's face remained blank, her eyes steady. "How did she die?"

"She was murdered, Ms. Greenway. In 1974. We never found the man—or men—who did it."

"I'm sorry."

"I was the officer first called to the scene. The perp took everything that wasn't nailed down. Jewelry. Cash. Electronics. Even the toaster. He tied her up and strangled her in her bed." Diamond crossed his arms over his chest, still clearly bothered by the memory.

"Where was Glen when it happened?"

"Out of town. On the road. He got back the day after she died. I've never seen a man so broke up." He leaned forward again, shaking his head. "A couple of weeks after it happened, I found him over by Caribou Lake. He was sitting on a fallen tree trunk with a gun to his head. Wanted to kill himself. I talked him out of it, but it wasn't easy. Took nearly the whole night before he gave me the gun and let me drive him home. I got to know him pretty well that night, Ms. Greenway. He was never the same after Bliss died. He put the house on the market the day after her funeral and left town as soon as it was sold. I never saw him again."

"Did you try to keep in touch?"

"What was the point?"

Sophie hated to ask the next question, but she felt she had no choice. "This may sound cold, but did you check out Glen's alibi? You said he was on the road. Were there any witnesses?"

"Yes," said Diamond. "Believe me, friend or no friend, it was the first thing I checked out. Not because I thought Glen was a bad guy, but in murder cases, we always look hard at the people closest to the victim. My superior thought Glen was guilty, alibi or no alibi, but I disagreed. I think it's pretty clear it was a robbery that turned ugly. From what I remember of the case, Bliss wasn't supposed to be home that night. She planned to stay with a girlfriend in town."

"Did Glen and Bliss live out of town?"

He nodded. "In the country. Like I said, I was their closest neighbor."

So much of this story reminded her of what she'd found out about Morgan and Laura Walters. "Tell me, what did you think of Glen? As a person? A husband?"

Diamond pressed his lips together. "You think he ran out on your friend, huh?"

She nodded.

"Well, it's not consistent with the man I knew. He was a decent guy. A little wild sometimes. Liked to take the path less traveled, if you know what I mean, but I know he loved Bliss. She told me so a hundred times. Said he always cooked the meals when he was home, always brought her gifts if he had to be gone a long time. He pampered her like crazy and she thought he walked on water. I know she missed her family, felt pretty lonely every now and then, but she had her work to keep her busy."

"What did she do?"

"She was an artist. A painter. She hoped that one day, she'd sell some of her canvases. See, Bliss and I were both originally from Detroit, which is where Bliss's family lived. After Glen married her, they moved to Claremont."

"Why did they move?"

"Detroit was too far away from Glen's route. It just made more sense for them to live in Claremont. Houses were cheap. So was land. Glen didn't like big cities. Can't say that I blame him."

"So you saw nothing . . . dangerous about him?"

Diamond held her eyes. "You really don't like him, do you." It wasn't a question, but a statement. "He must have hurt your friend bad."

"He did," said Sophie. She saw by the way he shifted in his chair that he was getting restless. "Look, I really do appreciate you stopping by. Before you go, let me ask you one last thing. Do you remember if Glen Taylor had a tattoo?"

"Sure. He had one on his upper arm. Can't remember which side, but it was a snake with a single red eye."

Sophie had forgotten the red eye part, but she remembered it now—remembered staring at it the day she'd gone riding with him.

"Did your man have a tattoo?"

"Yes."

"A snake?"

She nodded.

"Then he must be the same fellow. Was he using a different name when he married your friend?"

Again, she nodded.

"Mind telling me what it was?"

"Morgan Walters."

"Walters, huh? Never heard of him." Rising from his chair, he continued, "I'm sorry I can't be more help. I came down to the Cities to visit my grandson, so I thought maybe I'd stop by while I was in town and see what that poster was all about. All I can say is, the man I knew wasn't the kind of guy who would just leave a woman, walk off and never come back. But, you're putting so much effort into it, I hope you find him."

"Thanks," said Sophie. "I hope so, too."

21

Angelo sat in his rental car and waited for Bernice to come out of the hospital. The Washburn family had taken to visiting John now in shifts. Bernice took her turn in the afternoons. She hadn't confirmed Angelo's theory, but he figured nobody in the family wanted the old man to be alone ever again. Someone had to be in the room to protect him—from the police and from himself—at all times. There would be no more chicken scratches on slips of paper admitting to a murder. If no further admissions were allowed, Bernice said the family lawyer would demand that the note be thrown out as evidence. If that didn't work, plan B was to say that John wasn't in his right mind when he made the admission. Since no one could deny his impairment, that meant he wouldn't be legally bound by anything he'd said.

However it worked out, Angelo figured John was off the hook for Runbeck's murder. He was guilty, of course, but that had little meaning if the police had no proof.

And that's where Angelo came in. He'd saved John Washburn's neck. Not that he could tell Bernice what he'd done. He'd lied to her the other night, told her he hadn't been inside her parents' house. The truth was, he had. It was a simple favor from one guy to another. If

Angelo ever needed to call in his marker, he would, but for now it was enough to know that he'd saved Bernice and her family a shitload of grief.

Pulling the book he'd lifted from the old man's study out of his glove compartment, he opened the cover and read the title page. *Total Resistance.* It had originally been published by the Swiss government, released during the Second World War. The point was clear enough. The government wanted the citizenry to fight against Nazi aggression with every means at their disposal. In essence, it was a terrorist manual. A small American press had reprinted the book, and that's where John must have gotten his hands on it. It sold mostly to survivalists and white supremacists. The question Angelo wanted answered was why did John have a copy of it in the first place? Was he *that* kind of guy?

Angelo found a recipe for nitrogen tri-iodide midway into the book, the substance the police suspected had been used to blow up Kirby Runbeck's truck. How had Angelo found out that bit of information? He smiled at his reflection in the rearview mirror, lifted his hand to smooth the side of his wavy black hair. He prided himself on knowing how to get information. Sometimes it took doing favors for the right person; sometimes it took money. Angelo's father had given him one good piece of advice. Everything in life came with a price tag. Angelo could have anything he wanted if he was willing to pay. In his fifty-two years, that advice had never failed him.

If the police had discovered *Total Resistance* in John's study, his fate would have been sealed. By removing the book before the police arrived to search the house, Angelo had saved the old man's ass. It was a good thing the Washburn family didn't lock their doors; otherwise Papa

Washburn would have to recover from his stroke in a prison hospital. Angelo couldn't imagine why he hadn't burned the book, or at the very least, tossed it in a dumpster behind the Piggly Wiggly. It was a mistake that could have cost him his freedom. But then, before Runbeck's death, Washburn didn't seem to be a man who was thinking straight.

Angelo had met him for lunch the day before Runbeck's untimely demise—if you could call it lunch. The restaurant/vitamin store/sprout emporium served nothing but rabbit food. Kefir. Tofu. Organic cheese and whole wheat sandwiches. The smell of ozone from the air purifier was so strong, it nearly gagged him. Everyone in the place seemed to know Washburn. They called him Mr. Mayor, and smiled broadly. He was clearly a well-loved man in his hometown. Good for him. He still had an enemy. Halfway through the meal, Runbeck had shoved his way through the front door, then stomped up to the counter and demanded his money back on some herbal remedy for thinning hair. Everyone in the place heard him. They stopped what they were doing to see how the clerk would respond.

That's when Angelo noticed a change come over John Washburn. He'd been friendly and relatively relaxed as Angelo explained why he'd come to town. But as soon as Runbeck entered the room, his face flushed and his eyes narrowed. For all practical purposes, he stopped listening to what Angelo was saying. Stopped eating. Started fidgeting with his napkin. Playing with his water glass. It didn't take a rocket scientist to identify Runbeck as the cause of the old man's discomfort. If Angelo had to define it, he'd say that John's reaction was a mixture of fear and anger. And when Runbeck sauntered up to the table, stuffing the money the clerk had returned to him into his back pocket, Angelo sensed that John wanted to get up and knock the old guy on his ass.

Instead, he sat on his hands and didn't move. Before Runbeck could issue his opening salvo, Washburn said, "I thought you were coming by the house yesterday."

Runbeck just smiled, showing his crooked yellow teeth. "Did you?" he said.

"That's what you told me."

"Well, I guess I changed my mind." He glanced at Angelo. With his skinny chicken neck, his overalls, and his gray stubble, he looked like one of the Clampetts. "Those letters you lent me are pretty interesting. I think I'll hang on to them for a while longer."

"That wasn't our agreement." Washburn looked as if his entire body were being squeezed in a vise.

Runbeck casually picked up one of the carrot sticks from John's plate and said he'd catch him later.

As he drifted out the front door, Angelo asked who the old guy was.

All John would say was that he was a loathsome creature, a lowlife with no principles or human feeling, and if there was a God, he'd be struck dead before he reached his truck. Washburn was shaking, the hatred in his eyes unmistakable. Angelo decided there was more to the story than Papa Washburn was willing to tell, and since he had a personal connection to the family now, he decided to pay Kirby Runbeck a little visit later in the afternoon.

He found Runbeck in his front yard, picking up broken tree branches from a recent storm. Angelo got right to the point. What the hell was he doing messing with John Washburn? Runbeck denied he was messing with anybody, but Angelo could tell he'd startled the old guy. For one thing, he was probably twenty-five years younger and seventy-five pounds heavier than Runbeck. John Washburn might have the body of an undernourished pencil, but Angelo's girth was menacing. He liked it that way.

Angelo had grown up in Brooklyn in a tough Italian neighborhood. If you didn't show a little bravado, whether you felt it or not, you got your face kicked in on a daily basis. He still liked to swing his weight around, especially when it came to assholes like Runbeck. So he threatened him. Told him that if he didn't leave Washburn alone, he'd regret it. He made it sound ominous. And then he asked Runbeck if he understood. He wanted to hear the old guy croak out an affirmative. As it turned out, Runbeck was a typical bully. When faced with a situation that called for courage, he caved. Angelo never laid a finger on him, but when Angelo left, Runbeck was about to piss his pants.

As Angelo sat in the car now, still waiting for Bernice to show, he realized that life had been good to him. He wasn't a handsome man, but he'd never wanted for female company. His money and his sports car talked louder than his paunch and his big nose. But life had been a bowl of cherries for so long that he was sick to death of cherries. The kind of woman he attracted wasn't the kind of woman he wanted to settle down with. And at fifty-two, Angelo felt he was finally ready to settle down.

His mother had pressured him his whole life to find a good woman, buy a house in the Hamptons, and make grandchildren. But that had never appealed to him. The grandchildren part still didn't. But the good woman . . .

that did. Especially now that he'd found the proverbial diamond in the rough. Bernice wasn't somebody he could let get away. No matter how hard she fought against it, they were fated to be together. It was the romance of the century. They were star-crossed lovers. In another life, they'd gone down on the Titanic, locked in each other's arms, that song by Celine Dion playing in the background. Funny how love worked. Bernice wasn't a looker, like the other women he'd dated. But she was smart. And clever. And beneath that gangly, intellectual exterior beat a heart as passionate as his own. She was Lara to his Dr. Zhivago. Scarlett O'Hara to his Rhett Butler. Rhea Perlman to his Danny DeVito.

Angelo wasn't the kind of man to let anything stand between him and what he wanted. Like his father said, you just had to pay the price. And where Bernice was concerned, he was willing to ante up whatever it took.

22

On Friday night, Sophie and Bram took in an early movie. The only show that appealed to both of them was at Centennial Lakes in Edina, so that's where they ended up. On the way home, the subject turned to John Washburn. They were still discussing him when they entered their apartment at the Maxfield Plaza around eight. Ethel greeted them at the door with a green tennis ball in her mouth.

Bram tugged it free and rolled it playfully into the dining room.

Ethel gave him a look of pure loathing.

"What's up with her?" he asked, disappearing into the kitchen.

Sophie stayed by the door to pat Ethel on the head. "She's not into exercise this late in the day, honey."

"Since when?" he called.

Sophie could hear the refrigerator door open. "Since her last birthday. I think the big thirteen really hit her hard."

"She's a dog."

"Your point is?"

Bram appeared in the doorway with two glasses of ice tea.

Ethel cast a dour eye on him.

"Should I get the ball for her?" he asked, his exasperation showing. It had hit the table leg and rolled under a chair.

"Maybe you should."

Bram pulled it free with his foot, then gave it a tap, rolling it straight for Ethel.

Instead of grabbing it with her mouth, she glared at it as if it were made of plutonium.

"Now what's wrong?" he asked.

"I think she wants you to pick it up and hand it to her."

"Oh, *pullease*. If we'd raised our kids this way, they'd both be in jail." Still huffing, he handed Sophie her glass of ice tea, then picked up the ball. Crouching next to Ethel, he held it up to her nose, and said, "Forgive me, oh great dog spirit. I have sinned."

Ethel stared at the ball for a few seconds, then gave his hand a tiny lick.

"I think you're forgiven."

"Lucky me."

Clamping the ball in her teeth, Ethel stood up and seesawed forward, dragging her weary body around the corner into the living room.

"So," said Bram, making himself comfortable on the couch. He patted the spot next to him, waiting for Sophie to sit down. "You've gathered all this information about John Washburn's past. What are you going to do with it?"

"I don't know," she said, kicking off her shoes and joining him. "If I'm jumping to conclusions, expressing my concerns to Bernice would be a total disaster. But what if her father really did murder those two women?

The idea that he got away with it makes my blood boil. And if he murdered twice already, maybe he did it again."

"Runbeck."

She nodded. "I just wish I had more insight into the kind of mind that could assume false identities and marry more than one woman."

"He had to be clever. And inexhaustible. I wonder how he came up with those aliases? Did he just pick the names out of a hat?"

Sophie shrugged.

"Hey, why don't you talk to Helen Domrese?" He glanced at his watch. "It's not late. Maybe she's home."

Helen was a psychotherapist with a thriving practice in downtown St. Paul. She also happened to live at the Maxfield Plaza in one of the hotel's penthouse apartments. "Do you think she'd mind if I called her?"

"With the story you've got to tell, I think she'd be fascinated."

Fifteen minutes later, Helen was sitting in their living room listening to Sophie explain what she'd learned about John Washburn. Bram stood by the drinks cart mixing a pitcher of martinis.

Helen was in her middle forties, with dyed red hair, bright-red lipstick, and—out of the office—a rather ribald sense of humor. She listened attentively and didn't interrupt. When Sophie was finally done, she said, "That's quite a tale of woe. You know, I've been in practice for over thirty years and I've known more than one bigamist in my time, but I've never heard anything to rival that." She sipped her drink and thought for a few seconds. "If what you say is true, my first inclination is to wonder if the man isn't a sociopath."

"Define sociopath," said Bram. He was sitting on the arm of a club chair, fishing an olive out of his glass with his finger.

"In a nutshell, a sociopath is someone who thinks he's the center of the universe. Everyone else was put on earth to service his needs and desires. In fact, some personality theorists actually believe the sociopath thinks of other people as less than human. You can see why they make such great dictators and CEOs. Sociopaths are often highly successful, productive citizens. They aren't hampered by normal human guilt. If there's a problem, they externalize—it's always somebody else's fault. John Washburn might be a sociopath, but it's also possible he simply has sociopathic traits. Most abusers do."

"Could you elaborate?" asked Sophie. "What are some other sociopathic traits?"

"Oh, things like failure to conform to social norms— like a bigamist. They often walk a thin line between the legal and the illegal. They con others for personal profit or just for pleasure. They're impulsive and aggressive. They usually have problems with anger. They aren't able to sustain personal relationships and they often don't honor financial obligations. They also have a distinct lack of remorse for having hurt others. The flip side of the coin is, these people can be highly seductive and charming. If you meet a sociopath, I can almost guarantee you'll like him—at least initially, until you get conned or swindled. If the sociopath is highly intelligent, and many are, he may never get caught. Outwardly, he may seem like a success story. But again, once you start looking a little more closely, you see the dysfunction. One caveat. Once you start discussing personality disorders, you see pathology everywhere—and I mean *every-*

where. And that can be misleading. Most people have some negative personality traits, but it doesn't make them inflexible or unable to change. What I'm saying is, it doesn't mean they have a full-blown disorder."

"That's good to hear," said Bram, looking relieved.

Sophie grinned at him.

Helen set her martini glass down on the coffee table, then continued, "Just for your information, my personal expertise is in the areas of spousal abuse—both psychological and physical—and also religious cults. At first glance, you might think those two are worlds apart, but they're not. What they have in common is mind control. Psychological manipulation. The manipulator, whether it's a spouse or a religious guru, uses similar techniques to persuade, often to the detriment of the person being persuaded. Whether or not John Washburn is a true sociopath, if what you tell me is accurate, he may have used some common mind control techniques on his various wives."

"Like what?" asked Bram, rising to refill the martini glasses.

"Well, speaking about cults in general terms, the forms most often used are control of information, which then limits alternatives from which the members can make choices. Also, outright deception. Group pressure. Intense indoctrination into a belief system that considers the world outside to be threatening, evil, or in error. Isolation from social supports, especially friends and family. And, in my opinion, the most effective tool in the mind controller's arsenal is alternating threats of physical violence with human tenderness, love with harsh disapproval. It keeps the members off-balance, and makes them yearn to do whatever is necessary to feel they're once again basking in the glow of acceptance and love. It's the same with spousal abuse."

Helen held her martini glass as Bram poured. "I've thrown a lot of theory at you. Let's get down to specifics. One of the key points in your story about John Washburn is that, with the exception of his current wife, he seems to have isolated his wives, either by moving them away from their family, or moving them out to the country. He also lavished them with love and attention. It's not a huge leap to assume that when he withdrew that love, it had a big impact. It's what I call 'tending and narrowing' behavior. You bombard the person you're after with total adoration. You literally whisk them off their feet. Then you slowly begin to isolate them, cut them off from opinions that might differ from yours. This ultimately leads the victim to second-guess her own thoughts and opinions. If the victim is a woman, society has already programmed her to blame herself for problems in a relationship. If the family of the victim should happen to suggest that her loved one is less than saintly, the victim takes the blame herself. It's her fault if he gets angry. Her fault if he hits her. And perhaps even more importantly, her fault if he withdraws his love. It becomes an insidious cycle. The more abuse, the more guilt the victim feels. I've seen it so many times, but it still surprises me."

Sophie mulled it over. "Maybe Laura Walters did commit suicide. Her husband drove her to it."

"The problem is, Sophie," said Helen, taking a sip of her drink, "if your man did marry all these women, if he did have a hand in two deaths, it's going to be virtually impossible to prove so many years after the fact. Your theory might be correct, or you could be way off base. There's no way to know for sure."

"But what about the tattoo?" asked Bram.

"It proves the bigamy, but it hardly proves Washburn was a murderer."

"But he admitted to a murder," said Sophie. "He killed a man in his hometown because the man was blackmailing him. I'll bet a million bucks it has to do with his past."

"That's highly likely," admitted Helen.

"Isn't the bigamy bad enough?" asked Bram.

"It's illegal," replied Helen. "But in the scheme of things, it's certainly possible to love more than one person at the same time. If it was love, not manipulation, it doesn't make him a monster, just a felon. There's a lot of room for interpretation."

Sophie immediately thought of Nathan. Her own life was living proof that a person could love two people at the same time. And if two, why not three? Or more? Sophie loved Bram deeply, passionately, but that didn't erase her feelings for Nathan, as hard as she willed it to be so.

"I'm sorry I couldn't be more helpful," said Helen, finishing her martini. "But hopefully, I gave you some psychological context."

When Sophie looked up this time, she saw that Bram was watching her, his eyes narrowed, his expression intent. Had her face given something away? Did he know she was thinking about Nathan? Perhaps, in the end, nobody's life was free of secrets. Or maybe that's what she wanted to think to rationalize her own disgusting behavior. "No, Helen, you've been a huge help." She forced a smile.

"I'm usually around evenings and weekends if you need any other questions answered."

"Or a little family therapy," said Bram. The comment was obviously meant as a joke, except that the smile that accompanied it didn't quite reach his eyes.

After almost ten years together, Sophie still wished she could read her husband better. There were times when she had no idea what he was thinking. Bram probably had moments when he wished he understood her better, too. If she wasn't mistaken, this was one of them.

23

Milton settled himself into a green plastic chair in his brother's hospital room. Before John's therapy session today, his nurse had decided to let him sit up in a chair so that he'd be ready for breakfast. He spent the better part of each morning in physical therapy, and every afternoon he saw a speech therapist. Slowly but surely, he was returning to life. There were tears in Milton's eyes when he looked at him now. He was so glad that, for the moment, John was out of danger. He couldn't imagine a life without his big brother.

The Washburn family had been taking turns to be with him, just in case he felt the urge to talk about the Runbeck murder again. They couldn't allow that to happen. Mary stayed nights—from eight in the evening until seven in the morning. That left the breakfast, lunch, and dinner shifts to be divided up among Milton, Bernice, and Plato. Bernice was taking the afternoon shift today—twelve to four. John would be whisked away right after breakfast and when he got back, he'd be too tired to talk, so this was the best time to do it. Because it was Saturday, there were fewer people around. Right now, before the food arrived, Milton had a green light.

Pulling his chair directly in front of John, Milton sat forward, trying on his friendliest expression. "How are you feeling today, buddy? You're lookin' so much better." He could tell his brother was tired, but happy to be out of bed and sitting up.

"I'm o . . . kay," said John, nodding. The right side of his face lifted easily in a slight smile.

"Listen, Johnny, I know this might not be the best time, but I need to talk to you. It's about Kirby Runbeck."

The smile faded. He looked away.

Milton felt his brother's resistance, but plunged ahead. "Why did you admit to the murder? That was so . . . so incredibly stupid."

"Mm . . . be . . . I . . . um . . . shtupit."

"Of course you're not. Don't get all melodramatic on me now."

Again, John looked away.

"They say Kirby was blackmailing you before he died."

"Nnnn . . . a . . . your . . . bish . . . nush."

"Of course it's my business. Ten minutes after you found out the guy was dead, you had a goddamn stroke."

John shrugged his right shoulder. "Co . . . ennn . . . shi . . . dence."

"Don't lie to me. That was no coincidence. I saw the look on your face, saw how agitated you got. He was blackmailing you, wasn't he?"

John looked over at the bed. Finally, his eyes averted, he nodded stiffly.

"Why?"

He puckered his mouth, then said, "We . . . all . . . shinners, right?"

Milton folded his arms over his chest. "Look—"

"No," John said with surprising vigor. "E . . . nfff."

"I won't let you squirm out of this. We've got to put our cards on the table. It's the only way out of this mess."

John gave his head a determined twist.

Milton was at a loss. If his brother refused to open up, there was no way he could figure out what to do next.

They sat for a few moments just looking at each other. To Milton, it felt like a staring match, like when they were kids. Who would blink first? But Milton wasn't the gullible kid brother any more. He'd be damned if he'd give in.

Finally, John's eyes dropped to the tray table in front of him. After a long moment, he raised his chin. "I . . . love my . . . kilren. I love . . . my wife. En . . . I love . . . my bro . . . er. You . . . are all my . . . life."

"We know that, John. We all love you, too."

"Do . . . ou?" He met Milton's gaze directly. "I know . . . wa . . . you'f done, Mil . . . en. I . . . know the truff."

Milton's mouth tightened. "What are you saying?"

Before John could answer, the nurse pushed through the door with his breakfast tray. She was early. Damn it all.

"They're all ready for you down in physical therapy," she said, setting the tray in front of him. Removing the plastic dome covering the plate, she added, "Since the trays came up a little early, I thought I'd bring yours in first. Give you a head start."

John looked up at her. "Gooh," he said, the right side of his mouth curling into a smile.

"We've got your favorites today. Low sodium chicken broth, a big glass of apple juice, and some chocolate pudding."

John raised his eyebrows, glancing at his brother. "My . . . favoritesh," he said.

Milton could read the sarcasm in his tone, even if the nurse couldn't. For a man who'd been living on wheat grass and carrot juice for the past year, hospital food must feel like torture. Not that John wasn't taking it all in stride. His characteristic humor had even returned, something he'd lost entirely before the stroke.

"Here, let me fluff that pillow behind your back before I go."

"Th . . . ank . . . uo, Ca . . . ol," said John, easing forward.

"You're welcome. Remember, if you need anything, just push your call light."

Milton turned his head and watched her go. As she pushed out the door, he saw that there was a cop standing outside. Why didn't they leave his brother the hell alone? He wasn't going anywhere. It was harassment, pure and simple. When he looked back, he saw that John had seen the cop, too.

"I'm a . . . fwight rishk," said John, a twinkle in his eyes.

Milton shook his head. "We're not done with our conversation."

"Yesh . . . we ah." He picked up his spoon. "Wou . . . you care to . . . join me?"

"Are you kidding? I'm not eating that pig shit."

The right side of John's mouth spread into a grin.

"I . . . for . . . give ou, Mil . . . en. We won't shpeak of . . .
ish . . . again. Come on. Dig in."

"You're something else, you know that?"

"I do . . . know . . . that. Thass my pro . . . blem."

24

Homicide. The word had a smell to it. It was dirty. Urban. Not the kind of thing that happened in Rose Hill. Plato had seen the headline in the morning paper, and the word was so huge and black and ugly, it nearly jumped off the page and punched him in the gut.

Plato stormed into Byron Jenny's office shortly after ten on Saturday morning. He'd made it crystal clear last Wednesday that no further mention of his father was to be made in the *Rose Hill Gazette*. Jenny had thumbed his nose at him. He'd connected the blackmail to the murder with the headline GRUESOME HOMICIDE TIED TO BLACK-MAIL OF EX-MAYOR JOHN WASHBURN.

"Can I help you?" asked Jenny, looking up from his tea.

Plato flung the crumpled Saturday edition across the desktop.

Jenny turned the paper around. "Today's edition. One of our better efforts."

"I gave you a direct order. No more coverage of my father's legal problems."

"Is that what you call murder? A legal problem?"

"I'm your boss. You do what I tell you."

Jenny pursed his lips. "I'm a professional journalist,

Mr. Washburn. I don't take orders that compromise my judgment."

"You *have* no judgment, you pedantic prig."

"I beg your pardon?"

"You've got the execrable instincts of a tabloid hack."

Jenny rose from his chair, meeting Plato's eyes. "Careful. You're about to exhaust your vocabulary."

"I want your resignation."

Slowly, Jenny pulled open the top desk drawer. He slipped his hand inside and took out a typed sheet of paper. Crumpling it into a ball, he tossed it at Plato's chest. "There it is."

Plato had expected an argument. A little healthy groveling. But Jenny wasn't about to give him the satisfaction. Fine. It was his funeral. "Don't expect a letter of recommendation."

Jenny glared at him, then threw his head back and laughed. And he kept laughing. Louder and louder. His face contorted. Tears leaked out of his eyes. He was a braying mule. A human gargoyle.

Plato stuck a finger in each ear to stifle the sound, but the laughter was like a virus seeping into his brain, making his instincts boil out of control. Before he knew what was happening, he had his hands around Jenny's neck. He was squeezing and squeezing, enjoying the sensation of power, the look of Jenny's face as it turned a deep purple. Jenny fought to push Plato away, but nothing could stop him. If he wanted, he could snap Jenny in two.

And then he let go.

Jenny fell backward into his chair, gasping for breath. "You're insane," he said, ripping his bow tie off and massaging his neck.

Plato loomed over him. "Maybe I am," he said mildly, even cheerfully. "If you're right, you better not mess with me or my family again. You got that?"

Jenny looked up at him, swallowing with some difficulty. After a moment, he gave a grudging nod.

"Clean out your desk and get out."

Half an hour later, Plato pulled his car into his parents' backyard. As he trotted up the back steps, a delicious smell tickled his nose. He'd been secretly hoping that nobody would be around today, that he'd have the house all to himself, but with Bernice still in town and his mother spending her days at home now, he knew it was unlikely.

After his run-in with Jenny, he felt uncharacteristically loose and lighthearted. He'd always shied away from confrontation before. Who knew it would be so much fun?

"Oh, good," Bernice said as Plato entered the kitchen. "You got my message."

"What message?" he asked, noticing that his mother was sitting at the kitchen table next to a man he'd never met before. Both of them had plates of food in front of them.

"I'm testing meat loaf recipes again today," said Bernice, getting another plate out of the cupboard. "I called your house last night and talked to Kevin. You weren't home, so I told him to be sure and tell you that I needed you to stop by this morning. I need another taster."

On the counter, Bernice had lined up six plates of meat loaf. As he bent over to sniff the first one, he said, "I'd be happy to help." The fact that he hadn't received the message was just more proof that he was invisible at home.

"Oh," said Bernice, handing him the plate and a fork. "I should introduce you to a friend of mine. Plato, this is Angelo Falzone. Angelo and I met while I was doing research on the New York club scene for my latest book." The two men shook hands.

"You from New York?" asked Plato, taking in Angelo's shiny gray suit and gaudy gold jewelry. People dressed a certain way are never wrong, he thought to himself. Angelo was that kind of man. He looked rich and confident—and connected. He looked like a mobster.

"I was born in New Jersey," said Angelo, resuming his place at the table. "But I was raised in Brooklyn."

You could cut the New York accent with a knife. Plato took an instant dislike to him.

"Dish yourself up some food," said his mother. "I know which one I like best."

"How are you feeling today, Mom?" asked Plato, breaking off a piece of each loaf.

"Remarkably fine," she said, dabbing a napkin at her mouth. "Your father had a good night. When he sleeps peacefully, so do I."

Bernice watched expectantly as Plato tasted each piece. "This one," he said, finally, pointing his fork at the first loaf.

"We all agree then," Bernice said with a triumphant smile. "Good. Now, I've got six more meat loafs coming out of the oven in a few minutes. You'll stay, won't you? I really need your help."

"It's a dirty job," Angelo said with a smirk. "But somebody's gotta do it."

Trite, Plato thought, setting his plate down. He leaned back against the counter. He might not have Angelo's easy self-confidence, but he was feeling pretty pumped this morning. He'd dealt with one asshole; he might as well deal with another. "How come you're in Rose Hill?"

Angelo shrugged. "I like to travel. I've never been in Minnesota before, but Bernice made it sound like a place I should visit. So—" He spread his arms. "Here I am."

"That's it?"

"What more do you want?"

"What do you do? For a living, I mean?"

"I own laundromats."

"In New York City?"

"In and around, yeah."

He looked pretty flush for a guy who owned laundromats. "Must be a good business."

"I do all right." He adjusted his diamond pinky ring.

"Mr. Falzone has been entertaining us with stories of his childhood," said Plato's mother, flashing him a look that said "stop the third degree."

"I've had a . . . colorful life," said Angelo, smiling at Bernice. "What can I say?"

Plato watched his sister. What was this guy to her?

"Well, I'll let you get on with your stories. I've got a few calls I should make. If you need me, I'll be in Dad's study."

As he walked past his sister, he could see the relief in her eyes. She was glad he was going. My God, he thought. She's sweet on the guy. Bernice was totally inexperienced when it came to men, and this proved it. Falzone was too slick to be anything other than a shark in pimp's clothing. What did she think she was doing, getting mixed up with a man like that?

Charging purposefully through the living room, Plato

was filled with disgust. He was the black sheep in the family, and yet here was his sister, bringing a man like that into their parents' house. Was nothing sacred? It irritated him to no end that Bernice and his mother were buzzing around Falzone like bees around a flower. But then, if they were occupied, it gave Plato the opportunity he was looking for.

Entering the study, he stepped up to the bookshelf that ran in back of his father's desk. Pushing the desk chair out of the way, he ran his finger down the first row of books. Then the second.

He was halfway through the third row when a voice behind him said, "Looking for something?"

Plato whirled around. It was Falzone. He was leaning against the door frame, chewing on a toothpick.

"Yes," said Plato testily. "I'm looking for a book." He bent back down and resumed his search.

"Not having much luck, huh?"

"It's here. I'll find it."

"What's the title?"

"Not that it's any of your business, but it's called *Total Resistance.*"

"No kidding?"

Something in Falzone's voice made Plato turn around. "You've heard of it?"

"What's your father doing with a book like that?"

Plato felt his neck retract into his collar like a turtle's into its shell. Why hadn't he made something up, said he was looking for *Harry Potter and the Magic Vacuum Cleaner,* or whatever the hell those books were titled. Now he had to give him an answer. In this case, the easiest way out of an uncomfortable situation was to tell the truth.

Sitting down in his dad's office chair, Plato stretched his legs out and crossed them at the ankle. "It's like this. Before my father's stroke, he was into organic food, alternative medicine, vitamins. He even thought he might start grinding his own wheat. He began sending away for mail order this and that, started getting interested in storing food in bulk, just in case we were ever overrun by starving Canadians or Mexicans demanding their fair share of wheat berries. Over time, he got on a few really crazy mailing lists. That book was sent to him with a bunch of information on building a secret food bunker. I'm sure he never read it. He just stuffed it in his bookcase and forgot about it."

"And so . . . you're looking for it. Why?"

Because I'm a fraud, thought Plato. Just like my dad. "Because, when I grow up, I want to be a terrorist."

Falzone reacted with a slow grin. "I guess it's always good to have a goal."

November, 1965

Dear Gilbert:
    She's dead, man. My wife, Laura. She's gone. Just got back from her funeral. I'm sitting here at the kitchen table and I feel like I'm suffocating. My bags are packed and in the car. I have to get out of here. Her sister looked at me with such hate today. I think she might know the truth, but hell, I'm not going to confirm it for her!
    What am I going to do, Gil? I screwed everything up. I'm just like my dad. God, I never wanted this to happen. I loved her so much. I wanted to protect her. But, the truth is, I hated her, too. I've never said that out loud to a living soul. I told you about our problems, didn't I? What's wrong with me? I can't do anything right.

    J. D.

25

Late Monday afternoon, Cora was back, rumbling down the county road to Melvin DuCharme's cabin. This time, she was packing not only a shotgun, but a metal detector. She'd driven to Marshall on Saturday, rented the detector from Jiffy Rents on Pearl Street. No way was her little adventure going to get back to her friends in Rose Hill now. This was private business, and Cora intended to keep it that way.

Pulling up to the cabin shortly after two, she got out and walked around for a while, the loaded shot-gun tucked under her arm. It was one of Kirby's. She'd never paid much attention to his gun collection before, thinking that all he owned were fancy rifles. She was pleasantly surprised to find an old shotgun in the gun cupboard, one very much like her father's. She knew how to use a shotgun. If there were any more Peeping Toms or bears in the woods, they'd be messing with an *armed* old woman this time.

Finally, feeling confident she was alone, she yanked the metal detector and the shovel out of the backseat and headed for the dead willow. She could hear the crows making their usual racket long before the tree came into view. "Knock it off," she yelled, but they kept right on.

They probably thought she was invading their territory. She probably was, but if she got lucky, she wouldn't stick around long.

It was another hot day. Sunlight fell slantingly through the hazy trees. The sharp tang of drying mud greeted her as she leaned the shotgun and the shovel against the willow and slipped her arm into the cuff of the metal detector. After switching it on and adjusting the dials like that man at the store had told her to do, she took the map and a compass out of her pocket. She paced it off just as she'd done last Friday, then held the round search coil two inches above the dirt and dried leaves. She watched the needle on the viewfinder as she walked slowly around the area. If Kirby had used a wooden box, or something plastic, she was up the creek without a paddle. But it hardly seemed likely he'd bury greenbacks in anything other than completely water-tight metal.

Halfway through her first pass, the needle twitched. Cora backed up and covered the area again. The needle moved into the red. "Bingo!" she shouted. It was only four feet or so from where she'd been digging on Friday, but four feet was the same as a mile.

Rushing back to the tree, she disengaged herself from the metal detector and grabbed the shovel. A few minutes later, she was the proud owner of a mud-encrusted jackknife. "Fudge," she growled angrily, tossing it away. She'd never even considered the possibility of other metal items out there for her to find.

An hour later, she counted up what she'd discovered. Six beer caps. Three shotgun casings. A nail clipper. A rusted hand trowel. An Indian head penny, a quarter, and two bent nails. And, of course, her biggest find of the day: the jackknife.

Sitting down with her back against the willow, she studied the map again. What was she doing wrong? She must be missing something important. And that's when she saw it. It was a little scratch at the bottom of the page. Something she'd overlooked before because it meant nothing to her. Now she wondered about it.

B K W D S

It was written so small, she could hardly make it out. But it meant something, she was sure of it. She repeated the letters out loud. "B . . . K . . . W . . . D . . . S." She stared at them, scrunching up her face in thought. And then it hit her.

It was an abbreviation for "backwards." If she reversed every direction, that's where she'd find the buried treasure!

Pushing herself up with some difficulty, she slipped her arm into the metal detector cuff and repeated the directions, only this time, she reversed them. "Sixteen paces due south of the Devil's Tree. Due west four paces. Northwest nine paces. X marks the spot." She walked it off, using the compass as a guide. Then, turning on the detector, she felt a rush of excitement as she started her search again.

This time, the needle hit red almost immediately.

Cora began digging. About two feet down, she hit something hard. Using the rusted hand trowel, she carefully removed the earth from around it. She wasn't positive, but it looked like a thick metal pipe, about fifteen inches long and maybe eight inches in diameter. Each end was enclosed by a rounded metal cap. By the time she'd freed it from the dirt, she realized it was extremely heavy.

It was just like Kirby. He loved muscling things around. Even from the grave he was trying to make her feel puny.

Cora took the shovel and leveraged one end of it out of the hole. The cap appeared to be screwed on, so she tried to twist it off, but it wouldn't budge.

Out of pure frustration, she stood up, grabbed the shovel, and gave it a whack. Her fingers stung and she felt the metal reverberate all the way up to her shoulders. But when she tried to twist off the cap a second time, it moved in her hand. A second later she was pulling money out of the hollow cylinder with both hands.

"Pay dirt!" she shrieked. The crows shrieked with her. Easing down onto the dirt, Cora counted the packages of hundred dollar bills, ten of them in all. Each package contained one hundred bills. One hundred thousand dollars. She was breathless! Ecstatic! Sure it was a rotten shame that Kirby had to die over it, but at least it wasn't lost for all eternity.

Reaching one last time into the cylinder to make sure she'd gotten every last dollar, Cora realized there was something else inside. She carefully drew out a large manila envelope. Inside, she found a bunch of smaller envelopes with letters inside, all written to a man named Gilbert Struthers.

"What's all this about?" she whispered, deciding to read the one postmarked July 1960. The letter was from a man named J. D. What he wrote wasn't particularly interesting. He talked about getting married, becoming a salesman. Just newsy stuff. Looking back at the envelope, she realized this Gilbert Struthers was in prison. Interesting. These letters must be the goods Kirby had on John Washburn.

Cora might have opened a couple more, but she was

starting to get nervous. Here she was, sitting out in the open with one hundred thousand dollars in her lap. She could read the rest of the letters later.

Scrambling to her feet, she cradled the money in her arms and hurried back to her car. She wished now that she'd brought a bag. After tucking the bills safely away in the trunk, she returned to the willow, lowered the metal cylinder back into the ground, then covered it with dirt and leaves. She tossed the bits of metal junk she'd found into the river, saving the penny for good luck, then hustled back to the car.

She was really on edge now. She should be on top of the world, but she was just plain scared. She had to get home and find a good hiding place for the bills. An odd thought crossed her mind briefly. She wondered whether the money would turn out to be a blessing or a curse. But how could one hundred thousand dollars be anything other than fabulous?

26

By five, Cora was home searching through the basement, looking for a place to hide the money. On the drive back from Melvin DuCharme's cabin, she'd decided to split it up, hide it in several different places just in case. Just in case *what*, she didn't want to think about. She was a whole lot jumpier now than she'd ever been before, but that was to be expected, she told herself. Her husband had just been blown up. And furthermore, she'd encountered a Peeping Tom in the woods. Since she was about to become privy to the secret that had gotten Kirby killed, she needed to be especially careful. Maybe it was time to get out of town.

As she packed the last of the money behind a loose brick in the laundry room, she heard the doorbell ring upstairs. "Fudge, fudge, and double fudge," she muttered to herself, trudging up the basement steps. The last thing she needed right now was company. True, she hadn't visited with her women friends much lately. They were starting to wonder what was going on. The reason she knew was that on Saturday afternoon, she'd had her hair done at Nola B's Beauty Nook and that's what Nola B had told her. Cora needed to invite a few of them over for coffee one morning soon. But that meant she'd have to run down to the bakery to get a coffee cake. Clean the house. It was always something when you were a woman. Cooking. Cleaning. Shopping. Laundry. Staying attractive.

"Hold your horses," she called, hearing her visitor bang on the front door. When she drew it back, she found a strange man standing on the front steps. She quickly made sure the screen door was locked. "Can I help you?"

"I hope so," said the man. He had chilly eyes. "My name's Angelo Falzone."

"You're not from around here." He wasn't tall, but he was still imposing. Thick neck. Hair combed straight back from a hard face. The milky-tea-colored sport coat and black polo shirt made him look like a million bucks. And even through the screen, she could smell the expensive aftershave.

"No, I'm from New York. I'm in Rose Hill . . . on business."

"Business," she repeated, inspecting the word for its true meaning. "Anyone ever tell you you look like Tony Soprano?"

"Who?"

"On HBO. *The Sopranos.* Don't you ever watch TV?"

"Not if I can help it."

Suddenly, she recognized him. He was the same man she'd seen the other day at the Prairie Lights Cafe—the one who'd been out in the front yard talking to Kirby the day before he blew up. "What do you want?" she asked curtly, backing up a step.

"To talk. Privately."

"About what?"

"John Washburn."

The name struck her like a blow. There was no way on earth she was letting a man who looked like him into her house. "Sorry. I'm busy."

"It'll only take a minute." He put his hand up to the screen.

Now she was frightened. "If you don't go away, I'll call the police." She closed the door, one note short of a slam. Watching through the picture window in the living room, she saw him trot back out to his car. She gave an involuntary shudder.

After he'd driven away, she walked around the house making sure all the windows were closed and locked, and all the blinds pulled. There was no use taking any chances. Passing a mirror, she saw that just above her wiry eyebrows, her forehead was smudged with dirt. So were her arms. The first order of business was to take a shower and change into clean clothes. She couldn't think when she wasn't tidy.

After getting out of the shower, she put on a freshly pressed cotton housedress and white cotton ankle stockings, tucking her feet into her pink terry-cloth slippers. She spent a few minutes in the kitchen fixing herself an egg salad sandwich and a cup of Folger's Instant, then she sat down in the TV room with her cat next to her in the chair. She lifted her feet up on the footstool and took the letters out of the envelope—the one she'd found buried with the money.

There were eight letters in all. Munching on her sandwich, she sorted them by date. Except for the first one, they were all written to a man named Gilbert and signed by someone named J. D. John D. Washburn, no doubt. These letters must have represented some sort of threat to him, so much so that he was willing to pay one hundred thousand dollars to keep them under wraps.

Winthrop settled in for a nap as she began to read through them, but each time she came to an important revelation, she cried "Oh—my—God!" waking him up. It seemed that John Washburn had been involved in a bank robbery in his youth. His friend, Gilbert, had killed a man and gone to jail for it. John had escaped capture and become a traveling salesman. He'd also been married to at least three women besides Mary—at the same time! And even more startling, from certain inferences in the letters, Cora concluded that he may have murdered two of them. "Oh—my—God!" said Cora, again and again. No wonder he didn't want these letters made public!

She read them through a second and third time, just to make sure she had all the salient points straight in her mind. By now the sandwich plate was empty. Taking a last sip of coffee, she stuffed the letters inside the envelope and leaned her head back. Kirby was a fool. He should have been more careful. John Washburn was a dangerous man whose entire life was based on deception. The Bible had plenty to say about a man like that, and none of it was good.

Poor Kirby, thought Cora, stroking her cat. As much as he liked to think otherwise, he wasn't a smart man. Cora might not be an Einstein either, but she was cagey. She had to come up with a plan to protect herself from the Washburns, and she had to do it fast. But her eyelids were so heavy. She usually took a nap in the afternoon, but today she'd missed it. Before she knew it, her eyes had closed and her mind began to drift to thoughts of dancing hundred dollar bills.

* * *

When she finally woke, it was dark. She was disoriented for a few seconds, not sure where she was. Then she remembered. She was in the TV room with the packet of letters still in her lap. The lighted clock next to her said that it was nine-twenty-seven. She usually turned lights on in the evening, but tonight the house probably looked like nobody was home. She wasn't sure if that was good or bad.

As she was about to switch on a lamp, she heard a noise. Winthrop jumped off the chair with a yowl, as if he'd been touched by a live wire. It sounded as if someone was rattling the back door. My God, Cora thought, somebody was trying to break in!

Tucking the envelope under her arm, she rushed down the hall to the kitchen. Sure enough, someone was outside, twisting the handle. Cora could hear her heart thump inside her chest.

And then the noise stopped.

Standing in the dark, Cora fiddled with her hearing aid. Where'd he go? she thought, creeping to the kitchen window overlooking the back porch. She peeked through the curtains, but nobody was there.

She swung around as she heard a clunk followed by a scrape. Someone was trying to get in through the TV room window! Her hand flew to her mouth, stifling a scream. Think, she ordered herself. Don't be a silly old woman. Where's the shotgun?

Her heart sank when she realized it was outside in the trunk of the Chevy.

Screw the money. It was time to call the police. She grabbed for the kitchen phone and dialed 911, then pressed the receiver to her ear. "Oh, no," she whispered.

"Oh my God, oh my God, oh my God!" The line was dead. Whoever was outside had cut the phone line. She was all alone!

Her mind disconnected. She rushed out of the room, up the stairs, and into her bedroom. She had to hide. But where?

The closet! It was long and narrow, stuffed with clothes, but at the end, there was a crook in the wall where she could fit herself. He'd never find her there.

That's when she heard the glass break. Where was her cat? "Here, kitty kitty," she whispered, knowing it was useless. Winthrop had dozens of places to hide. He'd be fine. She was the one who had to disappear. Fast!

Furiously messing up the bed covers, Cora balled up some of Kirby's old clothes and stuffed them under the blankets, then grabbed the wig she wore when her hair wouldn't cooperate and draped it over a pillow, covering it with more blankets. She stood back to see if she'd succeeded in making it look like someone was sleeping in the bed. As she did so, she heard a muffled crack downstairs in the living room. He was inside! An instant later the stairs began to creak.

Grabbing the manila envelope off the bed, Cora mashed herself into the closet and closed the louvered door. She held her breath, but instead of pushing all the way to the far end, she peeked through a crack in the louvers. She knew it was stupid, but she had to know who was after her. It couldn't be John Washburn, not unless he'd had a miraculous recovery.

Holding her breath, she saw an arm thrust itself through the doorway. Three quick bullets struck the sleeping form. Cora had seen enough TV shows to know a silencer when she heard one.

Instead of fear, her eyes lit with rage. If she only had her shotgun, she'd show him what she was made of. Inching slowly toward the rear of the closet, she could hear the intruder start to take the room apart. He was looking for the letters. He was right about one thing. She'd have to be dead to part with them now.

27

"When are you leaving for Rose Hill?" asked Bram. He was lying on the couch in Sophie's office.

Sophie was busily digging through her filing cabinet, looking for the notes she'd made for her next restaurant review. Sometimes, her biggest work-related problem was keeping her two jobs separate. This morning, she wished she had only one office and only one set of filing cabinets. "I've got some work to do here at the hotel, so probably later this afternoon."

"I wish I could come with you."

"You do?" She was a bit surprised.

"Can't trust a bigamist around a pretty woman."

"I don't think you've got anything to worry about."

"You never know."

"I'm only going to be gone one night." She walked over to the couch and looked down at him.

"So? Can't a fella miss his best girl?" He took hold of her hand and pulled her down next to him.

She loved the attention, but she couldn't ignore the feeling that something was wrong. "What is it, honey? I feel like there's something you're not telling me. I don't mean just today, but for the past couple of weeks."

"There is."

"What?"

"You're going to think I'm overreacting."

Now she was really getting worried. "To what?"

"My age. Sophie, I don't want a birthday party this year."

She was so relieved, she started to laugh. "But you love parties, especially when you're the center of attention."

"I'm not joking. I'd like to forget them from now on." He sat up. "I'm too old for a birthday party. It's pathetic the way I dote on them."

She still had the sense that he wasn't giving her the full story. "If that's what you want."

"It is." He pushed off the couch and stepped over to the chair where he'd draped his sport coat. Fishing in the front pocket, he removed a roll of Tums and popped a couple into his mouth.

"Another greasy grilled cheese?" asked Sophie.

"Why do you insist on this notion that I eat grilled cheese sandwiches. I don't. I haven't had one in years."

"Then why the Tums?"

"It's just a little heartburn."

"You know, sweetheart, Rudy had a bleeding ulcer a while ago. Maybe you—"

He cut her off. "I don't have an ulcer."

"Okay, okay. Don't bite my head off." She paused, watching him press a hand to his stomach. "Look, I promise I'll let everyone in the family know that there won't be a birthday party for you this year *if* you agree to see a doctor."

"That's blackmail."

"It's a simple request."

He sat down next to her. "For your information, I saw a doctor."

"When?"

"Yesterday afternoon."

"And?"

He brushed a strand of strawberry-blond hair away from her forehead. "The usual. The receptionist flirted with me. I flirted back. The nurse flirted with me. I flirted back. Same old same old."

"You know what I'm asking."

"You want the blow by blow?"

She elbowed him in the ribs.

"All right. The doctor looked in my ears. Apparently, I have unusually lovely ear canals. He tapped my knees, shined a light in my eyes, asked me how I felt. Oh, and he had a different nurse take my blood."

"Did she flirt with you?"

"I suppose you could call it flirting. She bit my neck instead of using a syringe, which I thought was a little odd, but what the hell do I know about all these new medical techniques?"

It was difficult to get a sense of what really happened from all his silly blather. "Are you healthy?"

"We'll know in a week when the tests come back. You'll call me when you get to Rose Hill tonight, right, Soph?"

"When I'm out of town, do I ever *not* call you?"

He kissed her nose. "Stay out of trouble."

"Don't I always?"

Instead of his usual comeback, something to the effect that she rarely made any attempt *whatsoever* to stay out of trouble, he just looked at her, frowning slightly. She knew that he often deflected his fears and frustrations with humor. Whatever was bothering him at the moment, Sophie had an intense desire to protect him, to keep him safe from harm.

As she sat wrapped contentedly in his arms, it struck her that perhaps he was thinking about Nathan. She didn't want to say Nathan's name out loud. Instead, she took her own less-than-direct route. "I love you, sweetheart." She squeezed him tight. "That will never change."

"I won't let you go," he whispered.

"To Rose Hill?"

He pulled back and grinned. A good sign. When he refused to be playful, that's when she got really frightened.

"No, you have my permission to go."

"Kind of like a hall pass from the teacher when we were in grade school."

"Right. But I may have something to say about other places you might want to go. In the future."

"I'm happy right where I am."

It was the kind of conversation married people often had when they didn't want to spell something out, but they wanted to get their point across. Message received, thought Sophie. She traced the line of his jaw, pressing a finger into the dimple on his chin. "My handsome, sophisticated, complicated man."

"That's right," he said, nuzzling her hair. "And don't you forget it."

When Sophie breezed back into her office after lunch, she found an unexpected visitor standing by the window.

"Nathan," she said, coming to a full stop just inside the door.

He turned around. "You never returned my phone calls or answered any of my letters. Why?" There was no preamble. No hello, how are you? He just launched into what was on his mind. He didn't seem angry, just baffled.

He looked tired, thought Sophie. His brown hair was shaved short, and his hands appeared rough, like he'd been doing a lot of physical work. Other than that, he seemed fit. He was wearing his usual jeans, chambray work shirt, boots, and thick leather belt. If she had her dates right, he'd been out of prison now for several days. She had expected to hear from him, but she hadn't figured on him showing up at the hotel.

"You know why I didn't answer your letters or return your calls," she said, wishing they'd had a few seconds to greet each other first, to normalize the situation. But Nathan had never been one to beat around the bush. He wasn't polished or urbane, like Bram. He didn't use words to hide behind. He said what he thought, unless there was a good reason not to. It was something Sophie had once loved about him. Now, it made him seem dangerous.

"You told me we could be friends," said Nathan, taking a few steps toward her. "I know I hurt you last spring, but I've explained all that. You said you forgave me. Can't we put it all behind us and start fresh?"

"You don't want a friend, Nathan, you want a lover."

"I want you to be my wife, Sophie. We'd be married right now if you hadn't been sucked in by that crazy Jesus Freak cult. And then, when you were finally free, you went and married somebody else."

"Nathan, when I married Bram, I hadn't seen or talked to you in over twenty years."

"I know it's not simple."

"That doesn't even begin to cover it."

"But you love me. I know you do."

It might be love he saw in her eyes, thought Sophie, or it might just be a bad case of indecision. Nathan thought he knew her, but he didn't. She was a middle-aged woman with an entire life behind her, not the seventeen-year-old blank page he'd fallen in love with. As much as she still cared about him, as much as she was still attracted to him, she didn't need this kind of complication in her life.

"You know, Sophie, I spent years cooking in France and Italy. Women there get married, settle down. Then they take a lover. It's commonplace, even expected."

"It's not commonplace in Minnesota."

"Europeans aren't tied heart and soul to all this puritanical crap Americans are so fond of. They don't have the same love-hate relationship with pleasure. It's a healthier way to live." He hesitated, then reached out to touch her hand. "We were close last spring. Why can't we be close again?"

"You get right to the point, don't you?"

"I've been locked up for months, Sophie. What do you expect?"

"I expect you *not* to come on to me like a character in a soap opera. I expect a little civility, a little understanding." She moved behind her desk and sat down. Seated, Nathan didn't tower over her in quite the same way. She hated being a shrimp. "We've already had this conversation. I'm married, and I love my husband. If you can't respect that, then you need to leave."

Nathan lowered himself into a chair. "Okay. I'm sorry. I shouldn't have exploded at you like that. I've made mistakes in my life, but loving you isn't one of them. Don't ask me to stop, because I won't." Pausing for a moment, he added, "But I do respect your feelings for your husband. Your loyalty is . . . admirable."

"It's more than loyalty, Nathan. That's what I need you to understand." He hadn't given in, she knew that much.

His expression lightened, signifying a change of subject. "I did a lot of thinking these last few months, about you, and about New Fonteney."

She nodded, wondering where he was going.

"I wondered for a while if I should open my own cooking school, but I'm not a teacher, Sophie. I'm a chef. And I've been away from it far too long. I want to get something going for myself again. I spent the past few days talking to people about renovating the main hall at the monastery, turning it into a spectacular dining room. I can finally put everything I've learned to use. I've got a great architect now, and I'm working with a contractor. It's time."

"A restaurant," she repeated. It didn't come as a complete surprise, and yet now that it was about to become a reality, she could feel the excitement growing inside her.

"I'd love for you to come out to the site and see the plans. We're going to break ground in late October."

"That's . . . incredible."

"I know." He grinned. "I want to call the restaurant Chez Sophia."

She just stared at him, feeling both touched and alarmed.

"It's just an idea, but I love the sound, the feel of the name. It's exactly right for the image I want to project. A mixture of French and Italian cuisine. Classic, yet warm, approachable. Like you. And . . . it's a way to honor what we once had. That's very important to me. It makes me feel like we're still connected on a deeper level than mere friendship. Not that friendship isn't good. I mean, it's great to have friends. You can never have too many."

He was babbling. He was also manipulating her and she knew it, but she was flattered nonetheless. "I think you better give it some more thought."

"Sure," he said lightly. "Nothing's written in stone. What do you say? You want to drive out to the site with me sometime soon? I should get my first set of blueprints by the end of next week."

It was tempting. But before she could answer, her cell phone rang. "Give me a second," she said, finding her purse and clicking the phone on. "This is Sophie."

"Is this Sophie Greenway?" asked a man's voice. "The one who works for the Minneapolis *Times Register*?"

"Yes. Can I help you?"

"The name's Morey Hall. I met your son last week. He was asking about Jim Newman, a guy I used to know. Had a picture of him from way back."

Sophie had to quickly change gears. "Yes, Mr. Hall. I'm delighted you called."

"Your son, Rudy, asked me to find out any information I could on Viola Newman. Her maiden name was Little. Viola Little. She was our town librarian from the late fifties to the late eighties."

Sophie picked up a pen. "Is she still alive?"

"Sure is. My wife knows for a fact that she's living in a nursing home somewhere in the southern part of the state. I checked around a little, but I couldn't locate her."

"Don't worry about that. I'm just grateful to know she's still alive. Do you have any idea how old she'd be?"

"Well, let me think. Oh, I suppose maybe eighty. Maybe a tad older."

Sophie wondered if her memory was still intact. "This information is a huge help, Mr. Hall."

"I understand from your son that you're trying to find her husband. I always thought he was a decent guy, a hard worker, but when he took off on her like he did, my thoughts changed. I started seeing him for the slicker he was."

"Slicker?"

"You know. Con man."

"Do you know anything about their marriage?"

"Just what I told your son. When Newman married Viola, he moved into her house in town. Nice little colonial on a quiet street. The place was torn down a while back. Viola was a classy lady, Mrs. Greenway. Way too good for the likes of Newman."

Sophie could hear a horn honk in the background.

"Oops. There's a customer. I gotta run."

"Thanks so much, Mr. Hall."

"If you find that Newman, give him a kick in the rear from me."

"I'll do that." She smiled. "Good-bye, and thanks again." When she looked up, she saw Nathan studying her.

"What are you up to now?" he asked.

"Nothing."

"Just an inquiring mind, huh?"

"It's business."

"Right. Are you going to answer my question?"

"What question was that?"

"Will you come out to the monastery one day soon to see the plans for the new restaurant?"

She felt the familiar trap door open beneath her feet. "I'll . . . think about it."

"I hope beyond the shadow of a dream."

"Excuse me?"

"John Keats."

"I take it you still read poetry."

"We like to think we change, but we don't."

"Is that Keats, too?"

A mischievous grin spread across his face. "No, Sophie. That's Nathan Buckridge. Feel free to quote me."

28

"Get out here!" shouted Cora. She was standing in the Washburns' backyard, the shotgun gripped tightly in her hands, the butt resting against her shoulder. "Get out here or I'm going to blow a hole in your goddamn picture window!"

The first person to step out onto the back deck was Milton. He was holding a coffee cup in one hand and had raised the other to shield his eyes from the bright afternoon sun. "What the hell do you want?"

"I got something to tell you, all of you. Anybody else in that house better come out now."

After her near-death experience last night, Cora realized she should be scared, but instead she was furious. The man who shot her in the head—or more accurately, in the wig—as she stood in the closet watching, had prowled around her house for nearly an hour before finally leaving. Thankfully, he was a fool. He never checked to see that she was dead. He either thought he was a crack shot, or he didn't like the sight of blood up close and personal.

Cora had spent the night in a cheap motel. She hadn't slept much, but she had done some important thinking. She should probably report what happened to the police, insist that they find out who the intruder was, that they protect her. But if she did, there was always the chance that they might find out about the hundred thousand dollars and make her give it back. That money was *hers*. She'd earned it.

The bottom line was, Cora—not the police—was the best captain of her fate. The Washburns had interfered with her life long enough. It was time she interfered with them.

Plato stepped out on the deck next. "What do you want?" he demanded, slipping on his sunglasses.

He'd turned into a real pork pie in his middle age, Cora thought, eying him critically. His mother and father were as skinny as a rail. So was his sister. What on earth had happened to him? "Is that it? Anybody else in there?"

"Why don't you lower the shotgun, Mrs. Runbeck?" said Milton. "Put it away in your car, and then we can talk."

She was standing in front of her Chevy Malibu, which she'd parked next to a derelict-looking vegetable garden. The cornstalks were high, but dry as sticks. The beans and tomatoes were lying flat in the dirt. "You think I'd come near this snake pit without protection? You must figure me for an idiot." She planted her feet firmly and regripped the gun. "I want you to know, I got your message last night."

"Message," said Milton. "What are you talking about?"

"One of you came to my house and tried to kill me. I imagine the fact that I'm standing here, alive and well, is causing one of you some real psychic pain."

"What do you mean, one of us tried to kill you?" said Plato. "That's ridiculous."

"Let's not play games."

"I'm calling the police," said Milton, turning toward the door.

"Stay put!" Cora thundered. She waited for him to do as he was told. "I got two big barrels here, and believe me, I'll use them both if I have to."

"She's insane," said Plato, looking a little shaken.

"Here's the deal. I've got the goods on John. I've read all the letters several times. I know what he did. I know what he *is*. Shame on *all* of you for trying to protect a man like that." She glared at them with as much venom as she could muster. "If anything should happen to me, copies of those letters will be sent to the police. Do I make myself clear? You harm one hair on my head and John Washburn will end up behind bars."

"What *letters*?" demanded Plato. "I don't know what you're talking about?"

"Neither do I," said Milton, with more indignation than his nephew.

They were a real pair, thought Cora. The son and brother of a bigamist and a murderer. One of them was a murderer, too. The very idea that something as evil as that could happen in a good Lutheran town like Rose Hill made her blood boil. And *they* had the gall to be indignant. "Ask John to explain it. Now, let's recap. I've got the goods. I've also come into some money recently, if you catch my drift. Leave me alone and I'll leave you alone. Oh, and one more thing. Just for my edification, what's John's middle name?"

The two men exchanged confused glances.

"Arthur," Milton replied finally. "John Arthur Washburn."

Hmm, thought Cora. That didn't fit. Maybe J. D. was a nickname.

"Why do you need to know that?" asked Plato.

"None of your business, boy," snapped Cora. "Just stay away from me. We'll do our own little version of a Cold War standoff. Peaceful coexistence. Just remember, I'm the one with the intercontinental ballistic missiles."

October, 1970

Dear Gilbert:
　It's just after one in the morning, but I can't sleep, so I thought I'd write you a letter. I'm in Fond du Lac, Wisconsin, at a Best Western motel. I spent the morning calling on accounts. I was supposed to head up to Green Bay this afternoon, but the fall weather is so beautiful, I decided to take the rest of the day off. I ended up in a park walking around an old lighthouse. I guess I'm still a loner at heart. I'm with people so much of the time that I can't wait to get in the car and drive away. Anywhere, just to be out in the open, by myself, with nobody wanting anything from me. It's funny, but the longer I live, the more responsibilities I seem to acquire. They feel awfully heavy, sometimes, but I gotta keep on pluggin, right? Can't let the assholes get me down.
　I guess maybe I haven't told you everything about my life. I am not, as they say, an open book. I know times are tough where you are, but it's not all wine and roses out here on the outside either. I figure there are all kinds of prisons, Gil. Sometimes I think the ones we make ourselves are the worst.

But, hey, I can't complain. I got a nice pay hike last month. Bliss is proud of me, and that always feels great. She made a special meal for just the two of us a couple of nights ago. She's been working real hard on her paintings. You know what I think of all that. She's talented, but she needs a break. When I go to drug shows and sales conferences in other parts of the country, I always try to talk up what she's doing. I even bring photos along. Before we got married, I promised her that I'd help her get a show at one of these hot new galleries. Maybe I was just shooting off my mouth. Sometimes I do that. Hell, I'm a salesman. I do it all the time. I thought I could sell her just the way I sell sunglasses, but so far, no go. And she wants it so bad. I guess I don't know the art biz the way I know drug sundries.

Anyway, I better try to get some sleep. I've got to make up for lost time tomorrow. Hang in there, Gil.

Your friend,
J. D.

29

All the way from St. Paul to Rose Hill, Sophie fought an internal tug of war. Should she get involved with Nathan Buckridge again, even on a very limited basis? She was genuinely intrigued by the prospect of watching him develop a restaurant at New Fonteney. She'd be fascinated to see *anyone* develop the space. From her brief experience of the old monastery, she knew the dining room would be amazing. And knowing Nathan, the food would be, too.

And yet, since it had nothing directly to do with restaurant reviewing, how would Bram interpret her interest? She'd examined the situation from every angle, her personal feelings included. If Nathan could just get it through his thick skull that Bram came first in her life, if she didn't have such a clear sense that Nathan was simply biding his time until he could make another move on her, it might be possible to remain friends. But the way it stood, any connection between them seemed very foolish indeed. The question was an old one. Could an erstwhile beau ever become a friend? Or more accurately, could an old boyfriend who didn't want to leave romance in the past ever be trusted?

Finding Nathan in her office today had been a shock,

but perhaps a necessary reminder that the sexual electricity between them hadn't gone away. She didn't want it to be there, but it was. She was probably playing with fire to even consider getting together to look at the blueprints. She might as well drink liquid drain cleaner or throw herself in front of a bus.

It was dusk by the time Sophie pulled her car into the Washburns' backyard. She cut the motor and sat for a few moments drinking in the small-town quiet. She was a city person, born and bred, but she appreciated the change of pace. As she opened the door and was about to get out, her cell phone squawked. Grabbing it off the passenger's seat, she clicked it on.

"Hello?"

"Mom?"

"Rudy!" She hadn't heard from her son for several days. "How's everything going?"

"Fine. I should be back home by Friday night at the latest."

"Where are you now?"

"I'm eating my way south from Duluth."

She smiled at the image.

"I just had dinner at the Blue Ox in Kettle River."

"How was it?"

"Great. I took lots of notes. They have a battered fresh walleye in cornmeal and ground hazelnuts that's to die for. It's served with wild rice pilaf mixed with dried cranberries, fresh rosemary, and lightly sautéed fennel. Really terrific food. The place was packed."

"How many cafes have you visited?"

"Oh, probably thirty you could call legitimate, not a franchise or glorified bar. I'm getting tons of new recommendations as I go along, so I've been altering my route accordingly. I could easily stay out here another month, but I'm getting kind of homesick. I've got lots of material we can use, so I think I've done my job."

"Admirably."

"Listen, I was wondering if you'd heard from that old guy I talked to last week—Morey Hall. Did he ever call you with the information you wanted?"

"He did." She went on to explain what he'd told her about Jim Newman, a.k.a. John Washburn, and one of his many wives, Viola Little. "Have you run into anybody else who recognized Washburn from the photo?"

"Actually, I have. Three people, to be exact, all in Pearl, Wisconsin. And all one-hundred-percent positive they remembered him. But they knew him as J. D. Washburn, not John."

"Interesting. He probably used his initials back then."

"You've got three other names, right?"

"Morgan Walters, Jim Newman, and Glen Taylor. Washburn either has three separated-at-birth doubles, or he led an active social life."

"That's an understatement."

"You've been a huge help, Rudy."

"Have you decided yet what to do with the information?"

"Not really. Actually, I just got to Rose Hill. I'm sitting in my car in the Washburns' backyard. I'm spending the night. Tomorrow morning, Bernice and I are going to put our heads together about that recipe contest, see if we can come up with the winners."

"Good luck," said Rudy. "I'll call when I get in."

"Be safe, sweetheart."

"You, too. Later, Mom." The line clicked off.

Sophie stuffed the cell phone into her purse, retrieved

her overnight bag from the trunk, then walked through the thick grass to the steps leading up to the back deck. As she was about to ring the doorbell, she glanced at the picture window directly next to her. The heavy drapes were pulled, but a crack in the center allowed her to see inside. It was almost dark out now and there was a light on in the living room. Sophie's eyes bulged in horror as she saw Milton take Mary into his arms and kiss her passionately.

"Oh, Lord," she whispered, looking away. But she couldn't resist. Her gaze swung back to the window. Stop it! she ordered herself, but she wasn't listening to her boring inner voice anymore. Obviously they hadn't heard her drive in. If she rang the doorbell now, would they wonder if she'd seen them? What were they doing! This was just one more complication in an already complicated family.

Sophie waited. After a minute, she looked again. This time, Mary and Milton were sitting down on the couch. Milton held Mary's hands in his.

Giving it another full minute, Sophie finally rang the bell.

Milton appeared at the door a few seconds later. "Sophie, hi," he said, welcoming her inside. "Bernice told us you'd be arriving this evening."

"Is she here?" Sophie asked, waving to Mary. The air inside the house was deliciously cool. Outside, the temperature was still in the low nineties.

"No. She's at the hospital. And when she's done, she's meeting her friend, Angelo, for a drink. She asked me to make sure you got settled in. You can use the same room as before. Clean towels are in the bathroom. You know the drill. Oh, and help yourself to anything in the refrigerator."

"Thanks," said Sophie.

"I was just about to give Mary a lift over to the hospital."

Mary appeared in the kitchen doorway, looking tired. "Good to see you again, Sophie. We've been eating a lot of meat loaf since your last visit."

Sophie smiled. "I'll bet you have." And that's when she saw it. The tattoo.

Milton noticed her looking at it. "It's a snake," he said, pulling up the sleeve of his shirt.

"With a red eye," said Sophie, feeling a jolt of adrenaline rocket through her body. When she looked back at Milton, she tried to find the young Morgan Walters in his whiskered and aging face. It was impossible.

"Something wrong?" Mary asked.

"Wrong?" Sophie repeated, stepping back against the kitchen counter for support. "No, nothing's wrong." Her gaze returned to the tattoo. "It must hurt a lot to get one of those done."

"Nah," said Milton, "it's not bad. Course when you're young and full of yourself, you don't admit that anything hurts. Tattoos are something that can make a guy feel more daring than he really is. They're silly, but that's an old man's perspective."

"We better get going," said Mary. She was holding her own overnight bag.

"Here, let me take that," said Milton. As he headed for the door, he looked back over her shoulder. "Don't expect me home right away, Sophie. I'll probably stay at the hospital for a while."

"No problem." She felt dazed. Confused. Like someone had changed the rules on her in midgame.

"Are you sure you're all right?" Mary asked, looking concerned.

"Don't worry about me. I just need to eat something." At least she could still lie convincingly.

"Try the meat loaf labeled number four," said Milton. "It's my favorite."

"I'll do that," said Sophie, her mind reeling at the idea that a man with *his* history could stand there and offer her something as prosaic as dinner suggestions.

From this moment on, Sophie would forever associate meat loaf with Rose Hill, snake tattoos, bigamy, and murder.

30

It was nearing midnight when Bernice and Angelo walked silently down a dusty dirt road toward Ice Lake. On such a sultry summer night, with the smell of freshly cut grass lingering in the air, Bernice couldn't help but feel that the lake's name had the kind of irony only a Minnesotan could truly love, living as they did half the year in tundra, the other half in a sauna.

In the dark, Bernice couldn't see Angelo's face very well, but she could feel his hand wrapped gently around hers. When she left New York in June, she never expected to see him again. She'd made a decision. She had her reasons. And yet, here she was, her unruly hair sprayed into submission, her mouth painted a deep mulberry, wearing her feminine clothes, as she thought of them—a long flowing Indian print skirt, a brightly colored cotton shawl, and a neckline that revealed just a hint of roundness. She was still the nearsighted daughter of the ex-mayor, the big-boned, awkward intellectual, the middle-aged woman in clunky shoes with a full-blown case of frowziness, but for some unknown reason, she felt softened around Angelo, and strangely content.

In the last few months, Bernice's life had come untethered, like a balloon escaping from a small child's hand.

She could see it floating over the trees, tossed by whatever air current happened to come along. She hated not
being in control of her emotions. She preferred thinking
to feeling, action to passivity. Her psychological slide
had started in New York, and then because of her father's problems, she'd slid still further, if possible even
more wildly, with no end in sight.

"What are you thinking about?" asked Angelo, leading her to a bench by the water.

"Nothing," she said, sitting down next to him, keeping a few protective inches between their bodies.

"It's not *nothin'*," he said, kissing her hand.

"Why do you say that? I was just enjoying the quiet."

"You're grinding your teeth, Bernice. You only do that
when you're upset."

How could he love her? She was such a klutz.

"Come on, you can tell me. I'm here to help."

You're here to complicate my life, thought Bernice.
You're here to get your way. But she didn't say it out
loud. That fact that she didn't made her feel even more
like a bowl of emotional mush.

"Is it about what happened this morning?"

She turned to him. "What happened this morning?"

"Cora Runbeck. She came to your parents' house with
a shotgun."

"She what? Who told you that?"

"Your Uncle Milton. He and Plato talked to her. Your
mom stayed inside. Seems someone broke into Cora's
house last night, tried to kill her."

"That's awful!"

"Yeah. Bad news all around."

Absently, Bernice lifted her hand to her teeth so she
could bite her nails. "Who'd want to hurt her?"

"Isn't it obvious? The same person who murdered Kirby is after her now. Cora said she had the goods on your dad, whatever that means. And if anything happens to her, the information will go straight to the police."

In the moonlight, Bernice searched his face. "Does that mean she thinks someone in my family tried to kill her?"

"Sure. She's not stupid. Except this time, it couldn't have been your father. My guess is, he didn't kill Kirby either."

"Of course he didn't."

Her indignation hung in the air for a moment, then he continued, "If she was thinking clearly, she'd go to the police *now* with what she knows. But from what Milton said, I got the impression she has the blackmail money and she isn't about to part with it. It makes her a sitting duck."

"But she said if anything happens to her—"

"Come on, Bernice. Use your imagination. There are a hundred ways around that."

"There are?"

He patted her knee.

"But . . . what does she have on my father?"

Angelo shrugged. "Don't worry. She won't use it."

"How can you be so sure?"

"Because I'll take care of it."

"As if you could." Bernice looked down, pressing her fists to her eyes. "This is all a dream. If I can just wake up, it will all be over."

"You are awake," said Angelo, slipping his arm around her shoulders, drawing her close.

They were such a ridiculous couple, thought Bernice. MTV should make them into a cartoon sitcom. She was a good five inches taller than Angelo, with all the sex appeal of a hubcap, while Angelo was thick and wide, with all the sex appeal of an Idaho baker. And yet that didn't prevent them from being madly attracted to each other. It must be some sort of twisted kismet.

"I adore you, Bernice." He nibbled her ear. "You're the most refreshing woman I've ever met. You're a real person. You're not just a facade."

If she could pick a facade, this wouldn't be the one she'd choose.

"I'd do anything for you and your family. We're in it together now."

"We are?"

"Sure. We have been for months. Since you agreed to be my wife. Only thing is, you left me standing at the altar, Bernice. You kicked me in the nuts . . . so to speak."

"I'm sorry," she whispered.

"I forgive you. I will admit, I was pretty PO'd back in June, but I cooled off. And to show you what kind of man I am, I'm giving you a second chance. You just got scared. Marriage is a big step."

She felt a little desperate. She'd fallen in love with him so quickly, so totally, but he was right. She *was* scared. "I can't marry you, Angelo."

"Why not?"

"Because . . . because—"

He drew back. "What? Tell me."

"I just can't." But he deserved an answer. She had to put it on the table once and for all. It was the only way out. "It's . . . your *business*."

He cocked his head. "Laundromats?"

"Don't lie to me."

"Lie to you? I own a bunch of laundromats, Bernice. Sixteen of them."

"You know what I mean. You're a rich man. You have an incredible apartment on the Upper West Side, a huge house in Connecticut. You drive a 1965 Lamborghini 400 GT with a Beretta in the glove compartment."

"How did you know it was a Beretta?"

"I looked it up on the Internet."

He grunted. "People have a right to protect themselves. And hell, I like vintage cars. Makes me think I'm James Bond."

She did a double take. "How does someone who owns laundromats get that kind of money?"

"Spit it out, Bernie. What are you saying?"

"That you're . . . you know . . . connected. I've seen enough movies to recognize the signs."

"You think I'm Mafioso? A member of the mob?"

"How else can you explain your wealth?"

"You're actually telling me that because I'm well off, I'm Italian, I own a gun, and I'm from New York, that I have to be a made man?"

"Aren't you?" she asked weakly.

"Are you nuts?"

"You aren't . . . laundering money in your . . . laundromats?"

"Is that what you've been thinking all along? *That's* why you wouldn't marry me?"

"You never talk about yourself, Angelo. Whenever I ask you about your family or your past, you clam up. What am I supposed to think? You must have secrets, things you're trying to hide."

He gazed up at the moon, looking solemn, hurt. And then he burst out laughing.

"What's so funny?" she asked, giving her shawl an indignant tug.

"You," he said, his laughter turning to giggles.

Now she was embarrassed. "I don't think being a mobster is all that amusing."

He wiped a heavy hand across his eyes. "Oh, Bernie. You're such an innocent. Sometimes I forget that."

"I *am not*."

"You may have traveled the world, doll, but you're still a small-town girl at heart. It's what I love about you."

"Why won't you tell me about your past?"

He cracked his knuckles. "There's not much to say."

"Give it a shot."

"Well," he said, crossing his arms over his chest, "you know the basics. I was born in New Jersey, grew up in Brooklyn. Never went to college. Never been married. And I own some laundromats."

"More."

He gave a frustrated sigh. "My family was dirt poor. I was one of six kids. I started working at a cleaners when I was thirteen, did mostly grunt work. But I liked it. I felt like I was doing something important, helping people take care of their fancy clothes. The guy who owned the business had a laundromat just down the block. By the time I was sixteen I was running it. Working a fifty-hour week, and making good money, too. I didn't give a damn about high school. I never got good grades. Hell, I couldn't be bothered. And I hated being home. My mother drank. Who wouldn't with six kids and a husband who thought he was Marcello Mastroianni."

"He was unfaithful?"

"He was a pig. Thank God he gave everybody a break and kicked the bucket fourteen years ago."

"I'm sorry."

"Don't be. He had testicular cancer." Angelo snorted. "Served him right. After he died, I bought myself a six-pack of Budweiser, sat under a tree in the graveyard and drank it, then pissed on his grave. It's what he deserved."

Bernice had never heard such anger in his voice before.

"Anyway, I was a natural at business. A real achiever. By the time I was twenty-four, I owned my own laundromat. By the age of thirty, I owned seven. I worked all the time. Night and day. Lived in a one-room dump and put everything I earned back into the business. And no, I never laundered money. Sure, I knew guys who were connected, but I didn't want any part of that. The farther I got from my parent's life, the better I felt about my own. When my parents divorced in '81, I bought Mom a house in Queens. Real nice place. Picket fence. Little blue-and-white checked curtains. I take care of her now, like my dad never did. By '81, I'd also started investing in the stock market. I had a few lucky breaks. And then when the nineties hit, well, I mean, you'd have to be brain-dead not to make money in that market. I made a shitload. Why shouldn't I have a house in Connecticut and a nice place in Manhattan? Why shouldn't I drive a great car? I got nobody to spend my money on but me and my mom. I've got four assistant managers on my payroll now so I get to relax a little, live the good life. I do what I want when I want. Except, I got nobody to share it with."

Bernice thought of all the willowy blonds she'd seen on his arm, young women who swung their pelvises across the dance floor, more interested in how they looked in the mirror than in who they were with. Not that they weren't impressed with Angelo's money. But that wasn't the same as caring about him. Angelo was right. He didn't have anybody to share his life with. And that was sad.

"It's a fascinating story," said Bernice, snuggling closer to him. "I had no idea. Why didn't you tell me any of this before?"

"It's not interesting."

"Of course it is. It's rags to riches. The American Dream."

"It's more like the American nightmare. Pulling yourself up by your own bootstraps is only interesting if you've never had to do it. Being poor isn't fascinating. Working like a dog isn't fun. I never had a childhood. Until I turned fifty, all I did was chase the Almighty Buck. But I'll be damned if I'll let anything prevent me from enjoying myself from here on out. Nothing and nobody's going to stand in the way of *that*."

"I'm so glad you're not a gangster, Angelo." She sighed.

"Yeah," said Angelo, smiling into her cleavage. "Me, too. Does that mean you'll marry me?"

"Yes. But I can't even think about it until my father's legal problems get resolved. I mean, if Cora Runbeck is running around with a shotgun threatening my family, I can't exactly announce my engagement."

"No, I see your point." He attempted to brush the bangs away from her forehead but found that her hair was glued together en masse. "Don't worry about a thing, babe." He settled for a friendly nose tweak. "I came to town to talk to your dad. Don't get mad at me now, but I wanted to ask his permission to marry you. I know it's archaic. I know it's dumb, but I thought if I had him on my side, it would help me win you over."

"You're neolithic, you know that?"

"But lovably neolithic, right?"

From her comfortable position wrapped in his embrace, she nodded contentedly.

"Good. Because, see, I came to Rose Hill for selfish reasons, but I stayed to help your family. You believe that, don't you?"

"I do," she said, gazing down into his eyes.

"I'll take care of Cora Runbeck. You can take that to the bank."

Bernice felt a tiny quiver of apprehension, but dismissed it. A quiver of something far more exciting commanded her full attention.

31

On Wednesday morning, Angelo stood on Cora Runbeck's front steps and rang the doorbell. After her near-death experience on Monday night, he figured it would take a miracle to get her to talk to him today, but he'd spent some time on the phone after breakfast talking to a business associate back in New York, getting ideas. He felt he had it all worked out. Only thing was, Cora didn't seem to be home. He pressed the bell again, then banged on the door with his fist. He cupped a hand over his sunglasses and tried to peer in through the small window, but all he saw was darkness.

Crossing the front yard to the side of the house, Angelo passed an old Chevy Malibu on his way to the backyard. If her car was here, she had to be around someplace. He moved carefully past the charred hole where Kirby Runbeck's truck had blown sky-high. Yellow crime scene tape had been balled up and stuffed into a badly dented garbage can. He also noticed that parts of the screen on the back porch were ripped away and the yard was pockmarked and still full of debris. Nitrogen tri-iodide sure made a mess.

"Stop right there, sonny!"

Cora was standing on the screened porch with a shotgun pointed at his chest.

Angelo dropped the briefcase he was holding and raised his hands.

"Get off my property. Now!"

"I can't."

"What do you mean, you *can't?*"

"We gotta talk first."

"I told you the other night, I don't talk to mobsters."

"I'm not a mobster."

"Tell me another."

"Look, this is important. I wouldn't stand here facing down a gun if it weren't."

She raised an eyebrow. "If it's about John Washburn and his demented brood, you can save your breath."

Very carefully, Angelo lifted his foot and pushed the briefcase toward her. "I brought you something."

She eyed the case suspiciously. "What is it? Another bomb? What do you take me for? I'm not as stupid as my husband."

No, thought Angelo, but you're every bit as greedy. "Just come down here. I promise. I'm not armed." Very slowly, he dropped one hand and flicked open the button of his sport coat, spreading it wide so she could see he wasn't carrying. Then he patted down his pocket and pants. "I can't hurt you when you're the one with the firepower."

She thought about that for a moment. "Open it up."

He looked over both shoulders. "Not out here. It's too public."

"My closest neighbor is half a mile away."

"Just let me bring it up to you."

"Open it!"

Bending down, he pressed the button on the expensive Zero Halliburton aluminum case, then drew back the cover. He could hear an audible gasp from inside the porch.

"In case you're wondering, Mrs. Runbeck, it's fifty thousand dollars in small bills. I'm makin' you a deal you can't refuse." He figured she'd appreciate the idiom. Standing up, he shoved the case closer to the concrete steps.

She was silent for almost a minute. Finally she said, "What kind of game are you playing?"

"It's no game. All you've got to do is give me five minutes of your time. Come on, let's put our cards on the table. The money's my bargaining chip. You've got something I want. I've got something you want. I'm no threat to you. You're packing the heat and you can go on packing it. Just let me onto the porch so I can talk to you more privately."

Her eyes shifted between the money and Angelo's face. "What *exactly* do you want?"

"Information. That's it. Just information."

"On John Washburn?"

He nodded.

"And if I give it to you, I get the money?"

"That's right."

"Is it hot?"

"Hot?"

"Stolen. Pilfered. Swiped," she said, disgusted by his ignorance.

"No, ma'am. It's clean. Unmarked. I swear." He might as well use the jargon she seemed to expect from him.

"Okay, so continue."

"I've heard you've got the goods on John Washburn. You can keep whatever it is you found. I just want to look at it."

"How come you're so interested?"

"I been thinking about asking his daughter to marry me. But if her father is as corrupt as everyone says, I'm not so sure I want into the family. You don't just marry the person, you know; you marry the whole megillah."

"Tell me about it," said Cora.

"So help me out. I'll make it worth your while."

"You must really have it bad for Bernice."

"Not so bad that I'm not gonna be careful."

She nodded her approval.

"What do you say? Will you talk to me?"

"It's no skin off my nose if you find out what a bastard that John Washburn is. Bring me the money." She lowered the gun, but didn't put it down.

Once Angelo was up on the porch and Cora had fingered the bills, making sure they were the genuine article, she excused herself saying she'd be back in a second. She entered the house, shooing her little gray cat back with her foot, and locked the door behind her.

Angelo sat down on a metal glider, a satisfied smile on his face. You could always count on a human's baser instincts to help you get your foot in the door. He hummed "Satin Doll" as he waited, thinking that his years as a businessman had served him well. He knew how to play people like a concert violinist played the violin.

Cora returned a few minutes later carrying a brown manila envelope. She tossed it to him, then sat down on a wooden rocker. She was still holding the shotgun, not about to take any chances. "There they are," she said with a note of triumph in her voice. "The letters."

"Letters?" Angelo repeated.

"Eight of 'em. Proof positive that John Washburn was both a bigamist and a murderer. To be fair," she added, "I'm positive about the bigamy, but not totally positive about the murder part. You can draw your own conclusions."

"He actually had more than one wife?" Of all the evils Angelo had imagined, bigamy wasn't even on his list.

"Yup. And I think he killed one of 'em. He was a traveling salesman, you know. They're notorious. Let me tell you, those letters are hot stuff. Somebody in that family of his tried to murder me over them just the other night. I nearly had a heart attack right there in the closet."

"You hid in the closet?"

"You bet your boots I did. Whoever broke in ransacked the place. But they didn't find what they were looking for," she said with a twinkle in her eye.

Angelo drew out the packet of letters and looked at them. All handwritten. All clearly originals. "If I were you, I'd put these in a safe deposit box."

"Think so?"

"You're not safe as long as they're here. Even if you made copies, you'd want these if you ever had to go to court."

"Maybe you're right."

"While we're on the subject, who do you think broke into your house?"

She hesitated this time, sitting back in her chair and rocking for a few seconds before answering. "You're not going to like it, so brace yourself. I think anybody in that family is capable of murder. The apple doesn't fall far from the tree."

"You're not suggesting Bernice—"

"Sure I am. Bernice. Mary. Milton. Plato. Any of them could've done it." She lowered her voice. "The gun had a silencer on it. Made my legs turn to jelly just to hear that sound in my house. I can't get it out of my head. It's a terrible thing when a woman doesn't feel safe in her own home."

"A silencer, huh," Angelo repeated. "But . . . you didn't actually see anyone?"

"Sonny, I was so far back in the closet by the time that ghoul came into the bedroom, you couldn't have pried me out with a blowtorch."

Angelo grinned. He didn't know if it was the right reaction, but her feistiness amused him. "Look, while I'm thinking about it, let me give you my card." He pulled one out of his vest pocket. "I've written the number of my cell phone on the back. You can reach me day or night."

He stood up halfway and handed it across to her.

She took it and studied it briefly, then used it to fan her face. "Can't imagine why I'd ever need to call you, but thanks."

"Don't mention it."

"Go ahead," she said, nodding to the letters. "Read 'em. I suppose I should offer you something to drink, but it seems kind of funny—you sitting here drinking my coffee while I've got a shotgun pointed at you."

"I had plenty of coffee at breakfast."

"Good. Then . . . go on. Let me know what you think. I'll just sit here and count the twenties. Not that I don't trust you, you understand. Just . . . just don't do anything funny. I'm not taking my finger off the trigger."

"In case you hadn't noticed, Mrs. Runbeck, I'm not a stupid man." He smiled at her, then opened the first letter and began reading.

32

Sophie sat at the Washburn's kitchen table, doodling on a piece of notebook paper. The morning had been spent with Bernice, taste-testing what she considered to be the twelve best meat loaf recipes. Bernice had baked them all in the past few days and then reheated them for Sophie's evaluation. She'd also prepared small sandwiches of each. A cold meat loaf sandwich was part of the necessary equation.

To make the recipe selection easier, Bernice's assistant had typed out every single submission on a separate sheet of paper, numbering them from one to nine hundred and seventy-eight. She'd sent the typed sheets to Bernice without the person's name or address attached, just to keep everything on the up and up. It made the selection so much easier. Bernice didn't have to read all the personal notes attached to the recipes or decipher hard-to-read handwriting.

Sophie expected the submissions to cover the gamut of what was being served today in American homes, but even she was amazed at the variety. She and Bernice lamented the fact that they hadn't divided the contest into Best Traditional Meat Loaf, Best Ethnic Loaf, and Best

Poultry Loaf. The only point that was non-negotiable for both of them was that a meat loaf should contain meat. Vegetarian loafs could be wonderful, but they didn't qualify for the contest. That decision eliminated a good hundred and fifty recipes from contention, which was just fine with Bernice. After an exhaustive examination of the submissions, she didn't care if she ever looked at another meat loaf recipe again. Most were fairly derivative, so she quickly pared the list down to thirty-six, then twelve, and this morning, they'd picked the best three.

After the final decisions had been made, Bernice phoned her assistant in Minneapolis and asked her to pull the winners' names. In a matter of seconds, they had the results. First prize went to Sally Halverson of Two Harbors, Minnesota. Second went to Ronald Kellogg of Rochester. But the third prize was the kicker. Cora Runbeck of Rose Hill, Minnesota, had won with her recipe, "No-Nonsense Meat Loaf."

Bernice wasn't happy. As a matter of fact, for just a moment, Sophie could see her toying with the idea of throwing third prize to someone else. But her sense of fairness—and her appreciation for the ironic—finally won out. She asked her assistant to type up letters of congratulations to the winners.

As soon as she was off the phone, Bernice begged Sophie to take over for her, handle all the events the paper had planned to help celebrate the winning recipes. Bernice said her father was too ill for her to return to work right now. Besides, she couldn't possibly deal with Cora Runbeck personally, not after everything that had happened. The powers that be at the paper might not like it, but nobody could make her do something she didn't want to do! Her voice rose to an emotional crescendo. Sophie assured her she wouldn't need to come in contact with Cora, that she'd handle it. By noon, Bernice had calmed down enough to drive over to the hospital. She needed to relieve her brother by twelve-fifteen.

And that left Sophie, sitting at the Washburns' kitchen table, wondering if she'd made a big mistake. All morning, she'd been dying to tell Bernice what she'd learned—that her father was totally innocent of any wrongdoing. That Milton was the culprit and John was just trying to protect him. Sophie was positive now that Milton was the man she'd known as Morgan Walters. The snake tattoo cinched it. She'd simply jumped to the wrong conclusion when she'd found that snapshot. Instead of John, Milton had been standing with his arm around Mary. And he still had his arms around her.

Sophie wondered how long their secret romance had been going on. She guessed that John didn't know about it; otherwise he wouldn't be trying to protect his brother. She assumed that John knew about Milton's past, and yet he clearly still loved him. Maybe, thought Sophie, he didn't know everything.

On the scratch paper in front of her, she'd written three names. Laura, Viola, and Bliss. Three of Milton's wives. Perhaps there were others. He had another wife in St. Louis, though Sophie didn't recall her name or when they'd married—not that it mattered. Everything bad that had happened to the Washburns in the last month all came down to Milton. He was the bad penny. The manipulator. The bigamist. The murderer. He'd not only killed Kirby Runbeck, but possibly one or more of his wives. He was an evil man and he had to be stopped.

The one big question Sophie still had was, why had Kirby Runbeck blackmailed John instead of Milton? From what Bernice had said, Milton had far more money than his brother. More to the point, why not go straight to the man who had the most to lose? Why try to squeeze money out of a relative?

"Where'd you get those women's names?" came a voice from behind her.

Sophie turned around to find Angelo standing by the sink. For such a big man, he had the stealth of a cat. Last she'd heard, he was on his way to the bank and would be gone most of the day. She'd met him for the first time at breakfast and could tell right away that he and Bernice were an item. They were an odd couple. Then again, it was a good thing physical attraction wasn't limited to people with movie-star looks or nobody would have a sex life.

Angelo seemed like a nice enough guy, very solicitous of Bernice. Sophie was pretty sure he was the same man she'd seen across the street from the house two weeks ago, the night that she'd spent in Rose Hill because of the storm. The fact that he could have starred in *The Godfather* gave him a menacing patina, although he was probably just an average guy with nothing dangerous about him.

He cracked his knuckles and repeated his question. "Where'd you get those names?"

"I didn't hear you come in."

"I'm light on my feet." He poured himself a cup of coffee and sat down at the table. "I didn't think you knew Bernice and her family all that well."

"I don't."

"Then how come—" He stopped before he finished the sentence, his gaze dropping once again to the names on the scratch sheet.

In that instant, Sophie realized his question wasn't just idle curiosity. He must have recognized the names. That meant he knew about Milton. When he looked up, she could see by the serious frown on his face that she was right. "You know, don't you? About the bigamy. About all the rest."

"Does Bernice?" he asked, his tone a mixture of eagerness and worry.

She shook her head.

"God, I'm so glad." He hesitated for a few seconds, as if he wasn't sure he should go on, then plunged ahead anyway. "This is going to kill her."

"How long have you known?"

"I suspected the worst ever since Runbeck died. But I didn't learn the details until this morning. I've been walking around for the last hour, wondering what I should say to Bernice—wondering if I should say anything at all. How did you find out?"

"I spent a night here at the house a couple of weeks ago. While I was sitting in the living room, I came across an old snapshot of what I thought was John and Mary on their first anniversary. Except, I knew the man in the photo by another name. Morgan Walters. He was married to a woman named Laura. I recognized his face, as well as the tattoo on his left arm."

"Tattoo?"

"A snake with a red eye." She paused. "How did you find out?"

"I paid off Cora Runbeck to tell me what her husband had on Washburn. She still has the letters."

"What letters?"

"The letters that the bastard wrote to a friend in prison. It's all there. How he and this buddy of his robbed a bank in the late fifties. The friend got caught and sent to prision, but Washburn made off with two hundred thousand dollars. Then his many wives. Maybe even a murder or two." He filled her in on all the details. "Runbeck must have discovered the letters and used them as blackmail. Cora's holding on to them for dear life because she thinks they're the only thing keeping her alive. She may be right. Somebody tried to kill her the other night. If Kirby had information on Washburn's past, whoever killed him must have figured Cora had the same information."

This was all news to Sophie. Clearly, she and Angelo had both discovered pieces of the puzzle, but neither of them had the entire picture.

Angelo took a sip of coffee, then set his cup down and pushed it away. "Bernice is so close to her dad. Always has been. She thinks of him as a saint. Well, I mean, until the last year when he went a little nuts with the vitamin pills. But that's small stuff."

"But . . . we're not talking about John Washburn here; we're talking about Milton Washburn, right? Milton was the bigamist. The one who robbed the bank. The one who may have murdered one or more of his wives."

Angelo narrowed his eyes. "Milton? The uncle? Hell no, I'm talking about *John* Washburn. The letters were signed J. D. Cora told me John's middle name was Arthur, but the J's got to stand for John."

"But Milton's the one with the tattoo."

They stared at each other.

"Maybe J. D. is a nickname," Sophie said finally.

Angelo looked off into space. "That doesn't make sense. It has to be John. He was the one being blackmailed."

"Let's go over this again," said Sophie. "Who do you think put the bomb in Runbeck's truck?"

"Plato," Angelo said flatly.

Now Sophie was even more confused.

"He was trying to protect his dad. And I can prove it. There was a book in John's library, a sort of terrorist manual. Inside was a recipe for nitrogen tri-iodide."

"The stuff that was used to blow up Runbeck's truck."

Angelo's eyes opened wide. "How did you know that?"

"I've got my sources, too."

"You've really been busy since you found that snapshot."

She shrugged. "I had to find out if I was right about the man in the photo."

"Well, I caught Plato searching for that book just the other day. I'll bet you he left it in his father's bookcase thinking nobody would ever look for it there. But after his dad confessed, Plato remembered where he'd left it and wanted to get rid of it. Except, I'd come across the title before. I grabbed it off the shelf the day before the police arrived with their search warrant. Thank God I did or they would have nailed John's hide to the wall."

Maybe Plato made a mistake, thought Sophie, just like she did. Jumped to the wrong conclusion about his father. After all, John did pay Runbeck the blackmail money. The fact that he'd withdrawn one hundred thousand dollars from his bank accounts proved it. He couldn't look any more guilty if he tried. But he wasn't the one with the tattoo.

"Who do you think murdered Runbeck?" Angelo asked.

"Milton," said Sophie, every bit as unreservedly. "He's the one with the past. If he robbed a bank, he probably used the money to start his business in St. Louis. It all fits."

"But in the letters, this J. D.—whoever he is—said he didn't even like being in the same room with the money, so he dumped it in the nearest gutter."

"What's that supposed to mean?"

Angelo scratched his head.

"Look," said Sophie, "in these letters, he did admit to having more than one wife, right?"

"Not exactly. But he talked about several women, and he was married to all of them. You could gather that much from the dates. See, this Gilbert Struthers got religion in prison. He'd saved some of the letters so he sent them back to J. D. and basically told him to repent before it was too late."

"Did he talk about Laura's death? Or Bliss?"

"Yeah, but again, he never admitted to killing anybody."

"Well, he wouldn't. But maybe he used those letters as a kind of confessional."

"Yeah, I thought about that, too."

"What are we supposed to do?" said Sophie, tossing her pen on the table. "We don't have absolute proof of anything, not even the bigamy. And we disagree on who murdered Runbeck."

Angelo leaned forward and rested his arms on his knees. "Somebody should pay for what happened to Runbeck."

"And Laura and Bliss."

"You think that tattoo's pretty conclusive, huh?"

"In my opinion, it's proof positive. Milton's our man."

"I'd be thrilled if that turned out to be the case. Bernice loves her uncle, but it's nothing like the way she feels about her dad. You know, Sophie, I used to have this idea that small towns were where the salt of the earth lived. In some ways, I still believe that. When I pay for something in a store here, people look me in the eye. Maybe they even smile. In New York, shopkeepers look at your hands. It's a different world. In Rose Hill, you don't get a lot of attitude."

"Scandinavians don't know how to give attitude. It's genetic."

He smiled. "Yeah, I've noticed. But if you ask me, Scandinavians could use a little Italy in their souls. The thing is, after I see what's happening around here, I'm beginning to think people are basically the same wherever you look."

"You're probably right." Sophie wrote her cell phone number on the edge of the scratch paper, then ripped it off. "I have to drive home this afternoon. Can we agree that if we learn anything new, we'll let each other know?"

"You got a deal." He shook her hand, then took out his own card and wrote his number on the back.

"I have a couple of leads that I think might be promising."

"And I've got an idea, something that might help protect Cora Runbeck." He took a final sip of coffee, then got up and dumped the rest in the sink. "An associate of mine used to call it the 'indirect direct' approach. I'll let you know if it works."

33

About half an hour out of the Cities, Sophie answered her cell phone. Laura Walters's friend, Rebecca Scoville, was on the line. She'd finally arrived home from her business trip and said she'd be happy to meet with Sophie. They made a date for three at Rebecca's office.

Sophie spent a few minutes gathering her thoughts. This was her one shot, and she didn't want to blow it. Shortly before three, she entered the Lamar Building. Northstar Investigations was on the third floor. A receptionist buzzed Rebecca's office and several seconds later, a white-haired woman dressed in jeans, a sweatshirt and running shoes appeared.

"I came into work today, but just for a couple hours," Rebecca said over her shoulder as she led Sophie down a long hallway to her corner office. She sat down quickly behind a large mahogany desk piled high with files. Behind her was an antique credenza filled with books. "I've been out of town, so I'm pretty backed up. But you piqued my curiosity, Ms. Greenway. Please," she said, extending her hand to a chair, "make yourself comfortable."

Sophie pulled the strap of her purse off her shoulder and sat down. Rebecca's grandmotherly features didn't fit the image of a private investigator. Or maybe Sophie was looking at Kinsey Millhone thirty years from now.

"Would you like a cup of coffee?"

"No thanks."

"Okay, so I understand you've got some questions about Laura Walters."

"I was told the two of you were best friends."

Rebecca sighed. "That was a long time ago. But yes, we were. We lived across the street from each other when we were growing up. We even got married around the same time. Laura stayed married, but I got divorced a year later." Her matter-of-fact speaking style reminded Sophie of the old TV show *Dragnet*.

"You knew her husband?"

"Morgan? Sure, we were good friends."

"I talked to Laura's sister recently. She seems to think Laura's death wasn't a suicide."

"You came here to talk about Laura's death?"

Sophie nodded.

"Why? It's ancient history."

"I have reason to believe that the man she married, the man you know as Morgan Walters, was an impostor. He used a number of aliases over the years, and was married to at least three other women at the same time he was married to Laura."

"Morgan?" She gave Sophie a skeptical look. "You can't be serious."

"I'm completely serious. The fact that he was a bigamist—"

"Wait a minute here, Ms. Greenway. Are we talking fact or theory?"

Sophie removed the snapshot from her purse and handed it over. "Do you recognize that man?"

Rebecca slipped on her reading glasses. After gazing at it for several seconds, she said, "It's Morgan. Who's the woman he's with?"

"Her name is Mary."

"One of his other wives?"

"No, she's married to his brother."

"Morgan didn't have a brother," she said, glancing down at the picture again. "He was an only child. Look, why all the interest in him now? Laura's been dead for what? Forty years?"

"It's a long, complicated story," said Sophie. "At this point, I can't give you any more details."

"Are you a P.I.?"

She shook her head. "Just a friend of the family."

"Morgan's family?"

"Something like that."

"Maybe you should let a professional look into it."

"We might do that, but for now, I'm hoping you can help me out."

Rebecca shrugged. "Okay. Go ahead. Ask your questions."

"If Morgan was a bigamist, it doesn't automatically follow that he was a murderer. But when I learned from Laura's sister that she was positive Morgan had killed Laura and then covered it up by making it look like a suicide, I have to wonder. Is there anything to it?"

Rebecca looked at the snapshot again. "I remember his tattoo now. It's got to be the same man." She glanced up. "And you're certain he was married to other women?"

Sophie nodded. "What sort of man was he?"

"Smart," said Rebecca, dropping the photo on her desk. "And surprisingly sweet for such a rough-and-tumble young guy. I thought he was good for Laura. She was a troubled woman, Ms. Greenway, with a lot of personal problems. Morgan told me once her problems were what had attracted him to her. He thought he could help."

"In what way?"

"This was all such a long time ago," she said, fingering a gold locket hanging around her neck. "Morgan and Laura met in a bar in Coleraine. You know where that is?"

"My grandparents used to live in Grand Rapids. I met Morgan and Laura when I was a teenager. He gave me a ride on his motorcycle. It's something I've never forgotten."

Rebecca smiled at the memory. "Yes, he sure loved that hunk of junk. I thought it was loud and smelly. He used to rev the motor when I was over at the house. He did it just to get a rise out of me. He was a real tease. Full of fun. Anyway, the night he and Laura met, they were both pretty drunk. Laura wouldn't tell him her name, so he called her Blue Eyes. I guess he was pretty closed-mouthed about himself, too, so she called him Jim Stark. She thought he was the spitting image of James Dean in *East of Eden*, her favorite movie. I guess that was the name of the character Dean played. To hear Laura tell it, it was love at first sight. I'm not sure Morgan—" She stopped. "What's Morgan's real name? Just for the record."

"Milton."

She made a sour face. "I'll stick with Morgan. I'm not sure Morgan felt the same way, but they hooked up pretty fast. Laura told me she didn't remember giving him her phone number, but she must have because he called her the next time he was in town. From then on, whenever he came through Grand Rapids, which was every couple of months, they'd go out on a date. They dated a few years and then announced their engagement. Laura was the happiest I'd ever seen her. Morgan wanted to buy this rundown old shack out in the country, fix it up. He hated cities, even small towns. In some ways, he was a loner. But so was Laura. They were very much in love, I can vouch for that. They both worked on the house, but because Morgan was gone a lot, most of the work fell to Laura. She didn't mind. It gave her a focus, kept her busy for almost two years. I remember helping her paint one of the rooms cherry red. Hideous color. They didn't have a lot of money, so Laura worked on and off in Grand Rapids clerking at Kremer's department store. Driving home one night, she wrecked the old beater Morgan had bought her. It was a '51 Thunderbird. Blue and white. Of course, it came out later that she was drunk. Her drinking got worse and worse over time until Morgan was simply beside himself. He didn't know what to do."

"Laura's sister said Morgan was the one who drank."

"I'm sure Morgan probably told her that to save face for Laura. If you want my opinion, Dotty Mulloy is an old prune. I think she was born that way. Laura loved her, but she didn't like her. That was one big reason why she jumped at the chance to put some distance between them. That way, her sister couldn't pop over whenever she felt like it. As time went on, Laura's drinking got so bad she couldn't even hold a part-time job. Staying home depressed her, so she started hitching rides with friends to bars. I'm not positive, but I think she started sleeping around. She already hated herself for so many reasons, it was just one more thing to add to the list. She was down in the dumps if Morgan was home, then back in the dumps when he left. Today, she could have gone to a therapist and gotten some help; but back then, if you suffered from depression, you were out of luck. She drank to deaden the pain, but in the end, it didn't help."

"So you're saying she really did commit suicide?"

"I'm positive of it."

"Why?"

"Let me give you a little background. First, you should know that I've investigated dozens of suicides over the years. Very often, families of suicides find it impossible to believe that their loved one could have done something so horrible. It makes them feel impotent, like they should have seen it coming, should have been able to prevent it. It's especially true if the person who dies doesn't leave a note. Laura didn't. It becomes easier on family members if they convince themselves that their loved one was the victim of foul play. And when it comes to suicide, the family has an uphill struggle if they want the police to investigate the death."

"But don't all suicides have to be investigated?"

"Yes, any unnatural or unattended death, which includes suicides, homicides, and accidents. But I'm talking about investigating a death as if it were a homicide. Dotty was treated fairly by the police, although I'm sure she didn't think so. Most suicides are just that—suicides. When there's no evidence to the contrary, and there wasn't in Laura's case, then the police don't want to waste their time investigating a dead end."

"Sure, I understand, but—"

"Sometimes Laura would call me late at night when she was drunk and Morgan was on the road. She'd tell me she was no good, that Morgan deserved so much better. By the fourth year of their marriage, he was urging her to take classes at the local junior college. She loved to read, even wrote a little poetry, so he thought she might like to take some writing courses. I offered to drive her, show her the ropes, but she just never got around to it. Morgan was so frustrated with her. We'd talk about her sometimes, although he didn't like to admit Laura was as sick as she was, even to himself. He desperately wanted to help, but she'd begun to shut him out. I think he wondered if she was seeing someone else when he wasn't around, and of course, that hurt him terribly.

"One hot summer night, a few months before she took her life, Laura and I were sitting on her front porch. Somehow or other the subject of suicide came up. Laura asked me if I'd ever thought about it. I told her I hadn't. She said she'd wanted to do it many times, but in her saner—or more sober—moments, she was glad she hadn't gone through with it. She knew her drinking made her depression worse. That's when she felt most like ending her life. The worst time for her was the dead of night. Everything was so painful then. I still remember the look on her face when she talked about it. In my entire life, I've never seen such . . . such utter desolation. But she said that she'd made herself a promise. If she was going to kill herself, it would have to be on a bright sunny morning, with the birds singing and sun shining. She couldn't have a hangover. She'd have to be completely straight. That way she'd know her feelings were real, that it wasn't just a passing mood, but a decision." Leaning forward, Rebecca continued, "Laura killed herself on a bright sunny morning. She waited until she knew it was what she really wanted, that for her, there was no other way."

The silence in the room closed in around them.

"Morgan may have been a bigamist, Ms. Greenway, but he wasn't a murderer."

June, 1974

Dear Gilbert:
Thanks for your note. Yes, you're right. This is a horrible time for me. It was almost nine years ago that Laura died. And now Bliss. It's enough to make a guy turn his back on the people who count on him and just run for his life.

Between you and me, I'm pretty sure the chief of police thinks I did it. Can you fathom that? He believes I murdered Bliss and then covered it up by making it look like a robbery. When he interrogated me last week, he said that in his experience, nobody got murdered so violently unless there was a huge amount of emotion involved. To him, that meant the victim knew her killer. There was no forced entry, no sign of a struggle, so in his mind, I was the most likely suspect. I feel like we're playing some kind of chess game. Thank God I found a guy in La Crosse, Wisconsin, who'd vouch for me. He gave the police a statement yesterday, said I'd been in town the night it happened. With him for a witness, I don't think there's much they can do to me. And I got at least one cop on my side. He's a neighbor, been a friend for years. *He used to know my wife when she was a kid. He's seen firsthand how much I loved her, and how much she loved me.*

It's love *that's important, Gil, not the other crap that happens. I've got to keep my eye on the ball, not let my wife's death break my spirit.*

J. D.

34

Sunlight flooded Byron Jenny's office, where Plato now sat, his feet up on the desk. He was making a paper airplane, something he often did when the world overwhelmed him. He found that mindless activity helped him to focus his thoughts. "Simplify," he whispered, knowing that his life was anything but simple. Folding the paper wings into place, he wondered idly if thinking could be carcinogenic. He supposed it could be, although that notion probably put him in the same health-obsessed camp as his father.

Plato wasn't depressed. If anything, he walked with a certain spring in his step these days. His father was no longer high atop the family pedestal, and that made Plato feel vindicated. As far as he was concerned, no matter what everyone said out loud, each family member knew in his or her heart that John Washburn had done something very, very, *very* bad. Plato remembered reading once that suicide rates always went down during wars. Perhaps that was why he was in such good spirits. His family was at war—with the anarchy of town gossip, with Cora Runbeck's evil threats, and with a police department intent on putting a not-so-innocent man behind bars. The whole situation inspired barrels of overwrought emotions. High drama. But the final outcome didn't matter all that much. In the end, everything turned to dust. The only question was, how long would it take?

In the midst of his nihilistic meditations came a knock on the door.

"Enter at your own risk," he called, waiting for the door to open. When it did, he propelled the airplane into the blue. It took an immediate nose dive and landed at Gloria Applebaum's feet. Gloria had been Byron Jenny's personal assistant. Now she was the temporary managing editor.

"Nice touch," she said, picking up the fatally flawed piece of origami and undulating toward his desk.

For the past few weeks, Plato had begun to experience certain moments in his day in a kind of weird slow motion. He closed his eyes and shook the wheels in his head, hoping to rearrange them. When he opened his eyes, Gloria was standing at his desk. She wants something, he thought silently. He hoped he wouldn't have to play twenty questions to find out what it was. Everybody had to be *someplace*, so that's why he'd come to the paper this morning. He had no intention of working, though it was important to look busy; otherwise people talked. All he really wanted was to be left alone.

Dropping the airplane on the desk, Gloria smiled.

"What do you want?" He frowned in an effort to look substantial.

"I'm hoping I can help you." She swiveled her hips into a chair.

"Oh God."

"Look, Mr. Washburn, the newspaper's in a bad way. Decisions are being left unmade. Our creditors are starting to get nervous. We need a leader, someone to part the Red Sea for us, like Byron used to do."

"Speak English."

"I want his job. Permanently. I need you to make the official announcement today. Without your backing, your clear and unequivocally stipulated confidence in my considerable, substantial, and weighty abilities, we're just spinning our wheels around here."

"How long did it take for you to memorize that?"

"Excuse me?"

She'd spent too many years with her nose in a thesaurus. Probably majored in adjectives in college. For all he knew, she couldn't even spell. "What the hell? Sure, you can have the job." Nobody else was beating down his door.

She seemed at a momentary loss. "Is that it?"

"Is what it?"

"I don't have to, you know, sell you on the idea a little more?"

"No, you made your point."

"Oh. Well, then, can we talk about salary?"

"Same as Byron was getting. How's that sound?"

"Really!" She shot out of her chair. "You're nothing like people say, Mr. Washburn. You're just an old pussycat."

Plato was growing more dyspeptic by the moment. "Have someone type up an interoffice memo and I'll sign it. You can put the announcement in the paper on Saturday."

"You won't regret this, Mr. Washburn. I'll work like a viper!"

"Do you know what a viper is, Ms. Applebaum?"

"Something strong and courageous and purposeful,"

she said, her eyes crinkling as she looked off in the distance. She was a walking B movie.

Plato noticed now that she was holding a small white envelope. "What's that in your hand?"

She looked down. "Oh, this. Somebody slipped it under the door this morning before we got in. It's addressed to you."

He plucked it from her hand. "Thanks."

"About my office—"

"We'll discuss it later."

"Yes, Mr. Washburn. Whatever you say, Mr. Washburn."

After she'd gone, Plato took Byron's letter opener and sliced open the top of the envelope. Inside was a folded sheet of typing paper with three short lines printed in capital letters:

I KNOW WHAT YOU DID.

IF YOU DON'T STOP, I'LL MAKE YOU REGRET IT.

VERY TRULY YOURS,

A CONCERNED FAMILY MEMBER

"What the hell?" Plato whispered. He examined the page, both front and back, then returned his attention to the envelope. His first name was printed on the front. That was it. No other marking. After staring at the message for a few more seconds, he refolded the page and placed it carefully inside the vest pocket of his wrinkled linen suit. He tossed the paper airplane in the trash on his way out.

Mary waited as Milton opened the front door for her. She felt devilish. They'd just returned from an afternoon movie. She was ashamed to admit she'd been off having fun while John was in the hospital struggling his way through another round of physical therapy. Even in the best of times, John didn't enjoy movies much, but Mary did. And so did Milton. Unfortunately, they'd made the mistake of going to a romantic weeper. When Mary thought of the ill-fated couple in the story, she started to cry. She cried so easily these days. It was as if all the walls she'd built over the years to help her cope with the stresses and strains of life had suddenly dissolved, baring her vulnerable soul for all the world to see. Except, the only person who ever looked was Milton. He saw her for who she really was.

Milton busied himself in the kitchen making them a bite to eat as Mary opened a window in the living room to let in the breeze. For most of the past month, the weather felt as though someone had turned on a furnace full blast and forgotten to turn it off. But today was different. For the second time in two weeks, the humidity had dropped and so had the temperature. The house could be opened to receive the blessing of a late summer breeze. Mary felt opened, too, on a day like this. Open to life. Open to love. On those increasingly rare moments when she and Milton were alone together, she felt wrapped in a protective cocoon, adrift on a deserted island where only the two of them mattered. But when she emerged, as she would in a few short hours when she returned to the hospital for the night, the weight of the world dropped on her shoulders again, all the heavier because of the respite.

Mary's mother used to say that guilt was God's way of telling you that you were doing something bad. Maybe loving Milton *was* wrong, but it seemed to Mary that marriage was an impossible situation. A man you might have loved when you were in your teens could hardly be expected to be the same man fifty years later. What if he changed into someone you didn't even like? In Mary's case, her love had been mixed with gratitude, an equally complex emotion. The minister at First Lutheran said that if married people had problems, they should try to work them out. And Mary had. But if she was forced to sit through one more conversation about organic strawberries versus conventionally grown fruit, she was going to scream.

Mary thought of all the fiftieth anniversaries she and John had helped friends celebrate over the years. As far as she was concerned, people who stayed married that long were an odd bunch. Either they lacked courage or they lacked imagination. Maybe that was a cold thing to say, but it was how she felt. She wouldn't fight her guilt or try to push it away. No, she deserved whatever judgment God chose to impose. And she'd pay the price gladly, if only Milton would stick around and not leave her all alone to care for a sick and aging man she'd long ago ceased to love. It was time to admit the truth. It wasn't the way she'd intended her life to turn out; it's just what had happened when she wasn't looking.

"Mary? Why don't you see if the postman's been here?" Milton called from the kitchen. "I'll be out in a sec with our meat loaf sandwiches."

Feeling the breeze ruffle her hair as she passed the open window, Mary stepped out onto the front steps and collected the mail.

"Anything for me?" asked Milton, setting a tray on the coffee table in front of the couch. "I poured you orange juice. I hope that's okay."

"It's wonderful," she said, touched that he was so eager to care for her. She'd spent her life taking care of others. It was nice to be on the receiving end for a change. She sat down next to him and flipped through the letters. "Nothing for you but this." She handed him a small white envelope. His first name had been printed in capital letters on the front. "It wasn't mailed. See?" She pointed. "No stamp. Somebody must have come by and put it in the box."

Milton took a bite of his sandwich, then opened the letter. Peering through his bifocals, he read silently.

"What's it say?" asked Mary, taking a sip of her juice. He stopped chewing.

"What is it?" His face had turned a deep, angry pink.

"Nothing." He crumpled the paper into a ball and jammed it into his pocket.

"It most certainly was not *nothing*," said Mary, searching his face for clues.

"Eat your sandwich," he replied, attempting a smile that fell flat.

"You can confide in me, Milton. Is it about John?"

"It's junk. Let's forget about it, okay? People should mind their own business."

She agreed with him, though she wasn't entirely satisfied that he'd told her everything. But she let the matter drop. She had so little time to share with Milton these days, she didn't want to spoil an otherwise perfect afternoon with unpleasantness.

35

Angelo promised he'd pick Bernice up outside the hospital. It had become their routine. He waited for her by the front doors, but when she didn't show by three-fifteen, he parked his rental car and headed up to John's room. He found Papa Washburn all alone, sitting up in a chair.

"Angel," said John, one half of his face smiling broadly, the other half a little less enthusiastic.

Angelo didn't really mind that he called him Angel. He figured it was an affectionate kind of nickname.

"You're looking for Bernice," said John. His speech had improved remarkably in the last few days. He still didn't pronounce things quite right, especially words with an "L" or an "S" in them, and he talked deliberately and slowly, but he was completely understandable.

"Is she here?" asked Angelo. "I was supposed to pick her up at three."

"Sit," said John, his eyes dropping to a green plastic chair. "She was hungry. I told her to go eat. I would entertain you until she got back."

On the table in front of him was a glass of water with a straw, and a plastic bowl of applesauce.

"My afternoon snack," said John, nodding to the bowl. "Yum."

Angelo laughed. "Not your kind of cuisine, huh?"

"I've mellowed. It's keeping me alive."

"Yeah, that's something."

"A miracle." He rolled his eyes.

"How are you feeling?"

"Better. Stronger. But this . . . is hard."

"I can only imagine."

"Did you pop the question to my daughter?"

Angelo's smile turned to a grin. "I did."

"She's glowing. She must have said yes."

"We're not telling anyone yet."

"But me."

"Right. Anyone but you."

Hesitating, John reached his right hand toward Angelo. "You be my angel, okay?"

Angelo wasn't sure what the old man was saying, but he took his hand and gave it a squeeze. "I will. I promise."

"Do you know Benjamin Disraeli?"

"The English politician? No, not personally."

"He said that most people die with their music still in them. Remember that, Angel. Don't let that happen to you. Or my daughter."

He was a sweet old guy. This was his fatherly advice, delivered with all the majesty he could muster in his current condition. Since Angelo's own father wasn't capable of giving much good advice, even if he'd been alive, Angelo was deeply touched. "You'll dance at our wedding, John."

"Damn right I will." He gazed forlornly at the applesauce. "My nurse told me I had to eat all of this. Want some?"

"Gee, I don't know."

"Help an old guy out."

"Well, okay. But I've never liked applesauce very much."

"Then don't get sick. Or old."

"You're full of good advice today."

"That's me. A font of wisdom." He pushed the spoon toward Angelo.

"Say, since I'm here, maybe you could clear something up." He took a bite, trying not to make a face. "Did you ever go by a nickname?"

"A nickname?"

"Yeah, you know. Did anybody ever call you Jake, or Jack, or . . . maybe, J.D?"

"My middle name is Arthur. Why would someone call me J.D.?"

Angelo shrugged. "Just curious. I mean, you call me Angel. That's kind of a nickname."

"You mind?"

"Not at all. Coming from you, I like it."

"You can call me Jake." He smiled. "If it makes you happy."

"But I suppose your brother, Milton, had tons of nicknames. Don't take offense, but Milton isn't exactly a cool name."

"You're right. Eat up," he said, pushing the bowl closer to Angelo.

"So, did he?" asked Angelo, choking down another mouthful.

"Some people called him Sonny. I called him Junior. Used to annoy the hell out of him. Mom called him Milt.

Dad called him Stupid, 'the little jerk,' and 'the gutless wonder.' He had some choice names for me, too."

When Angelo had almost finished the applesauce, a nurse bustled through the door. "Time to take your vitals, John."

Angelo quickly hid the spoon under his leg.

"Look," said John, smiling up at her. "I was a good boy. I ate it."

She beamed. "Just what you need to make you well and strong."

John winked at Angelo.

"Let me push your sleeve up," she said, inserting a thermometer into his mouth. "I'll get your temp first, then your blood pressure."

Angelo's eyes opened in surprise when he saw the tattoo on John's arm. The same one Sophie had seen on Milton's. A snake with a red eye.

The nurse waited, gazing intently at an electronic device attached to her belt. When it gave a beep, she smiled. "Perfect." She removed the thermometer, then pulled the blood pressure cuff away from the wall.

"You've got a tattoo," said Angelo casually.

"Silliness. When we were young, my brother and I got good and drunk one night in downtown Terre Haute. While we were wandering around, looking for a good time, we came across a tattoo parlor. I thought, what the hell? It was the manly thing to do, right? I had some cash burning a hole in my pocket, so I sprang for both of us. You got any tattoos?"

"Me? No."

"Shhh," said the nurse.

Angelo stared at the snake. So much for Sophie's infallible theory.

36

Three cows in a row meant death. On the way back from town, Cora had seen them, black as southern Minnesota dirt, grim sentinels standing in a gray-brown field. She'd never been a superstitious woman, but it wasn't smart to ignore a clear message from the great beyond. Maybe Kirby was trying to warn her away, or maybe her mother had sent the cows. Cora knew her sight wasn't all that great, but she could swear she'd seen their hollow, penetrating eyes staring at her as she sailed past. And once they were behind her, she could feel their gaze burning a hole in the back of her head. *These were no ordinary cows.*

But she was home now. Home and safe. Yesterday, a handyman had come out to repair the broken window. At the same time, he'd installed bars on all the basement and first-floor windows. Nobody was going to break into her house again, not if she had anything to say about it.

Cora had spent the better part of the afternoon at Lindstrom Travel, talking to that ninny Vern Lindstrom about Caribbean cruises. Even before the cow sighting, she knew it was time to make a graceful exit. Rose Hill could get along without her for a few weeks. Winthrop could stay with friends. She'd get someone to come in to water her plants. When she returned from her trip, she hoped everything would be back to normal. If she still didn't feel safe, there was always that "Fun-in-the-Sun Jamaica Vacation" package Vern had shown her. Vern, with his usual pitiful lack of good taste, had kidded Cora that she was about to become a Caribbean Mama. Good thing for him he had the only travel agency in town, otherwise she would have taken her business elsewhere.

Dumping the cruise brochures on the kitchen table, Cora poured herself a glass of apple juice and carried it into the living room. Winthrop wasn't asleep on the back of the couch as he usually was, so she called to him. "Here kitty kitty kitty. Winthrop, come here, sweetie. I'm home." He was doggier than most cats, and almost always came when she called him. His other favorite place to relax was the bathtub.

Cora sipped the juice as she walked into the bathroom, but again, Winthrop was nowhere to be found. "Winthrop, honey, where are you? I need to kiss my boy." He was getting to be such an old cat, he rarely went upstairs anymore. Maybe he'd been frightened by a noise outside. He was still recovering from the break-in the other night. Winthrop was a sensitive, shy, gentle cat, with the wide-eyed gaze of an insane prophet, but Cora loved him more than anything on earth.

She didn't feel like playing hide and seek, since he could be anywhere, so she sauntered back to the kitchen and set her empty glass in the sink. When she turned around, she saw that a piece of paper had been taped to the back door. She hadn't noticed it when she first came

in because it was almost the same yellow as the paint.
Now she pulled it free and gave it a look-see.

If you want to see your cat alive again, do exactly as I
say. If you fail to follow my directions, he'll return in a box,
no longer breathing.

Cora gasped, feeling her heart stop.

I want the letters, the originals. I don't care if you've
sent copies to everyone in North America. Put the
originals in a metal box and leave the box under the
wood steps at Melvin DuCharme's cabin. You must do
this by midnight tonight. Come alone.
I'll be watching, so don't think you can get away
with anything. Once you've done what I ask, leave
the area and don't come back. I'll know if you go to
the police. I think you already know you don't want to
cross me. If you do as I say, you'll get the cat back
unharmed, and I'll never bother you again. If you don't,
say good-bye to kitty.

P.S. In case you're wondering how I got into your house,
I found a set of spare keys the other night. You might
want to have your locks rekeyed.

Cora clutched her throat. Not Winthrop! Anything
but him! He was her baby. She could feel herself begin to

panic, thinking of her poor sweet kitty in the clutches of that horrible, horrible heathen.

"Snap out of it," she ordered herself.

Winthrop was such an ordinary, unassuming little kitty. His conception of the world was the inside of her house. He was as cherished, as dear and familiar to her as the smell of her own skin. How could something so sweet and innocent be in such danger?

Cora's fear turned instantly to fury. How dare the Washburns threaten her cat! They'd finally gone too far. This was all-out war. Cora wished she knew which one of them was harassing her. Like she told Angelo yesterday, it could be any of them. He seemed to think it had to be Plato or Milton, emissaries of the big bad kahuna, John Washburn himself. But Cora knew Bernice or Mary were equally capable of murder, and probably a lot more clever at it.

Picking up the phone in the kitchen, she took the card Angelo had given her and dialed his cell phone number. It rang three times before he answered.

"Falzone."

"Angelo, it's me. Cora Runbeck. I need to talk to you right away."

"You do? Why?"

"Something's happened."

"What?"

"I can't talk about it on the phone. We have to meet."

"Do you want me to come to your house?"

"No. It has to be someplace neutral—and quiet. How about the Coffee Klatch. You know where it is?"

"Sure, but—"

"Meet me there in half an hour. This is life or death, Angelo. Don't fail me."

* * *

Cora entered the coffee house wearing a pastel-blue sleeveless dress and her best straw hat. Before slipping on her white cotton gloves, she'd patted a drop of Evening in Paris behind each ear. The bottle was a relic of her youth. The clothes made her feel put-together. Spiffy. She could hardly do what needed to be done in a housedress.

Angelo was sitting at a table in the back, away from the windows. Cora thought it might be tempting fate to do this deal in full view of everyone in Rose Hill, but sometimes it was best to hide in plain sight. She nodded to him as she sat down.

"What's up?" asked Angelo. A half-drunk cup of coffee rested in front of him. He looked sufficiently solid and menacing in his dark suit and tan silk shirt.

Cora placed her purse on the table and leaned forward. In a low voice, she said, "You don't need an umbrella unless it's raining."

"Huh?"

"I need an umbrella, Angelo."

He stared at her blankly.

"I want to hire you. What's the cost?"

"For what?"

"I want to put out a contract on somebody's life."

"You're kidding. Whose?"

"Whoever broke into my house the other night. I pay you, you find the slime and then rub him out." Cora knew that if the person turned out to be Bernice, they'd have a problem, but she'd deal with it when the time came.

"You want me to make a hit?"

For a gangster, he was pretty slow on the uptake. "Yes. Now, I brought a hundred dollars with me in my purse.

That's just a down payment. I can get you more. What's it cost? Five hundred? Six?"

"Wait just a minute," said Angelo, lowering his voice to a whisper. "Are you nuts?"

"I see no reason to call me names. This is a business deal, plain and simple."

"Look, lady, I don't kill people for a living. I own laundromats."

She smiled conspiratorially, then winked. "Right." Opening the clasp on her purse, she removed the ransom note. "Read this."

Angelo took it and scanned it quickly. "When did you get it?"

"Today. Just before I called you. I found it taped to my back door."

He read it over again, shaking his head. "Where's Melvin DuCharme's cabin?"

"By the Cottonwood River, maybe forty miles away. There's nothing around it but woods."

"No other cabins?"

She shook her head.

He considered it a moment. "Did anyone follow you here?"

"Nobody. I'm positive. I went way out of my way, made all kinds of crazy turns, just to make sure."

"Well, Cora, I'd say you've just been checkmated."

"I realize that. That's why I'm hiring you."

He folded the paper and handed it back to her. "You know, babe, I'm gonna make you another offer you can't refuse."

She liked that. She smiled, looking expectant.

"Here's what we're gonna do."

37

Sophie sat cross-legged in the middle of her bed, scratching off the names of nursing homes as she phoned each one to ask if Viola Newman was a resident. There was no other way to locate her except with a tedious phone search. She'd found a Web site earlier in the day that listed all the nursing home facilities in Minnesota. If she hadn't found that site, she'd be knee-deep in alligators, as her father used to say. At least this way, she had up-to-date information. She'd been working at it since two. It was nearly four now and she still hadn't located the woman. Sophie was beginning to think she was searching for a needle in a haystack, and that just about exhausted her store of folksy sayings for the rest of the millennium.

Picking up the phone again, she punched in the number for Meadow Woods Manor in Windborne, a small town about seventy miles southeast of Rose Hill. A woman answered.

"Meadow Woods. May I help you?"

"Yes, I hope so," said Sophie. "I'm looking for a Viola Newman. Can you tell me if she's a resident at your facility?"

"Just a minute, please."

Sophie could hear a keyboard being tapped.

The woman came back on the line. "Yes, Ms. Newman is with us. She's in a private room on the fifth floor. Room 509."

Yes! mouthed Sophie, thrusting her fist into the air.

"Would you like to leave her a message? She doesn't have a phone in her room."

"Is Ms. Newman . . . I mean, would she be able to talk to me if I came to visit? Do you know what I'm asking?"

The woman laughed at Sophie's discomfort. "Honey, we're all gonna hit eighty one day, if we live long enough. To answer your question, yes, Viola should be perfectly able to talk to you. She's in our minimal care unit."

"Do you have visiting hours at Meadow Woods?"

"We just ask that visitors leave before bedtime."

"What time is that?"

"If you leave before nine, you'll be okay."

Sophie asked for directions. No sooner had she hung up than she got another call, this time on her cell phone. She reached into her purse and pulled it free. It couldn't be Bram, unless he was taking a break from his show. Maybe it was Rudy, calling to tell her he was home early.

"This is Sophie."

"Angelo Falzone."

"Hey, hi! What's up?"

"Something big. I think we're about to catch ourselves a murderer, Sophie. You got a minute?"

"Absolutely." She listened eagerly as he explained about Cora and the note she'd received a few hours ago. He went over the plan he'd formulated, how he intended to catch the bastard, whoever it turned out to be.

"Don't take this the wrong way," said Sophie, "but

you don't strike me as the kind of guy who knows his way around the woods, especially at night."

"If I can handle myself on the mean streets of New York, I can handle a few squirrels and jack rabbits."

Sophie wasn't so sure his equation worked. "Have you told Bernice?"

"I'm going to wait on that. I don't want her to worry."

"Yes, I suppose that's best. I still think Milton's behind everything. I'd even bet money."

"You might lose your bet."

Sophie was taken aback by his vehemence. "You sound pretty sure of yourself."

"I went to visit John Washburn yesterday and guess what? He's got the snake tattoo on his arm, too. They both have it. So, as far as I can see, all bets are off."

Sophie's surprise turned to frustration. For Bernice's sake, she'd hoped Milton was the bigamist, not Bernice's father. Now it was all up in the air again.

"Look, Sophie, the reason I called is, I was hoping you could drive down to Rose Hill tonight."

"You want me to come to the cabin with you?"

"God, no. I'd never put you in that kind of danger. But I'm in a bind here. I've got no backup. I can't tell Bernice what's going down, and, well, to be honest, I think Cora Runbeck has a few screws loose. I need you in town tonight. But I don't want you to go to the Washburns. There's a hotel on the edge of town. It's called the River Inn. I took the liberty of making you a reservation. Can you come? Please say yes."

"What time do I need to be there?"

"Ten at the latest." He spent a few minutes going over the particulars of his plan.

"I'll be there," said Sophie finally, glad to be part of

the posse. She had to think fast. What would she tell Bram? He was playing racquetball tonight after work, part of his effort to get into shape. Then he planned to have dinner with a work buddy. She could tack a note onto the refrigerator and call him when she got to the River Inn. He'd be home by then. She knew he'd miss her, but she'd been spending so much time with Bernice lately, it wouldn't come as a complete surprise. And if she left now, she might be able to see Viola Newman on the way.

"Make sure your cell phone is charged," said Angelo. "And keep it with you at all times. With any luck, we'll bag ourselves a bigamist tonight."

38

It was nearing dusk by the time Sophie made it to Meadow Woods Manor in Windborne. She checked in at the main reception desk, then rode the elevator up to the fifth floor. Walking down the wide central hallway, her heels ticking on the tile floors, she glanced up at the room numbers. She found Viola sitting in front of a TV set watching *Who Wants to Be a Millionaire*. The room was small and dimly lit but cozy, filled with furniture circa the 1940s. The hospital bed was the only object that suggested the space was anything other than a normal bedroom.

"Mrs. Newman?" said Sophie, knocking softly.

"Who's there?" said Viola, squinting into the open doorway. She was a heavyset woman, wrapped in a multicolored shawl, her thin white hair pulled back into a bun. She pushed her glasses up on her nose, patted the back of her hair, then started to get up.

"Excuse the interruption," said Sophie, stepping just inside the threshold. "We've never met before. My name's Sophie Greenway. I live in St. Paul, and I drove down this evening to see you."

"Me?" said Viola, looking baffled.

"May I come in?"

"Well, of course. Let me just turn this TV off." She used her remote, then sat back down with a thump. "There's nothing on television these days but junk." She had a high, rather nasal voice. "I remember when TV used to be good. Did you ever watch *Sugarfoot*? Or *77 Sunset Strip*? Now those were good shows."

Sophie didn't remember either show.

"You say your name is Sophie?"

"That's right."

"Please, sit down. I don't get many visitors." She switched on the floor lamp next to her, revealing hands heavily gnarled by arthritis.

On the table by her bed, Sophie saw a Bible, the latest *Newsweek*, a book about Leonardo da Vinci, and two novels—*Julian*, by Gore Vidal, and *Animal Dreams*, by Barbara Kingsolver. The walls were covered with dog photographs—one specific breed, to be exact. "What kind are they?" asked Sophie, looking up at the largest picture.

"West Highland terriers," said Viola. "I used to raise them. The one you're looking at is Zazu. She was my sweetheart. My first dog. My dear husband bought her for me on my forty-fifth birthday. He was out of town a lot on business, so she kept me company."

Sophie pulled a chair up close and sat down.

"Why did you come?" asked Viola, still looking at the picture of Zazu.

"Actually, you've already brought up the subject I'd like to talk to you about. Your husband."

"Jim?" She searched Sophie's face. "He's all right, isn't he? I haven't seen or heard from him in almost a month. I was starting to get worried."

"He visits you?"

"Every week. He only lives an hour away, in Rose Hill. Jim is thirteen years younger than me, but he's getting up there in years. Thankfully, he still drives, still takes care of me."

Sophie had expected anger, hatred, even rage. She could work with those emotions, use them to get the information she wanted, but she'd never anticipated this.

"Do you know him? Is he all right?"

"Yes, I . . . know him," said Sophie, not sure how to handle this turn of events.

Viola studied her. With her small black eyes, she resembled a bird eyeing a worm. Whatever she was thinking, she was making Sophie uncomfortable. "You know about Jim, don't you?" she said finally. "About us, his wives."

Haltingly, Sophie replied, "Yes . . . I do."

"Thought so." She winked.

"But I don't . . . know everything. That's why I came. I was hoping you could fill in some details."

"First, how do you know Jim?"

"I'm a friend of Bernice Washburn's."

"Oh, yes, Bernice." She nodded knowingly. "Such a fine girl. I've never met her, but Jim's told me so much about her over the years, shown me so many pictures, I feel like we're related. In a way, if you count love as a connection, we are." She smiled. "I can see I've surprised you."

"And then some."

"If you're a friend of the family, then you're not here to hurt Jim, or his loved ones. Go ahead and ask your questions. If I can answer them, I will. Actually, you're not the first person to come to me wanting information. A woman named Katherine Lang visited me about five

years ago. She was a niece of one of his other wives—
Joan Marie Harrison of Storm Creek, Iowa."

This wasn't one of the wives on Sophie's list, which
meant there were more than she'd originally suspected.
"How did she find out about you?"

"As I understand it, Jim must have left a letter lying
around the house with my name and address on it.
Somehow, she got hold of it and located me. I don't recall
all the details, but she must have gone to a lot of
trouble."

"What did she want?"

"The same as you. She discovered that Jim had a secret
life—many secret lives, I should say."

"Was she angry?"

"Yes. Especially when she arrived. But I think I helped
her to understand a bit better. At least, she wasn't
breathing fire when she left. She thought Jim was dead. I
let her go on believing that, just in case she wanted to
make trouble for him."

Sophie couldn't believe what she was hearing. "You
mean, you approve of what he did?"

"Approve?" She thought about that. "No. But I understood."

"But Bliss Taylor was murdered! Some people think
Laura Walters was, too."

Viola seemed horrified. "Yes, Bliss died violently, hor-
ribly, and Laura committed suicide. Jim may have
blamed himself for both deaths, but he wasn't responsible. He wouldn't hurt a fly."

Sophie wondered if the woman had ever seen the
movie *Psycho*. "How can you be so sure?"

"Because I know him. I know his heart. Oh, he could
be wayward and willful at times, but he's a kind man."

"Were you aware that he and another man had robbed a bank when they were young? A guard was killed."

She nodded, and kept on nodding. "Yes, I know all about that. Jim had nothing to do with the guard's death. And frankly, Sophie, you hit right at the core of the matter. That incident is what started Jim on the road he eventually chose to travel. Ever since that time, he's been trying to change his life for the good, to make amends."

Sophie had the urge to fire questions at her, but she had the sense that Viola wouldn't respond well to pressure. If Sophie didn't pass the patience test, her motives would look suspect. She knew her reasons for the visit couldn't stand close scrutiny. Viola appeared to be a kindly, slightly sentimental old woman who liked to see the good in people. That penchant had led her to draw the wrong conclusion about Sophie. Sophie might be a friend of the family, but she wasn't here to find proof of Jim Newman's goodness. She wanted the dirt. Or more accurately, she wanted the truth, without the patina of sympathy and compassion Viola attached to the story. But Sophie could read between the lines. From the look on the old woman's face, she could see that Viola was eager to tell her tale. The best thing Sophie could do now was offer a willing ear.

In her slow, deliberate way, Viola continued. "Jim should never have gotten mixed up with that Gilbert Struthers. He was a bad man. If Gilbert hadn't been caught and sent to prison, there's no telling what mischief he would have cooked up. I'm not saying Jim was weak-minded. He was just young. And he came from a family where there was very little love. Gilbert was his best friend. Jim's always been loyal to a fault, and it was no different with Gilbert."

"How many wives did Jim have?"

"I knew of six, including me. There may have been more. Jim didn't tell me everything, I suppose, although, of all his wives, he said I was his best friend. I was the only one who knew about the others. He confessed everything to me before we got married. It just slipped out one evening while we were sitting on the piano bench. I think he was feeling guilty. He was starving for someone to confide in. And also, he wanted to give me a chance to back out."

"But he was a bigamist, Viola. That's against the law. Didn't that bother you?"

Viola gave a grudging nod. "But with each marriage, he not only loved the woman, but he tried to help her answer the hard questions in her life. His motives were pure. His weak spot was that he'd get caught up in other people's problems and see himself as the solution. With me, I suppose he felt a kind of pity. I was considered an old maid when Jim came along. I was the town librarian, a confirmed old biddy in most people's eyes. Jim and I met because he loved to read. When he was in town, he'd always stop by the library. Eventually, we struck up a friendship. He was on the road and lonely, and he recognized that same loneliness in me. We were friends for many years before he asked me to marry him. I didn't find out until much later what prompted the proposal. You see, it seems that one night he was in a local tavern and he heard a couple of guys laughing about me. They must have made some pretty nasty comments because Jim threw a punch at one of them and knocked him out. I imagine it was the usual. Viola May Little was the town old maid. She was either frigid or a lesbian. Look at the way she dressed. What she needed was to smoke a little weed, take an acid trip, loosen up. It was the sixties, man. Nobody was wearing sensible shoes and Peter Pan collars in the sixties."

Sophie found herself laughing along with Viola.

"Jim hated ignorant attitudes like that. His solution was to pop the question. At first, I turned him down. I was so much older, it didn't make sense to me. I thought he should be with someone younger. I couldn't believe some woman hadn't already snapped him up. But I was greedy and I loved him, God forgive me, so a week later I said yes. Jim had left town by then, but he came back right away and gave me a ring. That was the night we sat on the piano bench and talked late into the evening. He told me everything."

"And you still married him."

"Yes. I've never regretted my decision. I believe I helped anchor him when Bliss died. It almost killed him, you know. He'd married her because he saw how talented she was, but also how scattered and undisciplined. Without nurturing and direction, he felt she'd never have a chance at her dream. He worked so hard to help her realize it. Her parents wanted her to become a nurse. Nothing wrong with that, I suppose. But they offered to put her through school on the condition that she stop wasting her time on art. I guess they didn't feel that painting would get her anywhere in life. By the time she was in her early thirties, she'd finally hit her stride. She was beginning to produce a genuinely impressive body of work. And then she was killed. It was a traumatic time for Jim. He was very much in love with her. Not only that, but the police were hounding him. They thought he was responsible. He'd called me the night Bliss died. He was in La Crosse, Wisconsin. I had the phone records to prove it, but he refused to bring me into it. He was terrified the police would find out about his other wives, about his real identity, that he'd go to prison."

"What was his real name?" asked Sophie.

"Why, I thought you knew. John Washburn. But he'll always be my Jim."

Sophie shivered at the revelation. "Who was his first wife? His legal wife?"

"Why, Mary Washburn, of course. But she wasn't his first love. He'd fallen for a girl up north the year before. Laura was her first name. I don't recall the last. But she was a real beauty, dark hair, dark eyes. Jim could see right away that she had a problem with alcohol and depression. He tried to spend as much time with her as he could. His eyes just glowed when he talked about her."

"Then why did he propose to Mary first?"

"Because she was pregnant and desperate. Plato isn't John's child. The biological father took off right after he found out Mary was in the family way, as we used to say. Jim cared about Mary a lot. He knew how scared she was. So he married her. And he loved her, but not the way he loved Laura. Laura committed suicide several years before I met Jim, but she was still very much on his mind. She was his true *grande passion*." She gave it the French pronunciation.

"But Bernice—"

"Yes, Bernice is Jim's child. His only child. He adores her, and she him. Plato was more of a problem. It isn't that Jim doesn't love him, but they're so very different. Plato is a passive man. He allows life to happen to him, doesn't try to change what doesn't work. Bernice is more like Jim. If she sees a problem, she wants to fix it. But then, you're her friend. You must know all about her."

Sophie wasn't sure what she knew anymore. "Yes, she's a fine woman. What about Jim's brother?"

"Milton? I met him once. He didn't know I was married to Jim. He thought I was just a friend. I liked him. He and Jim were very funny together. And Milton was a real success story, thanks to his brother."

"What did Jim have to do with it?"

Viola shrugged out of her shawl. "Would you open the window? It's getting a bit stuffy in here."

Sophie stood and rolled the casement window away from the screen, allowing the cool breeze inside.

"That's better," said Viola, folding the shawl into a neat rectangle as Sophie sat back down. "About Milton. After Jim and Gilbert Struthers robbed that bank back in the mid-fifties, Jim ended up with the money. Two hundred thousand dollars. He carried it around in a big suitcase for a few months, but he couldn't bring himself to spend any of it. It felt like blood money to him. His brother, Milton, was kicking around St. Louis at the time. He was working as a salesman for Lee Broom and Mop, and so he traveled a lot, too, but he and a pal of his had this bee in their bonnet to develop a new kind of trailer home. Jim decided to give Milton the money. He refused to tell Milton where he got it, and Milton didn't care. He wasn't about to look a gift horse in the mouth. It was just the break he and his pal had been waiting for. They patented their design, then started constructing the homes. By the mid-sixties, they'd built up a nice little business. And by the mid-seventies, they'd gone national and made their first million. Milton sent his brother money every month, as a way of paying him back. That's how Jim could afford the extra mouths to feed. And when the company went public in the early eighties,

Milton made Jim a major stockholder. Milton's company made them both rich."

So that's what happened to the money, thought Sophie. "Does Milton know about his brother's secret life?"

"Heavens, no. And you mustn't tell him."

"Did Jim ever refer to himself as J. D."

Viola frowned, shaking her head. "Not that I recall. You know, Sophie, as I think of it, I heard someone repeat a wonderful quote the other day on public radio. I liked it so much, I wrote it down. It's in that novel by Gore Vidal. Right inside the front cover. Pick it up and read it to me."

Sophie turned around and lifted the book off the nightstand. Opening the cover she found the quote scrawled in red pencil.

> We believe at once in evil. We only believe in good upon reflection. Is this not sad?
> —MADAM DOROTHEE DELUZY
> Actress, (1747–1830)

Gazing thoughtfully at a Mason jar of wilting daises, Viola continued, "In the end, everyone's life is a puzzle. Perhaps it's best not to try to decode motives. Our decisions are far more random than we like to think. Very little on this earth begins clearly, or ends neatly. If I've learned anything, it's that every person's story needs a preface and an epilogue. Maybe that's the librarian in me talking, but I believe it's more than that. I hope you understand Jim a little better now. He told me once that his wives were easy to please, but hard to protect. He may have broken some rules, but he has a good heart. In the end, that's what counts."

Sophie was touched by the old woman's words. Perhaps she had misjudged John Washburn, at least partially. "I'm driving to Rose Hill tonight as soon as I'm done here."

"Will you give Jim a message for me? Will you tell him that I miss him? That I hope he'll come by soon?"

Sophie was torn. Should she explain that John had suffered a stroke? It seemed cruel to tell her, and equally cruel not to. When she looked back, the elderly woman was staring at her.

"Is he dead?" asked Viola softly.

"No," said Sophie. She touched Viola's arm. "He had a stroke several weeks ago. But he's getting better every day."

Viola flinched, then closed her eyes. "Bless you for telling me."

"I'm sorry to be the bearer of bad tidings."

"Don't be. Now that I know, I can pray for him. I can do something useful. Will you give him my love?"

"Yes," said Sophie, feeling Viola squeeze her hand, "I will."

39

The moon rose, the crickets sang in a deafening choir, and night closed in around him. Tucked deep into the boughs at the base of a spruce tree about ten yards from Melvin DuCharme's cabin steps, Angelo waited. He'd spent the early part of the evening in Minneapolis, digging up a pair of night-vision goggles, handcuffs, and a bulletproof vest. Armed with a forty-five caliber Glock in a shoulder holster, Angelo had come prepared for a fight, one he intended to win.

Just before sunset, Cora and Angelo arrived at the cabin in her car. As Cora climbed out of the front seat, Angelo remained in the back seat covered by a blanket. He watched through the open door as Cora stuffed the envelope containing the letters underneath the steps. He wanted to make sure that once she'd stashed the goods, she got away safely.

On her way home, she let him off by the side of the road. He tramped a good mile through the woods, using a compass, and arrived back at the cabin just as the sun set over the Cottonwood River. Crawling slowly through the undergrowth toward the huge spruce, he took up his position, hoping he wouldn't have long to wait. Ever since he'd talked to Cora at the coffee shop, he'd been a man in motion, rushing from one place to the next. He hadn't had much time to think, only to act. But now the niggling worry he'd ignored earlier just about swallowed him whole. What if Bernice had put the bomb in Kirby Runbeck's truck? If she showed up here tonight, instead of Milton or Plato or even Mary Washburn, what would he do?

Angelo knew the answer. He'd wait for her to read the letters, then together they'd destroy them. He'd make her promise never to bother Cora again. Together, they'd wait it out. The police had no real proof that her father had murdered Kirby Runbeck. A confession given right after a major stroke would never hold up in court. Chances were, nothing legal would ever come of it and John would be free to live out the rest of his life in peace. The only matter that still bothered Angelo was the cold-blooded way Bernice had gone after Cora. That is, if she had. He still believed she had nothing to do with it. It was most likely Milton or Plato. Whatever the case, Angelo felt confident that whoever had stolen Cora's cat, demanding the letters as ransom, wouldn't wait long to pick them up.

By three A.M., Angelo was beginning to wonder if he'd been wrong about the blackmailer's impatience. It was possible that the letters could sit under the steps for days. Maybe the person he was waiting for was being ruthlessly careful, making sure no trap had been set. If so, Angelo would have to alter his plans accordingly. He'd been fighting sleep for the past two hours. Thank God for the mosquitoes. He couldn't believe an intelligent human being would willingly live in a place infested with such vile bugs.

Just before four in the morning, he heard grass rustle

behind him. His body tensed and his senses switched to high alert. He turned his head carefully to the side, but saw nothing. Quiet returned. Except, this time, he could feel alien body heat right through the branches. At all costs, he couldn't give his position away. He waited for what seemed like an eternity, controlling his breathing, eliminating even the smallest twitch. A mosquito landed on his nose. He could feel it boring into his skin, making a meal of his blood. He had an overwhelming urge to smack the life out of it, but he couldn't move.

Suddenly, a dark form burst past the pine tree headed for the cabin steps. Angelo assumed the person must have been waiting in the dark for a long time, creeping ever closer to the target. Through his night-vision goggles, he could see a long, hooded raincoat. Whether the form was a man or a woman, he couldn't tell. But it definitely held a gun.

Crouching near the steps, the figure looked around cautiously, then transferred the gun from one hand to the other and pulled a small flashlight out of the raincoat pocket. Angelo had instructed Cora to place the letters in a zip-lock plastic bag, then insert the bag into a large white envelope. Once the envelope had been placed safely under the steps, she was to pour a jar of honey over it. Angelo figured this would slow the blackmailer down, giving him an opening to attack.

And that's just what happened.

"What the fuck," came a low, feral growl. The figure dropped everything, trying to smear off the sticky goo.

Angelo blasted into action. Pulling his gun, he spanned the ten yards to the cabin steps in a matter of seconds. "Stop right there."

The figured whirled around.

"You!" said Angelo.

Plato looked startled. But instead of stopping, he lunged forward, knocking the gun out of Angelo's hand and slamming him to the ground. They rolled around in the grass and the dirt, grunting and swearing, each struggling to reach the gun before the other. Just as Angelo's fingertips touched the metal handle, Plato's knee jammed hard into his groin. Angelo doubled up, howling in agony.

"Get up!" demanded Plato, sounding both furious and out of breath.

Pain consumed him. He couldn't answer.

"Who do you think you are? This is none of your business!"

Angelo felt a heavy boot slam into his side.

"What am I going to do with you? Huh? Answer me!"

"Let's . . . talk," rasped Angelo.

"Right. Communication. The all-purpose emotional band aid. As long as we're communicating, all is well. What a load of bullshit. What if I don't want to talk? What if I don't feel like *communicating?*"

Angelo swallowed back his nausea and tried to clear his head. "You're so angry."

"Damn right I am."

"Why?" He propped himself up on one elbow, then hauled himself up off the ground.

"You changed the subject."

"Where's the cat?"

He snorted. "I ate it with some fava beans."

"Don't be so melodramatic. You're not Hannibal Lecter."

"Of course I am! Don't you get it? That's the whole goddamn *point!*" He was screaming now. "You have no idea what I've done in my sleepy, obscure little life. Nobody does. I'm the quiet guy who lives next door. The pervert who was such a good son and a sweet child. I'm fucking invisible!"

"If you kill me, you'll go to prison."

"I don't care. It's all over anyway." He raised the gun and fired three bullets into Angelo's chest. They didn't penetrate his vest, but the force propelled him backward into the tall grass. As he lay motionless, Plato fired three more shots, two into his upper body and a vindictive afterthought into his right thigh. Even though he was hit, Angelo had the presence of mind to play dead. With six gunshot wounds to his vital organs, Plato must have figured Angelo was a goner. From what Cora said, his pattern was to shoot, but not to look at his handiwork.

Plato kicked some sand into Angelo's face just for spite, then left him alone and sat down on the steps, looking up at the stars.

Angelo could feel the blood oozing from his leg. He might not be mortally wounded, but if he didn't get help soon, he could bleed to death. The cell phone was in his pants pocket, mere inches from his hand. But he couldn't use it as long as Plato hung around. He had to play another waiting game. And this time, the stakes were his own life.

40

Sophie was startled awake by the sound of her cell phone. Checking the clock she saw that it was a quarter to five. Still dark out. The last thing she remembered was switching on the TV to catch a little of Conan O'Brien's show. She'd settled herself on the lumpy motel bed, dressed in jeans and a University of Minnesota T-shirt, anticipating that Angelo would call when the culprit had been handcuffed and immobilized, ready for transport back to town.

Instead, after clicking the phone on, she heard a raspy voice say, "Sophie, I've been shot. Send paramedics. You've got the directions, right?" He sounded weak.

"Yes . . . but how bad is it?"

"Bad. I've lost a lot of blood. I'm lying in front of the cabin. Call Bernice. I want you to meet me at the hospital. Hurry!"

Sophie was so rattled, she forgot to ask who'd shot him. Using the motel phone, she punched in 911. She rushed through the information. The woman on the other end promised to send a police car and a paramedic van right away. After Sophie hung up, she called Bernice. She crossed her fingers and sent up a silent prayer that

Milton wouldn't answer. He could easily be the one who shot Angelo. Closing her eyes, she heard the line pick up. It was Bernice's voice.

"This is Sophie. Don't react, okay? Don't say my name or repeat anything I tell you. Is that clear? If it is, just say yes."

After a long moment, Bernice said, "Yes."

"Angelo's been hurt. He's all right, but he's being brought to the hospital by a paramedic van. He wants us to meet him at the emergency room. I'm in town, at the River Inn. I'll stop by the house in a few minutes to pick you up. Do you understand?"

"Yes."

She sounded uncertain, but Sophie didn't want to get into any more of it now. "Meet me on the front steps. Is Milton there?"

Hesitation. "Yes."

"Is he still asleep?"

"No."

"The phone woke him?"

"I think so."

"Damn. What can you tell him?"

"It's all right, Angelo. Let's just drive around and talk. It was a silly lover's quarrel. I'm sorry for what I said. I still love you."

Sophie hoped that would work. "Tell Milton to go back to bed. It's a private matter between you and your boyfriend. And I'll meet you downstairs in ten minutes."

"Yes. Good-bye."

Sophie dropped the phone back in its cradle, grabbed her purse, and hit the pavement outside the motel door running.

* * *

An hour and ten minutes later, Angelo was in the emergency room. The paramedics had already examined the wound and found that the bullet had pierced through the flesh of his thigh. He also had deep bruises on his chest where the bullets had struck the bulletproof vest. As soon as the emergency room doctor had cleaned the leg wound and bandaged it, Sophie and Bernice were allowed into the cubicle.

Angelo was a sight to behold. His face was scratched and bruised, and he had blood all over his clothing, but he smiled when he saw Bernice.

She kissed him tenderly. "Who did this to you?"

Sophie had filled her in on some of the details in the car driving over, but she'd left out the part about her father being a bigamist. Sophie wanted to talk to Angelo about it first, decide what was the best way to handle it.

Angelo coughed, then winced.

"Are you in a lot of pain?" asked Sophie.

"Some. I may have a cracked rib. Once they're done giving me blood, they're sending me to X-ray." His eyes rose to Bernice. "God, but you look like a million bucks."

"Flattery will get you anything you want. But tell us what happened first."

A nurse zipped in to check the bag of blood hanging next to the bed. "The doctor's ordered another unit. I'll bring it in when this is done." She glanced at the IV in his hand, then left.

Sophie asked her question again. "Who shot you?"

Still looking at Bernice, Angelo said, "Plato."

Bernice covered her mouth with her hand.

"He's behind everything. Kirby Runbeck's murder.

The attempt on Cora Runbeck's life. And now tonight, he tried to kill me."

"But why?" demanded Bernice, horrified. "I don't understand."

"He knew I'd discovered what he'd done. Yesterday afternoon, he broke into Cora Runbeck's house and swiped her cat. He left a note telling her that if she wanted to see it again, she was to hand over the information her husband had discovered on your father. He told her to leave it under the steps of an old cabin out by the Cottonwood River. I tried to catch him, talk some sense into him. I wanted to convince him to turn himself into the police, but he refused. He lost it, Bernice. He's a sick man."

"You mean he shot you? Just like that?"

Angelo nodded. "I was wearing a bulletproof vest. Without it, I'd be a dead man."

"But I can't believe this," she said, pulling away from him. "What you're describing is a thug. A cold-blooded killer. My brother is a businessman, a good citizen, a father. Plato is a thinker, not a doer. Everyone in the family knows that."

"Not this time," said Angelo.

"But what *was* the incriminating evidence?"

He glanced at Sophie, then back at Bernice. "I don't know. I never saw it."

So that was the way he wanted to play it, thought Sophie. He hoped to protect Bernice from the truth. But with Plato on the loose, it might not be possible. Plato must have read the letters by now. That meant he knew what his father had done. What he decided to do next was anyone's guess.

Suddenly, an alarm went off. A nurse rushed into the room. "We've been ordered to evacuate the building."

"What?" said Angelo, his head rising off the pillow.

"There's a man on the fourth floor with a bomb." As she unlocked the gurney, she glanced up at Bernice. "Say, aren't you Bernice Washburn? You're his sister!"

Bernice's jaw dropped. "Plato's here? *He's* the one with the bomb?"

"He's in your father's room. The police couldn't stop him. He's got dynamite strapped to his chest. That's why we've all got to get out of here."

"Do what the nurse says," ordered Angelo. He grabbed Bernice's hand as the nurse began to wheel him out into the crowded hallway.

Pandemonium reigned. Sophie was nearly knocked down by a man pushing a cart. She had to struggle to stay close to Angelo's gurney.

"Don't try to be a hero," said Angelo. "Whatever your brother's about to do, you can't stop him. Believe me, I know."

"But I'm his sister," said Bernice. "He'll listen to me." She looked up at the clock on the wall as they sped past it. "It's just seven. My mother's still up there!"

"Your brother threw her out of the room," said the nurse. "He wants to talk to your father alone. He gave instructions not to be disturbed—or else."

"See?" said Angelo, looking desperate. He wouldn't let go of Bernice's hand. "We've all got to get out. Now!"

Plato stood in the far corner of the room, watching his father. It felt like he was seeing him for the first time. This was a rare moment: two bastards recognizing each other in the forest of life. Watching his father stare back at him with those sharp evaluating eyes of his made Plato glance down at his clothing. He looked like a rumpled park-bench drunk. He smiled for a moment, remembering his old theory. To be truly evil, he would have to dress better and lose weight. So much for the musings of a fat, middle-aged failure.

Plato wondered what his father was thinking. Was he frightened? He didn't look it. If anything, he radiated a kind of peaceful calm. Perhaps he knew this was it: High Noon. The moment of truth. Blastoff!

Plato kicked a chair away from the wall and sat down.

"How are you this morning, son?" asked John conversationally, his speech slow and halting.

"I've been better."

"You want to talk about it?"

He'd given a lot of thought to how he would begin. First, he'd nail his father's hide to the wall with a litany of his sins. He'd call him every name in the book, make sure he understood that Plato knew he was lower than pond scum. And then, he'd laugh. He'd tell his father that the Bible was wrong. The sins of the fathers didn't condemn their sons unto the third and fourth generation, they *liberated* them. Plato was a free man now. He no longer had to pretend.

But instead of his rehearsed opening, Plato asked, "Why did you say you'd killed Kirby Runbeck?"

"I wanted to protect you."

He hadn't expected that. "But ... how did you know—"

"I saw you the day Runbeck cornered me in my office. I watched through the window as you walked out to your car. I assumed you'd been standing in the front hall, listening to us."

"But I heard a noise in the kitchen. Someone was in there, too. I'm sure of it."

John shook his head stiffly. "No, that was the refrigerator. It clunks when it turns off and on. I made sure I was alone before I let Kirby into the house. Your mother and Bernice were out shopping. Milton was playing golf. I couldn't take any chances, son. I didn't hear you come in, but I saw you leave. I wanted to talk to you about what you'd heard, but I wasn't sure what to say. I was ashamed of myself, of what you'd think of me. I waited too long." He paused. "You did what you did to protect me. How could I do any less for you?"

Plato could feel something deep inside him give way. "I didn't realize what you'd done until I read the letters. But I knew it must be bad."

"You have the letters?"

He nodded.

"But how did you—"

"That's my business, not yours."

"What . . . what will you do with them?"

"I haven't decided. Why did you sign the letters J. D.?"

"It was a nickname."

"What's it stand for?"

His father seemed embarrassed by the question. "When I was young, I looked like the actor James Dean. A few of my buddies called me J. D."

"James Dean, huh? I don't see it."

John dropped his eyes to the glass of water on his tray table. "Give the letters to the police, son. Tell them you read them and got upset, so upset you wanted to kill me. That's why you came here with the dynamite. You were temporarily out of your mind. You snapped. Whatever you say, make it good. Tell them that after talking to me, you realized your mistake. The police believe I killed Runbeck. Let them go on believing it. My life is over. With what little I have left, let me protect you."

Plato shot out of his chair with such force that it skittered across the floor. "What the hell's wrong with you? I don't want you to be a saint to the end! I want you to own the fact that you're a low-life slime. I was never good enough for you. Never clever enough, never a star athlete, a wiz at math. I was a disappointment to you from the day I was born."

"That's not true."

"You never loved me!"

"I did—and I do," said John, his eyes pleading. "But sometimes . . . you'd frustrate me. How can I make you understand?" He raised a shaky hand to wipe his mouth. "Look, you're a father. Think with that mind for a second. You don't always like your sons, right? It happens. A friend of mine told me once that the trick to being in a family is, you don't have to like everyone, but you have to love them."

"What the fuck kind of reasoning is that? If you don't like someone, it's apparent. They *get* it! I sure did. How on earth was I supposed to figure out—through all your visible loathing—that underneath, you really loved me?"

"I don't know," said John, closing his eyes. "You and me, we're so different."

"Like hell we are. The reason we couldn't live together is because two narcissists under one roof will never get along. You think marrying all those women was noble? What a load of crap! You did what you *wanted* to do, just like me. You don't have motives, you've got *appetites*. You were an evil bastard from the beginning. Like father like son."

"You're wrong."

"I felt smothered my whole life by petty obligations and worn-out rules. The rules you didn't like, you ignored. Well, same with me. I took my pleasures where I found them. For your information, before I moved to the hobby farm, I went to a therapist for almost a year. The two of us tried like hell to work out a different plot for my life. We tried to come up with different explanations for my actions, tried to fit everything into a prettier package. She loved issuing her nifty little insights, but in the end, I couldn't stand the monotony. I could predict what she was going to say before she said it. Why the hell pay someone you can fake out so easily?"

Plato stepped over to the window and looked down at the street. It was shimmering with people rushing away from the building. Police cars were beginning to form a barricade on the far end of the parking lot. "Don't you ever just yearn for . . . for lightness, Dad? To wake up and find it was all a dream?"

"Every day," said John softly.

"I thought, if that therapist ever made one unalterably true statement about who I really was, I'd stay and work on my problems. But she couldn't see me. Nobody can. I'm the invisible man." He turned around and gave his father a sunny smile.

"You need help."

"I need a new life."

"What are you going to do?"

"Yes, the big question. Should I blow us up or not blow us up? What do you think?"

"You want to kill me? Is that what this is all about?"

"Golly, no, Dad. I want to keep you around. With you in the world, I don't feel so alone."

"Stop it!" said John, closing his eyes and looking away.

"The truth is hard to take." Sitting down on the edge of the bed, Plato waited until his father looked at him again. "I'll tell you my truth, Dad. Are you ready? There's a crack in me. I can feel it. I've known it was there ever since I was a kid. It's a small crack, so other people don't notice it, but it's there. It's been growing for years. Getting bigger. Too much pressure and I'll shatter."

"What are you saying?"

"You look frightened. Don't be." He reached over to straighten the front of his father's bathrobe. "I'm going home now. I will walk out that door and leave the hospital. Quietly. Peacefully. If anyone upsets me, well . . . you're not deaf. Dumb and blind, maybe, but not deaf. If I shatter, you'll hear me break."

41

"We can work this out," Deputy Sheriff Doug said, following Plato down the hospital corridor. "I know we can."

"Leave me alone."

"I realize you're upset with your father. Who wouldn't be? Look, we've got a psychologist outside. He wants to talk to you."

"I don't want to talk to him."

"But he says he can help you. He's sure of it."

Wasn't that *it* in a nutshell? thought Plato. Optimism. The belief that wrongs could be righted, problems could be solved. At a time like this, optimism was just one more burden.

"You can't get away, you know. We've got the entire hospital surrounded." Doug glanced at the detonation device in Plato's hand.

All the way down in the elevator, the officer continued his patter. By the time they reached the glass front doors, Plato had a splitting headache. The sun was already white hot. Police were everywhere. People were running around; some had stopped to gawk. Car fumes choked Plato's throat. "I just want to be left alone."

"We can't allow that."

"You can allow anything I damn well please. I'm the one with the dynamite, Doug."

Just then, two teenage girls rushed around the side of the building. They were giggling, acting like they'd just heard a big joke. An officer across the street hollered for them to stop, to get back. But it was too late. Plato grabbed the smaller one and jammed her against his chest. Doug drew his gun, but he didn't fire. He couldn't.

Plato guided the girl toward his car and told her to get in. As everyone watched in abject horror, Plato eased into the driver's seat and rolled down the window. "Leave me alone and nothing will happen to—" He looked at the girl. "What's your name?"

"Brittany," she said, her eyes round with terror, her body pressed to the door, cowering.

"There you have it. Brittany. Leave us the hell alone and she won't get hurt!" He started the motor, then burned rubber. Glancing in his rearview mirror, he yelled "Damn it all!" when he saw that he was being followed.

Twenty minutes later, Plato and Brittany were inside his barn. He used an old rope to tie the teenager's hands and feet, and he slapped a piece of duct tape across her mouth to shut her up. Finally, he stowed her behind the baled hay. Speaking very slowly and clearly, he promised he wouldn't hurt her. Once he decided what to do, he'd let her go. But she had to stay until then because otherwise, there was no telling what the police would do.

Astrid was still in the barn. Plato led her out of her stall, sidestepping the cow dung, then dragged a barrel over next to her and sat down. He needed time to think. Astrid would help him figure it all out. Her big brown eyes blinked their sweetness at him. Her unconditional love enveloped him.

"Oh, hey," he said, reaching into his pocket and pulling out an Oreo. "I brought this for you. Here," he said tenderly, feeding it to her, then petting her head. People thought cows were lumbering animals, dim-witted and smelly. Astrid might be a tad smelly, but she was also delicate. She bared her teeth ever so slightly as she took the cookie. She loved her Oreos, just like Plato did. It was kind of early in the morning for a cookie, he supposed, but then this was a special occasion. A party. Except, Plato couldn't quite come up with the theme.

"The problem is, Astrid, you have to make so many important decisions in your life before you're ready to make them. Like marriage. I was incredibly hot to marry my wife, but I was twenty years old. What the hell does a twenty-year-old know about life? How was I supposed to guess she'd turn into the Farmer in the Dell? Not that I've got anything against farm life, you understand. If I hadn't come here, I would never have met you, but to be truthful, I don't belong on a hobby farm. I hate the out-doors, hate tramping through the woods and dales. Give me a book and an easy chair any day.

"And then, there's children. How did *they* happen? Well, I mean, I know how they happened, but . . . I don't know them. They don't know me. My wife and I are strangers. And nobody seems to notice except me. Or, if they do notice, they don't care. We all just continue with our lives as if nothing's wrong. But everything's wrong, Astrid."

Plato could smell the foul odor of car exhaust wafting in through the open door. He stomped over to look out-side. Sure enough, squad cars had ringed the barn, but they were at least seventy-five yards away. They weren't taking any chances.

Sharpshooters were standing by the trees, their rifles pointed at the barn door. A crowd was beginning to form, well behind the cars. All the bored townspeople were coming to watch a real-life drama as they sipped their morning coffee. Overhead, Plato could hear a helicopter. Scanning the assembly, he could pick out a few familiar faces. Sophie Greenway was there; so was his sister, Bernice, his uncle Milton, and his mother. Next to them, his wife was talking to a cop. They were all huddled together under an oak tree. His two sons stood about fifteen feet away, hands shielding their eyes from the sun's glare, the better to witness their father's demise.

As Plato continued to watch the voyeurs arrive, he noticed several vans pull in. Men scrambled out the back doors with handheld cameras and sound equipment.

"You should see this, Astrid. It's like a county fair." Just as he said the words, a minidonut truck drove in. "I'll bet we're live on CNN. Welcome to the twenty-first century, huh? Mass media can now capture a man's mental collapse right on camera, as it happens, for all the world to see."

Astrid mooed. With the acoustics in the new metal barn, it had a deep, metallic ring. She must want another cookie, thought Plato. He didn't have one. If he could just get his hands on a package of those minidonuts, they'd both be happy.

Doug's voice blasted through the air on a loudspeaker. "Plato, this is Deputy Sheriff Doug Elderberg."

"I know who it is, asshole," muttered Plato. "I didn't figure Dan Rather was here yet."

"We've got the place surrounded."

"Gee, I never would have guessed."

"Send Brittany out. You said yourself you didn't want to hurt her. She's just an innocent bystander."

"Aren't we all? No, I take that back. I've never been innocent. Maybe that's my problem."

"Plato, if you can hear me, make some sort of sign."

Plato took off his right loafer and heaved it out into the sunlight.

"Good," said Doug, a little dubiously. "Was that your shoe? Never mind."

They couldn't fire their rifles as long as the girl remained inside. Bringing her along had been a stroke of genius.

Plato returned to the barrel and sat back down. "You know what, Astrid? One day, this is going to be the great town anecdote. Where were you when that crazy Plato Washburn got cornered in his barn? 'Why, I was there,' the old men will say. 'Saw the whole thing with my own two eyes. He was a freak, all right.' " Plato stopped, looking the cow full in the eyes. "But what's the ending, Astrid? I can't see it. What should I do? If I give myself up, I'll go to jail for the rest of my life. I'm not sure I could stand that. It seems unlikely I could get out of the barn without getting shot. Unless I came up with a pretty amazing plan, that is. And I seem to be fresh out of plans."

"Plato, this is Doug again. How you doin' in there? We've got a man out here who wants to come in and talk to you. He's unarmed. He won't try anything funny, I promise. Like I said, he just wants to talk."

Plato rushed to the door. "No way," he shouted. "If he approaches the barn, I'll blow the whole place up."

"Okay, okay," said Doug. "Maybe he can just talk to you on the loudspeaker."

"I want to be alone! Go away!"

"We can't. Not unless you send the girl out."

"She's the only thing keeping me alive. Do you think I'm an idiot?"

The crowd began to shout insults.

"Ill words butter no parsnips!" screamed Plato, huffing his way back to the barrel.

Astrid looked glum.

"Yeah, this is a mess. I won't tell you what I've done 'cause you won't like it." One more being he could disappoint. But with Astrid, it was different. She didn't *really* care, so she was safe.

"Plato Washburn?" A woman's voice boomed over the din of the crowd. "This is Cora Runbeck. Where's my cat?"

He grunted. The cat was the least of his worries.

"I kept my part of the bargain. Now you keep yours."

The letters, thought Plato. With all the commotion, he'd forgotten about them. He hurried over to the wooden workbench, and pulled them out from under a box of gardening tools. "What am I going to do with these, Astrid?" Part of him wanted his mother to read them, to see just what kind of man she'd married, and part of him wanted to protect her. He took the letters and walked back to the barrel, slumping down on top of it. Deep inside, his heart felt like a wet, drippy piece of ice, melting not from the heat of the barn, but from the fire of his indecision.

"I'm melting," he said to Astrid.

"I want my cat!" Cora hollered again.

"Oh, shut up, you old biddy."

"Plato, it's your mother." This time the voice was close. Soft. Reassuring. Mary stepped to the edge of the barn door, her body caught in a shaft of sunlight. "Can I come in?"

Plato looked over at her, then dipped his hand into the pocket of his suit, where he'd put the detonator. "Go away."

"Don't shut me out. I want to help you."

"I don't need your help. I just need to think. I need to be alone."

"You spend too much time alone, dear."

"It's my life."

"Of course it is. Nobody's denying that."

"Did you hear what I did to Bernice's boyfriend? Maybe the police haven't found him yet. I shot him last night."

"I know," said Mary, stepping a few paces closer. "But he's doing fine."

Plato looked up sharply. "I shot him a bunch of times in the chest."

"He was wearing one of those vests, the kind that bullets don't go through."

"No shit?"

"Plato, your language. You don't need to talk like that."

Here they were, in a life-and-death situation, police with loaded rifles all around them, dynamite strapped to his chest, and his mother was scolding him for using profanity. Only in a small town.

"Why don't you let the girl go, dear? I'll stay here with you instead. It will work out just the same. The police can't do anything if they think an innocent person might be harmed. Maybe, after the girl leaves, we could ask them to bring us some breakfast. Would you like that?"

Of course, thought Plato. He could ask for anything he wanted. "Maybe I'll demand a limo to take us to the airport. And then a plane to South America. Throw in a million bucks and we've got ourselves a plan!"

"Be reasonable, dear. This is Rose Hill. The police are already falling over themselves trying to figure out what to do next. You can't put any more pressure on them. It wouldn't be kind, and you're not that sort of man."

"Mother, I killed Kirby Runbeck, and attempted to kill two other people."

She seemed startled. "*You* killed Kirby?"

"What do you think this is all about?"

"I thought you were angry at your father, and that it escalated into—" She spread her arms wide. "This."

"It did."

"But murder?"

He groaned.

"Plato, I demand an explanation."

"Look, the girl's behind the hay bales. Go get her."

"But—"

"No more talking. Take her and leave."

"But, son, what are you going to do?"

"I don't know!"

"Give yourself up. I couldn't bear it if something happened to you. You and Bernice are the lights of my life. You're still my little boy. I'd do anything for you."

He felt himself begin to crumble. "Get the girl, Mom, before I change my mind and blow us all up."

"You'd never hurt me."

"Get her!"

Hesitantly, Mary crossed to the back of the barn.

Crouching down, she untied the ropes, then helped the girl to her feet. "Plato, we can work this out somehow," she said as she passed slowly by him.

"Wait," said Plato gruffly. He stood and gave her a quick kiss on the cheek. "I love you, Mom. Don't worry. I'll be out in a little while."

She smiled uncertainly. "I'll be waiting."

Once they were gone, Plato spent a few moments petting Astrid's head. "You're a good girl," he said softly. "You're my cow."

He sat down to think. Every once in a while, his musings were interrupted by the annoying sound of Doug Elderberg shouting at him, but Plato didn't listen anymore. What was the use? He'd made up his mind.

As the sun reached midday, the heat in the barn was beginning to rise to an unhealthy level. Astrid was growing restless. She needed to get outside where there was a breeze, where she could nibble on some grass.

Moving over to the door, Plato called, "Doug? Are you there?"

"I'm here," came the prompt, booming response.

"I've got an unhappy cow in here. The barn's awfully hot. She needs to get outside. Will you let me walk her out to the pasture?"

No response. He was probably conferring with his henchmen. Finally, "All right, Plato. But stay to the south of the barn."

Slipping a rope around Astrid's neck, Plato tugged her to the door. With his hand on the detonator, he looked around. The air was still, the silence oppressive. When he reached the edge of the pasture, he stopped for a moment. A shiny new penny lay at his feet. As he bent down to pick it up, he heard the report of a rifle. Lunging forward, he slapped Astrid on her haunch, sending her away from him, then spun around and dodged his way back to the barn.

"At least she's safe now," he whispered, hearing a hail of bullets hit the metal walls. It was almost over. In one deafening blast, his pain would end forever.

Or would it?

Plato's father had always maintained that most solutions were only temporary. Since Plato believed in an afterlife, as his finger slipped over the detonator, he wondered if this solution fell into that category.

Epilogue

Sophie sat by the hospital room window, knitting a wool scarf. She hadn't done any knitting in years, but she needed to keep busy right now, keep moving, even if only barely. She'd made herself a cup of tea a few minutes ago, a variety that promised to tame her tension, but it wasn't working. In an effort to occupy herself with something other than worry, her thoughts turned to Cora Runbeck's cat. Winthrop had been found locked in a small cage in the basement of the *Rose Hill Gazette* two days after Plato had blown himself up. Plato had given him water and food, but by the time he was discovered, it was all gone. His plight had made headlines as far away as New Zealand. A veterinarian had checked him over and pronounced him frightened but fit, and Cora had taken him home to the cheers of cat lovers everywhere.

A lot had happened since Plato's death three months ago. It was late November now, a few days before Thanksgiving. The last Sophie had heard, Cora Runbeck was commuting to New York and L.A. on a regular basis. Her cat's odyssey had ended happily, and so had her own.

After being wined and dined in the Twin Cities as the third-place winner of the *Times Register*'s meat loaf contest, Cora had made a hit on *Good Morning with Bailey Brown*. So much of a hit that she'd been invited back three times. By the middle of October, she was a regular on the program. And by early November, she'd been a guest on *The Tonight Show, David Letterman, Oprah,* and *Rosie*. The latest scuttlebutt hinted that Cora would be the first person to land a regular berth on *Politically Incorrect* with Bill Maher. In three short months, she'd become a Minnesota phenomena, spouting her no-nonsense, small-town, Lutheran-inspired brand of plain talk on all the major networks. People couldn't seem to get enough of her.

Except for the Washburns. Sophie and Bram had driven down to Rose Hill in early October for Bernice and Angelo's wedding. Since everyone else in the country was talking and laughing about Cora, the fact that her name was never once mentioned didn't go unnoticed. And yet, nothing could get in the way of Bernice and Angelo's happiness that day. To everyone's delight, John was there, too, sitting in a wheelchair, thin as a reed in a new suit. He may not have been dancing at their wedding, but he was beaming with joy.

Later, when the happy couple was in Venice on their honeymoon, John had suffered a second stroke. He lived for two days before dying quietly in his sleep. Mary and Milton were at his side until the end. Mary called Bernice and Angelo when it was over, saying that John wanted to be cremated. His memorial service could wait until they returned from their trip.

Before Angelo left for Italy, he and Sophie had talked privately. He insisted that John's secrets be kept from the family. He'd already extracted an oath of silence from Cora. If Bernice or her mother ever learned the truth, it would only cause more pain. Sophie went along with him because she had no reason not to.

Angelo and Bernice were living in Connecticut now. And Milton and Mary were happily settled at the house in Rose Hill. Bernice wrote Sophie that her mother had fallen in love with Milton, never guessing that Sophie already knew. Bernice was happy that her mother wouldn't be alone, now that her father was gone. She approved wholeheartedly of the relationship, though she didn't think Milton and her mother would ever marry. They'd been down that road and didn't want to do it again. If they continued to live in the house without benefit of matrimony, it would become quite the scandal in Rose Hill. But Bernice said her mother had changed since her father's death. She didn't care these days what other people thought. What she thought was more important.

As for Viola Newman, the old woman in the nursing home, Sophie drove down to visit her every few weeks. Viola said she missed Jim, as she still called John Washburn, but she was glad he'd finally found peace. She talked to him every day now and felt he was listening, that he was waiting for her to join him. Sophie hoped that was true.

After taking a sip of tea, Sophie's thoughts turned to Nathan Buckridge. His dining room at Chez Sophia was finally under construction and he was busily at work with a commercial kitchen designer. She'd driven out one afternoon in late October to see the plans. Nathan was bouncing off walls he was so excited. She was happy for him. He wanted her to come back the following day to look at carpet samples, but she said she couldn't. He didn't press her and she was glad. Nathan had been a huge question mark tossed in the path of an otherwise happy marriage. But a few days ago, a new, more ominous threat had turned up. At this moment, all Sophie wanted was to spend the rest of her life with her husband. She wanted a *long* life with him, but that was up in the air right now.

Three days ago, while Bram had been doing his afternoon radio program, he'd begun to experience chest pains. As soon as the paramedics had been summoned, there'd been a mad scramble at the station to find someone to fill in for him. Sophie had been called and had met him at the emergency room entrance. The paramedics had already started him on oxygen and an IV in the ambulance. She's been so glad he was awake and able to talk that she'd burst into tears—not particularly helpful. Once he was stabilized, an emergency room doctor had come in to ask him some questions. Had he ever experienced chest pain before? Did he take any medications? Had a member of his family ever had a heart attack? Sophie was stunned to learn that Bram's father had suffered a heart attack in his early fifties, and that his uncle, his father's brother, had died of a heart attack when he was fifty-two. Bram had turned fifty-two in September. No wonder he didn't want to celebrate his birthday this year. If only Sophie had known. It explained so much about his recent actions. That's why he'd been trying so hard to get into shape. The physical he'd been given back in August hadn't suggested anything was wrong, but based on his family history, he must have had a premonition.

Bram was still sweating and in pain when they finally wheeled him off to do an EKG. Sophie spent the next hour in the waiting room, pacing in front of the window.

She couldn't believe this was actually happening. Finally, a different doctor, a man named Stoebel, came out to talk to her. He explained that they'd found blockages in two of her husband's major arteries and were prepping him for bypass surgery. Bram would be given a general anesthetic and wouldn't be awake during the procedure. The surgery would take anywhere from two to six hours. A bypass graft would be performed to reroute blood flow around the blockages. Dr. Stoebel felt that Bram would do just fine, but he wasn't offering certainties.

There had been no time for a second opinion. No time to check out Dr. Stoebel's medical references. Sophie had called her son, and he and his partner, John, had arrived just as the surgery began. Together, they waited.

That was three days ago. Bram had come through the surgery like a trooper. For the first twenty-four hours, his condition had been monitored closely in the cardiac intensive care unit. Because of a breathing tube, Bram couldn't talk, but his eyes spoke eloquently. He was scared, but incredibly happy to be alive. Yesterday, the tube was removed and he'd been allowed to sit up in bed. When he coughed, he used a pillow to cover the incision and lessen the pain.

And today, the third day after the operation, his nurse had helped him to get up. He moved slowly around the room for a few minutes, then sat in the chair and watched a little TV. He was so tired when he got back into bed that he'd been asleep ever since.

Hearing Bram stir, Sophie set her knitting down and went to make sure he was okay.

"Hi, sweetheart," he said, seeing her face loom over him.

With her diminutive height, Sophie rarely had the chance to loom over anyone, so this was a rare occasion.

"How are you feeling?" she asked.

"Like I got hit by a truck." His voice was still raspy and sore from the breathing tube. "But happy to be here."

She touched his face tenderly. "Dr. Stoebel was in a while ago. He says you're doing better than expected."

"That's me. An overachiever to the bitter end."

"This isn't the end, sweetheart. You're doing so well. You'll be home soon."

"We'll see." He coughed, then winced.

She took hold of his hand. "Bram? Why didn't you tell me about your father's heart attack? I thought he died of lung cancer."

"He did."

"Then—"

"The heart attack didn't kill him. My uncle wasn't so lucky. It seems the Baldric men have a fatal flaw. Not only do their hearts break easily, but they don't work very well."

"You mean you've been carrying this worry around with you all these years? I wish you'd told me."

"Why? So you could worry, too?"

"Yes," she said, squeezing his hand. "We're a team."

He searched her eyes for a long moment.

Finally, Sophie said, "You'll recover from this, honey. You're going to be better than ever."

His expression softened. "Frisky and feisty?"

She nodded.

"From your mouth to God's ears."

"That's right," she said, straightening his bed covers. "After all the time I put in with the Church of the Firstborn, I should get *some* points." She was about to adjust the pillow behind his head when he took hold of her sweater.

"I love you," he said, a heartbreaking urgency in his voice.

"And I love you."

"A team, right?"

She smiled to cover her tears. "Forever, sweetheart. You and me against the world."

Pinwheel Meat Loaf

First-prize Winner

1 pound ground beef
¹/₂ pound ground pork
1 egg
1 cup fresh bread crumbs
1 teaspoon salt
Fresh ground pepper to taste
1 cup finely chopped onion, divided
2 large celery stalks, chopped (with leaves)
6 ounces Bruder Basil cheese, grated
Ketchup

Preheat the oven to 350°F.

In a large bowl, mix together the beef, pork, egg, bread crumbs, salt, pepper and ¹/₂ cup of the onion. On a sheet of wax paper, pat the meat loaf mixture into an approximately 13 × 9 × ¹/₂-inch rectangle.

Spread the celery and the remaining onion over the flattened meat mixture; then cover that with the cheese, making sure to keep the filling one inch in from the edges. Starting with the wide end, roll the meat up, tucking in the sides.

Place roll seam-side down on a baking sheet, cover with ketchup, and bake until done, approximately 1 hour. Let loaf stand for 10 minutes before slicing.

Serve with garlic mashed potatoes and green salad.

Thanksgiving Meat Loaf

Second-prize Winner

1 ¹/4 *pounds ground lean turkey*
2 *eggs*
1 *cup crushed packaged dry herb stuffing (Pepperidge*
   Farm Herb Stuffing is great)
¹/2 *teaspoon salt*
Fresh ground pepper to taste
1 *tablespoon light olive oil*
1 *onion, chopped*
2 *celery ribs, chopped*
¹/2 *cup whole cranberry sauce*
1 *tablespoon prepared horseradish*

Preheat the oven to 350°F.

In a large bowl, mix the turkey, eggs, dry stuffing, salt and pepper together. Set aside.

Heat the olive oil in a medium skillet and sauté onion and celery until lighly browned. Add the vegetables to the meat mixture.

Pack the meat into a 9 × 5–inch loaf pan.

In a small bowl mix together the cranberry sauce and horseradish; spread this over the top of the loaf.

Bake for about 1 hour, until the loaf is firm and the top is caramelized and brown, or until a quick-read meat thermometer registers an interior temperature of 160°F.

Let the loaf stand for 10 minutes before slicing. Serve with twice-baked sweet potatoes and fresh steamed broccoli.

Cora Runbeck's No-Nonsense Meat Loaf

Third-prize Winner

1 *pound ground beef*
1/2 pound ground pork
2 eggs
1/2 cup bread crumbs
1/2 cup oats
1/2 cup ketchup
1 teaspoon salt
Pinch of pepper
Pinch of allspice
1/4 teaspoon nutmeg
1/2 teaspoon dry mustard
1/2 teaspoon dry thyme
3 tablespoons milk
2 tablespoons light olive oil
1 onion, diced
1 carrot, diced
1 large celery rib, diced
1 pat of butter
1 cup button mushrooms, sliced
2 teaspoons Worcestershire sauce
Salt and pepper to taste
1/2 cup chopped parsley (flat Italian is best)

Preheat the oven to 350°F.

In a large bowl, mix together the ground beef, ground pork, eggs, bread crumbs, oats, ketchup, salt, pepper, allspice, nutmeg, mustard, thyme, and milk, and set aside.

Heat the olive oil in a medium skillet and sauté the onion, celery, and carrot until tender. Add the vegetables to the meat mixture.

In the same pan, melt the butter and sauté the mushrooms with the Worcestershire sauce, seasoning with salt and pepper. Add the mushrooms to the meat mixture, and mix in the parsley.

Pat meat into a 9 × 5-inch loaf pan and bake for approximately 1 hour and 15 minutes. Serve with home-grown corn, fresh spuds, and a big glass of milk.

Praise for Ellen Hart
and her Sophie Greenway
mysteries

SLICE AND DICE
"Mouth-watering . . . A smorgasbord of devilment."
—*Alfred Hitchcock Mystery Magazine*

"The pace quickly bubbles from simmer to boil. . . .
The complexity of Hart's novel is admirable."
—*Publishers Weekly*

THIS LITTLE PIGGY WENT TO MURDER
"Strong characters and a rich Lake Superior setting
make this solidly constructed mystery hard to put
down. Another winner for Ellen Hart!"
—M. D. LAKE

FOR EVERY EVIL
"Another splendid specimen of the classical mystery
story, nicely updated and full of interesting and
believable characters."
—*The Purloined Letter*

*Please turn the page
for more reviews. . . .*

Praise for Ellen Hart and her Jane Lawless series

HALLOWED MURDER

"Hart's crisp, elegant writing and atmosphere [are] reminiscent of the British detective style, but she has a nicer sense of character, confrontation, and sparsely utilized violence . . . . *Hallowed Murder* is as valuable for its mainstream influences as for its sexual politics."

—*Mystery Scene*

VITAL LIES

"This compelling whodunit has the psychological maze of a Barbara Vine mystery and the feel of Agatha Christie. . . . Hart keeps even the most seasoned mystery buff baffled until the end."

—*Publishers Weekly*

STAGE FRIGHT

"Hart deftly turns the spotlight on the dusty secrets and shadowy souls of a prominent theater family. The resulting mystery is worthy of a standing ovation."

—*Alfred Hitchcock Mystery Magazine*

A KILLING CURE

"A real treat ... Secret passageways, a coded ledger, a mysterious group known only as the Chamber, experimental drugs, blackmail, sexual assault, betrayal: all the ingredients of a good whodunit."

—*Lambda Book Report*

A SMALL SACRIFICE

"A smart and shocking thriller."

—*The Minnesota Daily*

FAINT PRAISE

"Packed with mystery and scheming characters, *Faint Praise* is one of the year's best. It's no wonder Ellen Hart is everyone's favorite author."

—R. D. ZIMMERMAN